NEW YORK REVIEW BOOKS
CLASSICS

DISCARDED

THE KREMLIN BALL

CURZIO MALAPARTE (pseudonym of Kurt Erich Suckert, 1898–1957) was born in Prato, Italy, and served in World War I. An early supporter of the Italian fascist movement and a prolific journalist, Malaparte soon established himself as an outspoken public figure. In 1931 he incurred Mussolini's displeasure by publishing a how-to manual entitled *Coup d'État: The Technique of Revolution*, which led to his arrest and a brief term in prison. During World War II Malaparte worked as a correspondent, for much of the time on the eastern front, and this experience provided the basis for his two most famous books, *Kaputt* (1944) and *The Skin* (1949). His political sympathies veered to the left after the war. He continued to write, while also involving himself in the theater and the cinema.

JENNY McPHEE is the author of the novels *The Center of Things*, *No Ordinary Matter*, and *A Man of No Moon*. Among the works she has translated are books by Primo Levi, Giacomo Leopardi, Anna Maria Ortese, and, for NYRB Classics, Natalia Ginzburg's *Family Lexicon*. She lives in New York, where she is the director of the Center for Applied Liberal Arts at New York University.

D0963304

OTHER BOOKS BY CURZIO MALAPARTE
PUBLISHED BY NYRB CLASSICS

Kaputt
Translated by Cesare Foligno
Afterword by Dan Hofstadter

The Skin
Translated by David Moore
Introduction by Rachel Kushner

THE KREMLIN BALL

(Material for a Novel)

CURZIO MALAPARTE

Translated from the Italian by

JENNY McPHEE

NEW YORK REVIEW BOOKS

New York

THIS IS A NEW YORK REVIEW BOOK
PUBLISHED BY THE NEW YORK REVIEW OF BOOKS
435 Hudson Street, New York, NY 10014
www.nyrb.com

Library of Congress Cataloging-in-Publication Data
Names: Malaparte, Curzio, 1898–1957, author. | McPhee, Jenny, translator.
Title: The Kremlin ball / by Curzio Malaparte ; translated and with a foreword
  by Jenny McPhee.
Other titles: Ballo al Kremlino. English
Description: New York : New York Review Books, [2018] | Series: New York
  Review Books classics
Identifiers: LCCN 2017046485 | ISBN 9781681372099 (paperback)
Subjects: LCSH: Social classes—Soviet Union—Fiction. | Moscow (Russia)—
  Fiction. | Soviet Union—Social life and customs—1917–1970—Fiction. |
  BISAC: FICTION / Political. | FICTION / Historical. | GSAFD: Historical
  fiction.
Classification: LCC PQ4829.A515 B3513 2018 | DDC 853/.912—dc23
LC record available at https://lccn.loc.gov/2017046485

ISBN 978-1-68137-209-9

Printed in the United States of America on acid-free paper.
10 9 8 7 6 5 4 3 2 1

CONTENTS

FOREWORD

THROUGHOUT this unfinished work by Curzio Malaparte, the supreme chronicler of twentieth-century European decadence, Marika, Malaparte's sixteen-year-old secretary, translator, and lover, repeatedly calls him, in English, "You dirty pig." In this extraordinary, twisted, elegant, brutal, stark, revelatory, funny, prescient novel in progress, Marika functions as something of a Virgil to Malaparte's Dante as he wanders about Moscow in 1929, Stalin's Great Purge looming. Originally from Tbilisi, Marika is often, but not always, with Malaparte, yet her jaded, relentlessly hopeful, youthful, feminine perspective inevitably accompanies him wherever he goes. A foreign diplomat, Malaparte had access to the circles of society he called the "Marxist nobility," which included early Bolshevik leaders, Soviet generals, the People's Commissars and their wives, actresses, ex-soldiers, Bolshoi ballerinas, senior officials, and cronies of Lenin and Trotsky. Malaparte encounters them at the Bolshoi Theater, at dinner parties, and at embassy balls where Moscow's *haute société* share gossip, air suspicions, and do their best to tear one another apart.

Malaparte's meanderings also include attending gatherings of the Union of Soviet Writers, the Workers' Club, and the All-Russian Congress of Soviets. He eats in workers' cafeterias, visits Lenin's tomb in Red Square, and pays homage to the grave of the great Russian composer Scriabin in a small cemetery next to the Novodevichy Convent. He spends long hours in the library at the Lenin Institute. He befriends Mayakovsky and when Marika tells him of the poet's suicide, he immediately goes to see his room, finding there, among other things, images of Manhattan and Chicago tacked to the wall. Malaparte strolls with Bulgakov along Arbat Street and down Smolensky Boulevard where he observes former members of the aristocracy selling off their remaining possessions at a flea market. Everywhere on the streets of Moscow loudspeakers attached to streetlamps blare recitations of anti-Christian poetry, and everywhere banners blaze with the news that the Five-Year Plan has begun. But if Dante's descent into hell is suggested in these pages, Proust's dissection of social class is Malaparte's model. Alternative titles were, in fact, *Du Côté de Chez Staline* and *The Princesses of Moscow*.

Curzio Malaparte has been called a lot of things—opportunist; dandy; fascist; pervert; a fashionable reactionary; a traitor; a consummate storyteller who could take a kernel of truth and grow it into a vast forest of exotic trees; a precursor of Philip Roth, E. L. Doctorow, and Ryszard Kapuściński; one of the most remarkable writers of the twentieth century—but it is Marika's assessment that feels the most poignant: "You dirty pig."

I am sure that Malaparte had much to regret in his life, but if his considerable body of stunning work has a unifying theme, it is that we are, as citizens of Western civilization, through our vileness among other things, complicit in our own destruction, and that none of us, not even Marika, is fully innocent. He displays a disturbing fascination with violence and extreme rule—fascism, Nazism, communism—

and sees these phenomena as natural and inevitable aspects of our collective suicide. Nevertheless, as his thirteen novels, two collections of poetry, two plays, one screenplay, fourteen works of nonfiction, and prodigious journalism all attest in a unique style that is at once lyrical and devious, there is some mischievous fun to be had along our path to hell.

In 1925, the writer Kurt Erich Suckert invented for himself the pseudonym Curzio Malaparte after learning that this had been the original name of the Bonaparte dynasty. He thus took on evil as his raison d'être from the outset, leaving good behind for others to contend with. Malaparte was a prolific writer and for every project that eventually made its way into print, it seems another ten remained in the offing. *The Kremlin Ball* falls into that latter category. Malaparte put the book aside in 1950 in order to write for the cinema and theater; he died before he had a chance to return to it.

In the United States, Malaparte is chiefly known for two books: *Kaputt* (1944), a thoroughly gruesome—yet also glamorous in that uniquely Malapartian way—account of his experiences on the front lines of World War II as a journalist, army captain, and Italian consul; and *The Skin* (1949), a harrowing portrayal of Naples and the "liberation" of Italy at the end of the war when Malaparte was serving as a liaison officer to the Allied army. *The Kremlin Ball* has been considered the final work of a trilogy that includes these books, and indeed Malaparte began the novel in 1946 as an outtake from *The Skin*. Each book is a masterpiece in its own right, and together they capture the beauty and grotesquery of the entire mid-century European social, political, and physical landscape in catastrophic decline.

Malaparte, who figures as both the author and the main

protagonist of the books, called them "novels of autobio-graphical reportage," and rightly so, even if, as he writes in his preface to *The Kremlin Ball*, "everything is true: the people, the events, the things, the places." His truth, however, is inevitably accompanied by an aura of the incredible. His prose mirrors the incredulity elicited by the outlandish claims of politicians and their ideologies, by the horrendous events that had occurred and were unfolding at the time. Malaparte writes in a way that beggars belief, with a sneer and a leer, and in so doing takes the unreliable narrator to a new level. His unreliability as a raconteur is compounded by his own chameleon-like politics, which shifted at will depending on opportunity, circumstance, and whim. He encouraged his readers to see him for the flawed character he was, no better or worse than any of the many personalities he profiles and keeps company with in his novels. He was a writer who pushed the boundaries of every narrative form he tackled, but especially the novel, and his works go beyond neorealism and magic realism to the uncategorizable.

To read Malaparte, and indeed as I have found to translate him—his polyglot prose often veering, sometimes reeling, towards the absurd or the surreal—is to feel profoundly destabilized by his sentences while at the same time thrilled and intrigued as one is thrust into a quasi-hallucinatory state of uncomfortable surprise, awe, and disbelief. Did an aging Russian princess really try to sell her satin underwear at a flea market in Moscow? (*The Kremlin Ball*) Were the horses, escaping fire, really frozen to death where they stood in Lake Ladoga, becoming ghoulish ice sculptures until a spring thaw? (*Kaputt*) At an official dinner in Naples, after the fish from the local aquarium had been exhausted, was the American high command really served a dead baby girl on a platter? (*The Skin*)

Malaparte's lifelong fascination with Russia likely began when he went to Warsaw in late 1919 as a young diplomat. Communist Russia was banging on the newly constituted Poland's door, and the passion and power of the Soviet Revolution captured Malaparte's imagination. He would remain enthralled, if increasingly disillusioned, by Soviet Russia for the rest of his life, producing several books on the subject along the way: *Intelligenza di Lenin* (Lenin Explained, 1930), *Coup d'État: The Technique of Revolution* (1931), *Le Bonhomme Lénine* (That Good Man Lenin, 1932), *The Volga Rises in Europe* (1965), and the unfinished *The Kremlin Ball*.

The Russian Revolution was an inspiration to journalists, notably John Reed, Albert Rhys Williams, and N. N. Sukhanov, but its aftermath was less well-known, in part because it became increasingly difficult to find out what was going on. In writing about the Marxist nobility, Malaparte was challenging the claim that the revolution was in fact revolutionary at all. The old court had simply been replaced by a new one with all the same privileges and corruption. In his preface, Malaparte points out that Soviet writers "assume the only possible protagonist is the proletariat" ignoring "even the existence of a Marxist nobility," while European and American writers have suffered from some kind of "excessive discretion" or "mysterious circumspection" and so have avoided the subject.

The Kremlin Ball was first published in Italy in 1971 as part of an edition of Malaparte's complete works. In 2012, thanks to the painstaking work of Malaparte's sister, Edda Ronchi Suckert, and the scrupulous editorial and philological efforts of the literary scholar Raffaella Rodondi, Adelphi brought out an extensively annotated edition with appendices, including various versions of sections of the text. An excellent editor's note of a hundred pages provides a thorough history of the manuscript, its origin and odyssey, along with a robust explanation of Rodondi's methodology in organizing the book's six chapters. The first two chapters were identified as such by Malaparte himself before he died, the remaining four Rodondi determined using chronology as her principle guide. She aptly compares the text to a building under construction, with several floors, "each in a different state of completion. On some the work is nearly done, missing only the finishing touches; on others the work has barely begun or still has a ways to go, despite apparent progress." The book ends with an essay entitled "The Shame of Death," a brilliant analysis comparing the role of death in Soviet, European, and American society. In the interest of readability as we try to find Malaparte a wider audience in the English-speaking world, we have decided not to include Rodondi's philological annotations here, but we did want to bring her work to your attention.

Though *The Kremlin Ball* takes place in 1929, Malaparte tells this story from a retrospective distance of a decade and a half, looking back at his younger, more naive self ("Should there be a law prohibiting the young from having a romantic vision of men and life?") and with the hindsight of just how bad things would get in the Soviet Union under Stalin. In 1929, Malaparte's political sympathies were in the process of shifting from fascism to communism (he had marched on Rome with Mussolini in 1922, become a member of the National Fascist Party in 1925, and was a close friend of Galeazzo Ciano, Mussolini's son-in-law, but by 1933 he had been kicked out of the party and exiled to the island of Lipari). Malaparte's original agenda in going to Russia—he was working as a diplomat and a journalist at the time—was to describe a new ideal of government run with efficiency and enthusiasm by the working class. The resulting series of articles in praise of Lenin published in *La Stampa* at the time apparently so infuriated Mussolini that he suggested Malaparte apply for a job at *Pravda*.

In *The Kremlin Ball*, he instead describes how he found that a new aristocracy had simply replaced the old, that this new elite, even if they had overthrown the bourgeoisie, were themselves bourgeois to the core. They continued to enjoy all the customs and privileges of the former aristocracy, convinced nevertheless that they represented a new kind of superior humanity—and in this, too, they were no different than their predecessors. Unlike the aristocracy of the ancien régime, who assumed they would be in power forever, this new aristocracy was excruciatingly aware that their days were numbered and lived their lives drenched in fear.

Malaparte's cast of characters might have sprung from the combined imaginations of Fellini, Dalí, and Buñuel. There is Dimitry Florinsky, Chief of Protocol of the People's Commissariat for Foreign Affairs, "the most famous homosexual in Moscow," king of the Marxist court gossip, who parades through the streets of Moscow in his horse-drawn carriage, "all rouged and powdered, his little yellow eyes rimmed with black, his eyelashes hardened with mascara"; the "beautiful and mysterious" Lev Karakhan, possibly the handsomest man in all of Europe, a hero of the October Revolution, an adviser to Sun Yat-sen, who spoke with a perfect Oxford accent and played tennis only with balls flown in from Lillywhites in London; Marina Semyonova, the prima ballerina at the Bolshoi, the lover of Karakhan and possibly of Stalin, who regularly raided the Bolshoi's costume department in order to wear Schiaparelli gowns to embassy balls, a practice that was strictly forbidden; Madame Kameneva, Trotsky's sister and the director of Intourist, fat, swollen like a corpse, who carries the smell of death on her ever since her husband was arrested and her brother exiled; Anatoly Lunacharsky, the Soviet People's Commissar of Education and Culture, who took great risks to preserve Russian art and literature, but fell out of favor with Stalin, in part because of his inability to control his philandering wife, and was dismissed as commissar.

But perhaps the most resonant character of all is Lenin, lying in his great wooden mausoleum in Red Square, small, shrunken, and putrid, while every so often German specialists appear to "empty, scrape out, and disinfect the shell of that precious crustacean, that sacred mummy, the porcelain white face lit up by red freckles veiled by a greenish mold-like sweat." Malaparte indicates, in so many words, that practically from the start communism was rotting, dying, if not dead already, its practitioners the living dead.

Malaparte was convinced that Soviet communism was not unique to Russia but a fully European phenomenon. He did not, as many did, interpret Bolshevism as a debauchery of Marxist ideals but rather as an inevitable outcome of the European elite's failure to address issues of gross inequality and corruption. For Malaparte, the Bolsheviks simply took advantage of the people's malaise and acted as pretend revolutionaries in order to gain control of the government, allowing them to enjoy the same powers and privileges of the traditional aristocracy. Malaparte insists that the fates of the European and Soviet political systems are inextricably linked. "Since the Europe of tomorrow is to be found in the Russia of tomorrow," he writes, "it is equally true that the Europe of today is to be found in the Russia of today." Despite their disparate political systems, he believed the USSR and Europe shared a common corruption, identical social dynamics, a toxic misogyny, racism, and homophobia. Both systems craftily used the concept of "liberty" as a means of oppression. But he was genuinely afraid that the Marxist nobility in some form would prevail and if it did, one day in the not so distant future, he "and all of his readers would find themselves up against the wall."

Though Malaparte last visited Moscow in 1956—hoping perhaps that in the aftermath of Stalin, Khrushchev would open a new way forward for Soviet Russia—he was actually on his way to China, the communism of Mao Zedong his new obsession. Malaparte undoubtedly would have unleashed his pen on China if he hadn't returned from that trip already sick with the lung cancer that would kill him the following year. It is said that he seriously considered bequeathing his famous villa on Capri, the Casa Malaparte, one of the most remarkable examples of modern European architecture, to China.

So what does it mean for a work to be "unfinished" and why is the text qualified by the parenthetical "material for a novel"? First and foremost, Malaparte himself never deemed the novel finished. In correspondence with his publishers in both France and Italy, he promised to deliver the manuscript within a few months, sometimes days, but never did. After his death, many drafts and versions of the manuscript were found among his papers but none was clearly definitive or polished to the level of his published work; there are repetitions, inconsistencies, anachronisms, and abrupt breaks throughout the text. Malaparte's genius as a writer, however, is everywhere and it is a deep privilege, as a reader, to witness the nuts and bolts of putting a piece of writing together, to partake in the writer's beguiling process. Malaparte's flaws, weaknesses, vulnerabilities, and vices are all on vivid, raw display. He never smoothed the work into a perfection that works both to please the reader and to keep her at arm's length. Instead we get all of him, his considerable charm, erudition, wit, good humor, intelligence, and inspired storytelling along with his deep cynicism, snobbery, hypocrisy, prejudice, shameless name-dropping, and his amorality and immorality.

As Marika would say, affectionately, but without diminishing the accuracy of her accusation: "You dirty pig."

—JENNY MCPHEE

THE KREMLIN BALL

Moscow Society Is the Mirror Image of European Society but Dominated by Fear

IN THIS novel, a faithful portrait of the USSR's Marxist nobility, of Moscow's communist high society, of their *haute société*, everything is true: the people, the events, the things, the places. The characters did not originate in the author's imagination, but were drawn from life, each with his own name, face, words, and actions: Stalin, who watched the famous ballerina Semyonova prance about the stage every night at the Bolshoi Theater of Moscow; Karakhan (the same Karakhan Stalin later had killed), with whom Stalin was apparently competing for Semyonova; the celebrated beauties of the Marxist nobility, the Bs, Gs, and Ls with their lovers, intrigues, and scandals, their eager and restless faces basking in the ephemeral rose-tinted glow of glory, riches, and power; the extraordinary Florinsky, Chief of Protocol of the People's Commissariat for Foreign Affairs, who paraded through the streets of Moscow in his horse-drawn carriage; the fearful and resigned Madame Kameneva, Trotsky's sister; all of these *merveilleuses*, these *lions*, these *parvenus*, these ephebes are not invented but living people, real human creatures. What differentiates this novel, however, from a "court chronicle" catering to seventeenth-century French taste, or from a *mémoire* such as the one by Saint-Simon, or from a book of *moralités* like Montaigne's, and makes it a novel in the Proustian sense (not so much in style, but in its keen sense of *désintéressement*, or disinterestedness, so essential to the novels and characters created by Marcel Proust), is the fact that the characters, events, and episodes in this "court chronicle" are bound by a fatality propelling them all toward one end, toward a novelistic denouement. The protagonist, the hero of this novel, is not an individual, not a man or woman, but a social entity: the communist aristocracy that replaced the Russian aristocracy of the *ancien régime*, and in many ways resembled the revolutionary nobility that arose after the French Revolution, those who gathered around Barras during the Directory regime. Similarly, the protagonist of Proust's novels is no individual, no man or woman, not Baron Charlus or Swann, not Madame de Guermantes, Odette, or Langeron, but rather the French nobility, the Parisian nobility, the *monde de Paris*, in other words, a social entity, society itself. The author of this novel, however, has no intention of being a moralist—as in the *"plan de désintéressement"* or "framework of disinterestedness" Albert Thibaudet discusses in regard to Proust in which Proust infuses morality into his psychological analysis. This author emphatically declares that he is absolutely indifferent to the fate of his characters. As for their morality, whether they are on the side of the good or the bad, he's interested only up to a point. This author, instead, addresses disinterestedness not in terms of psychological analysis but in terms of how disinterestedness is infused in the social drama of politics and political unrest of his protagonists, ranging from Stalin to the young Marika. The most striking aspect of a Marxist society is not that it is Marxistically organized like Hitler's Germany (which the author defines as "feudal communism"), but how Marxist morality is dominated by fatalism. That historical materialism would lead to fatalism is odd. In reality, Marxism does not lead the individual to a collective sentiment but to the most absolute fatalism, to a total dedication to fatality—which is, of course, the sign of a society in decline. If the novel contains a moral it is this: Marxist society in the USSR is already in decline. And not only the Trotskyite nobility of 1929, but the Marxist nobility and the entire Marxist society are in decline. A distinct and dreadful sign of this decline is the fatalism that is the private rationale of every Russian man, even if disguised by activity and fanatic belief—these being characteristics of a Marxist society indifferent to its own destiny. Another factor is this: Russians suffer for others. The inducement to suffer for others is a form of fatalism. Only those who suffer for themselves take part in history, participate in the thrust of history, are the subject, not merely the object, of history. The destiny of any noble revolutionary is to wind up against the wall. This destiny is assured for a noble revolutionary in a Marxist society in which mankind, human life, has no value. A new Marxist nobility, which replaced the Trotskyite nobility exterminated in 1936, has been forming in these past few years around Stalin. It, too, will wind up against the wall if it doesn't succeed in imposing its morality, corruption, and ambition upon the entire Russian population, if it doesn't succeed in debasing all Russians. Accurate news does not come out of the USSR. But what is certain is that in all the European countries occupied by the Russians, in Poland, Hungary, Romania, Germany, Austria, among all the Allies, the most corrupt, the most susceptible to bribes, compromise, corruption, and money are the Soviets. And that's saying a lot if one thinks of the corruption among the English and the Americans in Europe! Nor should it be said that this Soviet corruption is due to a noncommunist, bourgeois environment into which these Soviets were suddenly transported. They must be very weak, these Reds, if they are so easily corruptible! And the communist morality must be very weak! The truth is that through these Reds one is able to gauge and become familiarized with the formidable decadence of the entire Marxist society—the leaders, the bureaucracy, the proletariat.

The intent of this novel is, then, to portray the dawn of this decline, to draw a picture of the truth by describing the communist nobility. By looking at the decline of the Marxist society in Europe—and not the decline of the bourgeoisie, which is already a thing of the past—one can see the reasons for the decline of Europe. Hitlerism was one of the most hideous aspects of the Marxist morality established in Europe. The decline of Europe consists in this decline of Marxist morality. And the decline also captured the USSR. The preeminent historian of the decline of the European bourgeoisie is Marcel Proust. The author of this novel is linked with Proust not by anything literary, but by the "framework" of disinterestedness involved in the novel's analyses and artistic representations. Using this framework of disinterestedness, the author shows and tells the story of the decline of Marxist society. It must be pointed out that a portrayal of the Marxist nobility has never been attempted before now, not by Soviet writers, nor by European or American writers. Soviet writers assume the only possible protagonist is the proletariat. They seem to ignore even the existence of a Marxist nobility, of a communist *haute société*. If they speak of a communist aristocracy in the USSR, they mean a workers' elite made up of Udarniks and Stakhanovites (workers who formed competitive brigades to increase production), war heroes, and heroes of the Revolution. Perhaps due to excessive discretion, or because of some mysterious circumspection, European and American writers, even those who have visited the USSR and experienced Russian communism firsthand, have carefully avoided discussing the Marxist aristocracy. Apparently, it is a subject of little interest to them. Compared to the *haute société* of Paris, London, New York, Berlin, Rome, Vienna, and Madrid, the Soviet variant is a very poor thing: *une noblesse de la roture,* a nobility of commoners. Its members speak mostly about Stalin, and always with a profound respect, as it should be. And it seems all that interests them is the life of the Soviet people, communist organizations, industrial and farming production statistics, schools, and so on. To read the writings of any one of them, it would seem that the USSR is an immense democratic and egalitarian society of workers.

The Soviet writers deserve a defense. In Russia, a Proust (or a Montaigne, a Saint-Simon) is inadmissible, unimaginable. The Marxist nobility does not tolerate being talked about, cannot bear having their ways and things discussed, and demands to be enveloped in silence. The Marxist nobility imposes certain subjects on Soviet writers and these compulsory subjects are the life of the proletarian masses, the struggle to construct socialism, the approbation of the state, in other words, the narrowest, blindest, most absolute conformity. One day while speaking with Lunacharsky, the author asked him if a Marcel Proust existed in Russia.

"Yes," Lunacharsky responded, "every Soviet writer is a proletarian Proust."

The author smiled politely at this response and refrained from pointing out that a proletarian Proust was nonsensical; that Proust was a product of a distinct European tradition—Western, French—ranging from Montaigne to Saint-Simon to Valéry and Bergson; that Proust was, as Thibaudet said, "A Dangeau who became Saint-Simon"; that Russian literature lacked the influences equivalent to those of Proust, lacked a *Cyrus* and a *Clélie* and the worldly novels of the seventeenth century. The author says this to defend himself from the inevitable accusation that he chose as his subject not the proletariat, but rather Soviet high society, Moscow's *gens du monde*, Moscow's Marxist Court with its courtiers and favorites, its profiteers, gala celebrations, balls, scandals, *lettres de cachet*, and palace conspiracies.

A portrait of the Marxist nobility, of the USSR's communist aristocracy—what an extraordinary subject! And what moral, social, and psychological virtues and lessons such a portrait would bring! Since the Europe of tomorrow is to be found in the Russia of tomorrow, it is equally true that the Europe of today is to be found in the Russia of today. The decline of Europe is the consequence of the decline of communist Russia due primarily to the corruption of the USSR's Marxist nobility. The subject is dangerous. And the author is profoundly convinced that if the existing Marxist nobility were to succeed in dominating Europe, the author and all of his readers would find themselves up against the wall—and not simply because they are criminals, or enemies of the people and freedom, but rather because both the author and his readers are free men. (The author remembers that during the tyranny of Mussolini and Hitler he suffered for a long time in fascist prisons—the experience, however, did not induce him to make a career of being a martyr for freedom, a profession that is very advantageous these days, with a guaranteed return.) The Marxist nobility, if it succeeds in dominating Europe, would exterminate not only communism's adversaries and the enemies of the proletariat, but all free men. The idea that all the free men in Europe and the world would be exterminated by that corrupt, brutal, greedy, and immoral Marxist nobility must be taken under serious consideration. The time for laughter is well-nigh over for the free men of our times.

I

The Black Prince

WHEN THE orchestra finished playing "Ich küsse Ihre Hand, Madame" (Viennese waltzes being *de rigeur* at the British Embassy balls, just as songs by Cole Porter and Noël Coward were ritually played at the German Embassy balls), Madame Lunacharskaya, wife of Anatoly Lunacharsky, the Soviet People's Commissar of Education and Culture, stood still in the middle of the room.

"I wonder where Lev Karakhan is?" she asked, looking around her. She placed her left hand on my shoulder while with her right she brushed a few loose black curls off her face. "Don't you think that Semyonova puts on a few too many airs, acting as if she were in the same league as Kschessinskaya?"

Kschessinskaya was the last great ballerina during the time of the czars and rumored to have been the lover of Nicholas II.

"What makes you say so?"

"She's late again tonight. She thinks it's *chic* to make everyone wait for her."

"I hadn't noticed she was late," I said.

"You're not in love with her anymore?" Madame Lunacharskaya asked, staring at me, her eyes full of amusement.

"You know very well," I said, "that it is you I am in love with."

"So they say around Moscow," Madame Lunacharskaya said, "but Moscow is a city of gossips."

The orchestra began to play "Wiener Blut," and Madame Lunacharskaya leaned languidly on my arm.

"When do you return to Paris?" she asked, abandoning herself in my arms, though her gaze remained fixed on the door.

"Perhaps I'll stay in Moscow for a few more weeks," I replied. "I should like to see the Russian spring in all its splendor."

"Spring in Moscow cannot compare to a Parisian spring," Madame Lunacharskaya said. "This past October, I went to Paris to select some dresses for the winter play. The one I'm wearing is Schiaparelli," she added. "I hope you won't tell on me as well."

Soviet theater rules forbade actresses from wearing theater costumes at any time other than while on stage. But Semyonova, Lunacharskaya, ———, all the most famous Soviet theater and cinema actresses, ignored regulations and wore dresses taken from the theaters' wardrobes in public—unaware that by doing so, more than defying the official rules, they were rejecting the universal poverty of the people.

The Schiaparelli dress was a little heavy, a little baroque, based on a design Madame Schiaparelli had devised by copying pleats found in Michelangelo drawings and drapery from Canova statues; the dress suggested the Domenichino style of Roman baroque, the colors those of Poussin's shadows, his shadowy trees, as well as Corot's turquoise shadows.

Madame Lunacharskaya was a brunette, pale, her facial features slightly enlarged as if viewed through a magnifying glass. Her black eyes were swollen with sensuality, malice, and lack of sleep. So unlike the clear glassy eyes of Russian working-class women, her eyes were eyes of the flesh in which images didn't reflect but appeared tattooed. Her black eyebrows were not plucked and thinned but rather accentuated by a touch of pencil and they cast a shadow on those cloudy eyes of the flesh, on those nocturnal eyes in which a lazy and sweet sensuality shone like *une veilleuse*, a night-light in a bedroom. She had a large pulpy mouth with thick lips across which an ironic and sometimes spiteful smile strayed like a ray of light through the crack beneath a closed door. There was something closed off about her, something in her manner, her gestures, her looks, her words.

In a hereditary aristocracy, the nobility's reserve, their simplicity, their natural decorum, their particular condescension in manner and words and even in smiles, their detachment, which is actually pride mitigated by good manners and self-respect, these things that are handed down through tradition, education, and custom, these things, in a true nobility, are innate. In a class newly come to the honors and privileges of power, these things, as everyone knows, are willful. And as in a bourgeois society of parvenus, in the communist nobility a sense of style is not innate but willful, and reserve, decorum, the proud simplicity of manners, these things are all replaced by suspicion. The chief characteristic of the communist nobility is not bad taste, vulgarity, or bad manners, nor is it the complacency of wealth, luxury, and power: it is suspicion, and, I would also add, ideological intransigence.

All of us in Moscow were united in our praise for the spareness and simplicity of Stalin's lifestyle, of his simple, elegant, worker-like ways, but Stalin did not belong to the communist nobility. Stalin was Bonaparte after the coup of 18 Brumaire: He was master, dictator, and the communist nobility was opposed to him just as the Directory's class of parvenus was opposed to Bonaparte. Among all the Red aristocrats, among all the communist nobles, one could feel a contempt that was not social but ideological. From a social point of view, actually, snobbishness was the hidden source behind the many worldly activities of that very powerful, and already corrupt, society, which had lived, up until just a moment before, in misery, suspicion, and with the uncertainty of secrecy and emigration. They had very suddenly risen up to sleep in the beds of the great women of the czarist nobility, to sit in the gilded chairs of the czarist officials, carrying out the same functions that until the day before had been carried out by the czarist nobility. Every one of those Red nobles studied how to imitate Western behaviors: the women studied Parisian styles, the men studied London customs, and to a lesser extent those of Berlin or New York. The most elegant women were actresses; the most elegant men were officers, especially the officers of the cavalry of the Proletarsky Division stationed in Moscow, along with a few of the diplomats from the Narkomindel, the People's Commissariat for Foreign Affairs.

The grand ballroom in the British Embassy was packed that evening with an unusually high number of Russian guests. The reason so many had rushed to the ball hosted by Sir Owen Stanley for Moscow's most scintillating inhabitants, both Russian and foreign, was the rumor that had suddenly spread throughout the worldly milieu of the USSR's capital contending that the prima ballerina of the Bolshoi, Semyonova, had spurned Karakhan and that he had tried to commit suicide. All heads were turned toward the door waiting for something extraordinary to happen: Semyonova had promised to come to the ball and her tardiness was beginning to arouse eager expectation in the guests, and most especially in the host Stanley Owen.

Everyone was by now used to Semyonova's lateness, her rivals accusing her of behaving like a grande dame of the *ancien régime* or, as Madame Lunacharskaya called her, "a Princess of the blood." But that evening she was even later than usual and Karakhan's absence only served to confirm the rumor that had rippled throughout Moscow in the late afternoon.

"You are a true Parisian," I said, smiling.

Madame Lunacharskaya turned her fleshy eyes toward me and smiled ironically.

"And to think," she said after a brief silence, "I am accused of having counterrevolutionary tendencies simply because I dress decently. Speak to me of Paris," she said, half closing her eyes.

I spoke to her of Paris. Of the city's gray and turquoise colors, of the autumnal pinks, the golden leaves of the *marronniers*, the horse chestnuts along the Seine, of the mist that rises in the evenings along the river, of the leaves crackling beneath the feet of passersby, of the Tuileries Gardens.

"Tell me about the Place Vendôme," Madame Lunacharskaya said.

I spoke to her of the Place Vendôme, of the harmonious silence of the Place Vendôme, of its gray stone color, that same gray-blue of the "pietra serena," the sandstone of Florence. I spoke to her of the Place Vendôme where there is nothing to suggest nature, no trees, grass, flowers, water, where everything is human, an entirely cerebral humanity like a Racine poem or a Cartesian idea.

"Imagine," I said, "a portrait of Racine painted in the Place Vendôme, imagine —— leaning against the Place Vendôme's column, imagine Pyrrhus shouting passionately as he crosses the square while Andromache huddles in a corner. Imagine the Place Vendôme's silence swelling Racine's poetry as the wind swells a sail, imagine Racine's poetry swollen with the wind sliding off the river and along the ground up rue de Castiglione:

S'enivrait en marchant du plaisir de la voir.

Imagine the Place Vendôme on a moonlit night, that silence, that profound and precise serenity like the silence that follows the last note of a symphony by Vivaldi, Lully, or Rameau.

"Tell me about Giraudoux," Madame Lunacharskaya said.

I spoke to her of Jean Giraudoux, of his manly voice that always sounded a little tired, of the sheer brilliance of his eyes, of his beneficent smile, and I told her about his dog Puck and the *camaraderie* that united those two beings born to understand each other. I spoke to her of Jean Giraudoux who went for walks without his hat or coat on brisk winter evenings, clear and cold, when Paris becomes glass, and the buildings, the monuments, the statues, the colonnades, the trees, become porcelain, lightly tinted, like Sèvres, when everything becomes fragile, exquisite, sparkling, and Giraudoux slowly walked along the *quais* of the Seine, between rue des Saints-Pères and Pont Neuf, speaking of Paris, its smells, silence, and mist. I told her about Giraudoux whom I left on Pont Neuf as he wandered slowly away disappearing into the mist, into the silence of Paris.

"I would like so very much," said Madame Lunacharskaya, "to be in one of Giraudoux's plays here in Moscow. But it's forbidden. Do you think that Giraudoux is truly a counter-revolutionary writer, a bourgeois writer?"

I laughed quietly and Madame Lunacharskaya corrected herself saying: "Baroque?"

So I told her about the baroque Giraudoux, the Giraudoux who modeled himself after the young Bernini; how he regarded France as precious, delicate, strange; of his ideas about men and women; of his graciousness. Madame Lunacharskaya put a hand on my shoulder: "Here in Moscow, one likes only what is liked by the workers. Do you really think that Giraudoux could teach anything to the workers?"

"But of course," I said, "most certainly," and began to laugh. "The workers of Paris," I replied, "the workers at Renault, the mechanics, the foundry workers, the lathe operators, the machinists, they all go to see Giraudoux because they understand Giraudoux better than the snobbish women of the bourgeoisie dressed by Paquin and Schiaparelli. In order to understand Giraudoux, one must have, in addition to the sensibility of certain French intellectuals, the sophistication of workers who know how to build and operate engines, who understand the precision of electrical lathes, the precision of gears. The same is true for Descartes or Pascal: on any given page of their work one encounters the mechanisms of image, thought, and logic from which French beauty is born, that particular beauty that only the French have, a beauty made up of precision, clarity, and boldness, a beauty also found in Baudelaire, Verlaine, Valèry, Ravel, Lèger, Segonzac, in the painters, writers, philosophers, precision workers, and artisans. I am sure that writers such as Giraudoux can educate workers better than revolutionary writers, better than Ilya Ehrenburg," I said. "In order to understand Giraudoux, one must be a refined man, intelligent, sensitive, like the French workers. The Russian workers..."

"Oh, the Russian workers," Madame Lunacharskaya said,

interrupting me, but she then stopped herself and fell silent. The orchestra began playing "The Blue Danube" and Madame Lunacharskaya stood up and said, "Let's go back into the ballroom." When she arrived at the door she looked around and said: "She's still not here." I understood she was referring to Semyonova and while on the threshold I asked her in a low voice if she believed what everyone in Moscow had been saying for the past few hours was true.

"It would please me no end if it were," Madame Lunacharskaya said, turning toward me. She placed her hand on my shoulder and I pulled her into a waltz, but just then the blond and ruddy Florinsky, Chief of Protocol of the People's Commissariat for Foreign Affairs, ran across the ballroom, dodging couples as he went, in order to greet Semyonova who was making her entrance alone. Madame Semyonova had stopped on the threshold and was glancing around for Lady Owen when Florinsky came up to her, kissed her hand, and exclaimed: "*Oh, daragaia, ma chère, enfin!* Oh, my dear, finally!"

At the sound of his voice, Madame Lunacharskaya turned around, saw Semyonova, and, detaching herself by pushing me away with a light shove of her hand on my shoulder, said, "Excuse me," then made her way to Tairov, the famous director and founder of the Kamerny Theater who was standing near a window surrounded by a cluster of young actors.

I remained in the middle of the ballroom observing those around me.

Seated in an armchair at the far end of the room, Madame Yegorova, the wife of Marshal Yegorov, spoke loudly and laughed with a few young officers from the cavalry of the Proletarsky Division, while out of the corner of her eye she watched Semyonova make her way to the buffet on the arm of Sir Esmond Ovey, the British ambassador. Semyonova, the prima ballerina of the Bolshoi Theater of Moscow, was a rather short woman with clear blue eyes and shiny blond hair severely pulled back behind her head. Soft white flesh covered her small, thin, very fine bones. In the white light cast from the lamps, her bare plump shoulders appeared to be made of snow. Her dress hugged her shapely hips and a rather low-cut back revealed the distinct curve of her spine. Made of white satin, its lower hem enlivened by a blue edge, the dress resembled a Byzantine toga, and I suspected a Lelong design. Around her neck, she wore a *collier* of pink pearls, and on her hair a diadem-shaped tiara similar to the *kokoshnik* headdresses worn by the women boyars of old, lending Semyonova's chubby pale face, big blue eyes, and frozen expression the same look as some of the female heads found among the ancient icons in the Rogozhskoye Cemetery, or in the possession of the "Old Believers." Leaning on the arm of Sir Edmond Ovey, she lifted the skirt of her dress with her left hand as she walked, just barely revealing those two small famous feet swooned over by all of Moscow, now squeezed into shoes covered in white satin, the excellent work of ——— in Paris, Pavlova's shoemaker. All eyes were on Semyonova, and I noticed how she smiled as she glanced to her left and right without actually seeing anyone, as if she were smiling at ghosts. She radiated an ineffable grace: not the grace of Degas's ballerinas, but rather the slightly ambiguous grace of a harlequin, like those by Magnasco or Picasso, or of some of the *pierrots* by Cubist painters, so full of remembered humiliations and gallant hope. But her gestures were brusque, and though they at first seemed instinctive, on further careful observation, they appeared not only deliberate but premeditated with arrogant malice. The look on her face conveyed cruelty, insolence, and a cold, calculating exaltation. To understand how much premeditation and calculation there was in the simplest of her seemingly natural movements, one only had to observe her whenever she turned her little head—she turned it with a quick jerk like a lizard—which was slightly squashed down into the nape of her neck. And the same was true for her prima ballerina tantrums, her mood swings, her fits of nerves, and her bouts of cold fury, all of which earned her considerable notoriety as a whimsical and tyrannical artist. Occasionally, because of some trifling mistake made by one of her colleagues, or due to the slightest hesitation on the part of the orchestra conductor, or to a violin being imperceptibly off-key, or to the creak of a seat at the back of the theater, or to the cough of an audience member, Semyonova would interrupt the ballet, stop in the middle of a pirouette, and stand center stage, cold and unmoving, like a marble statue before an audience silenced by terror.

The enormous proletarian audience thronging to the Bolshoi Theater of Moscow every night forgave her every whim, her rude and tyrannical behavior: they would stay silent, without breathing, holding their breath for fear of unsettling the nerves of their idol until finally a warm, passionate, endless applause melted that frozen marble statue. She would then give a slight, contemptuous bow of her head, her smile mischievously triumphant.

"She is the only being on earth who would dare to dance on a volcano," said the French ambassador, Monsieur Herbette, who for many years had been the director of *Le Temps* in Paris. He had remained a devotee of the *bon mots* fashionable among Parisian newspaper editors at the time of Fallières, of the witticisms bandied about the Quai d'Orsay since the time of the Duke of Gramont.

"You forget Karakhan," retorted the British ambassador, Sir Edmond Ovey.

During the winter, the long winter of 1929, the relationship between Semyonova and Karakhan was the predominant subject of conversation at every bridge table in Moscow's foreign embassies and at every gathering in the Spiridonovka Street mansion's immense ballroom where the People's Commissar for Foreign Affairs, Litvinov, the fat, pale, and jolly Litvinov, held his official dinners and dances. The men of the communist nobility favored Semyonova while the women favored Karakhan. The foreign diplomats also divided themselves into two camps, though in their case the women supported Semyonova and the men were for Karakhan. This was a clear sign of something new, but I'm not sure if the novelty said more about Russian communist society or about the old established well-mannered Western society, since men siding with men is an Eastern trait and men siding with women is a Western trait.

Karakhan was the handsomest man in the Soviet Union and perhaps, according to Frau Dirksen, the German ambassador's wife, the best-looking man in Europe. Times change, the ancient aristocracies fall into decline, the liberal European civilization is superseded by a Marxist society, but the standards of masculine beauty endure the tests of time, resist changes in fashion, political regimes, moral and social ideologies. A man or woman who was considered beautiful during the reign of Louis XV would have been just as pleasing to the eye at the time of the Directory. Lord Byron or the Count d'Orsay, with their beauty, splendor, and grace, would have equally charmed a society more crude or corrupt than their own. Without a doubt, Karakhan would have made the women at the court of Nicholas II swoon. The only thing that might perhaps have been an obstacle to his success with women in a hereditary aristocracy was his obscure origin—even if there are examples of men of obscure origin but of great beauty who have risen up to enjoy the highest worldly successes and to be held in the greatest esteem due to their exceptional good looks. In the early days of my stay in Moscow, when I hadn't yet realized how corrupt the communist aristocracy was, I marveled at the fact that even in Moscow, capital of the Soviet Union, beauty was a crucial factor in a man's success. I had arrived in Moscow believing I would find a tough, intransigent, puritan class in power, which had arisen from the working class and which abided by a Marxist puritanism (not unlike the Calvinist puritanism) in which only revolutionary values and a strict faith in Marxist theory mattered. And then I began to hear talk of this Karakhan, and all the praise and admiration for his moral qualities, for his contribution to the proletarian revolution (Karakhan was a hero, along with Borodin, of the Chinese Communist Revolution and of the Sovietization of Turkestan), every word of it inevitably accompanied by esteem, I would even say *engouement*, or infatuation, for his physical beauty, and I was scandalized, considering it beneath a proletarian society to place such importance on physical attributes.

But this was not the only symptom indicating the general corruption of the communist aristocracy—and in a revolutionary society corrupt habits are a sign of corrupt ideas, of a corrupt revolutionary spirit. In a communist society could beauty as a sign of worth, as a moral quality, ever be reconciled with Marxist austerity? Lenin had died only five years earlier and in that brief period of time the elements of corruption that already existed in communist society had developed, taking the usual forms of revolutionary corruption. My situation was not unlike that of a man who had left Paris during the years of Republican virtue and robust austerity, followed by the Reign of Terror, to find himself living under the Directory. "This is what has become of the puritan revolutionary society that I left only a few short years ago? Are these the same die-hards I left behind, all of them burning to the depths of their souls with the purifying flame of revolutionary zeal?" From the Porte Maillot along the Champs-Élysées on a serene, warm spring day he would hear, just as Chateaubriand had once heard upon returning to Paris, the singing, the music, the intimations of universal joy—all severe symptoms of the universal corruption of revolutionary aristocracy.

Nevertheless, I couldn't help but acknowledge a genuine fellow feeling for Karakhan. I was young, having turned thirty only a few months earlier, and the youthful enthusiasm that had brought me to Moscow to see for myself the heroes of the October Revolution, to mingle with the multitude of workers, with the Russian people, with the communist proletariat of the Soviet Union, naturally pushed me *tout entier*, as Phèdre would say, toward those men who represented in my eyes the genius and the will of the Revolution. Who today would fault me for having had something approaching passionate feelings for Karakhan? Giuliano Sorel was in love with Napoleon. My Napoleon in Moscow was Karakhan. Everyone contents himself with whatever Napoleon he happens to find. I must add that in my passion for Karakhan, for the hero of the Chinese Communist Revolution, there was something of my generation's revenge;

having returned from the war in 1918, we contented ourselves with the petty, pathetic, bourgeois heroes on offer—the likes of D'Annunzio, Mussolini, Barrès, along with Gide, Paul Valéry, and Paul Claudel. What I saw in Karakhan was an anti-bourgeois hero, a son of the Eurasian Steppe, hero of the Revolution, one of those who had knocked down the throne of the czars, flung into the mud the ancient, corrupt, and dysfunctional aristocracy, and brought onto the scene and into power the proletarian masses. Mine was a romantic vision. Should there be a law prohibiting the young from having a romantic vision of men and life? If, rather than Trotsky, Kamenev, or Bukharin, I had chosen Karakhan as my hero, the reason was this: he was the best looking and the least intellectual. There is always something feminine, though pure, in a young man's admiration for a hero that could not be farther from the defective passion of, say, Sorel or Fabrice del Dongo for Napoleon.

Karakhan was a tall, athletic man, his head proudly erect atop two broad shoulders. His facial features were a bit prominent like those of the peoples of the Caucasus—Armenians, Georgians, Ossetians, Circassians—who meet, clash, but never mix in that world of crossroads. Karakhan, in his language from the Eastern Steppe, means "Black Prince." Renowned for the role he played in the Communist Revolution in China, Karakhan was appointed Deputy People's Commissar for Foreign Affairs, and then ambassador in Ankara. The beautiful and mysterious Karakhan (these were the words most often used to describe him) was a middle-aged man, tall and thin, the kind of athletic thin that Pushkin called "Cossack." He had a pale visage, eyes of an indeterminate color, sometimes gray, sometimes very dark, inimitably flashing behind the glass of his spectacles. Contrary to what usually happens to the eyes of those who wear glasses, the lenses increased the magic of Karakhan's brumous yet alert eyes, reminding me of the glassy-eyed gaze of certain ancient Greek statues. He had a black, pointed goatee that made him look like one of the Spanish noblemen bent over the corpse of the Count of Orgaz in El Greco's painting in Toledo. He dressed in the somber English manner, with the modern predilection for grays and blacks that adorned the tailors' shopfronts along Savile Row. His clothes, his ties, his shoes, his shirts, his gloves all came from London by diplomatic courier from the Soviet Embassy in St. James's Square. Sir Edmond Ovey rightly observed that male fashion followed the dominant political ideas and that fashions changed according to whether the liberals or conservatives were in power: "William Pitt certainly didn't dress like William Fox, or Gladstone like Robert Peel." And he marveled that Karakhan dressed in the English style without knowing that by doing so he was wearing the prevailing English political ideas. He was a wonderful tennis player and he showed up every day on the courts at the Spiridonovka Street mansion, or on those at the British Embassy, dressed in an impeccable white flannel suit and wearing those red-rubber-soled white tennis shoes, called "Japanese shoes," that were so fashionable at the time. He played well, his movements fluid, *souple*, his demeanor smiling and calm.

All the diplomatic wives, all the actresses and "beauties" of communist high society, all the wives of the People's Commissars, of the senior officials, of the Soviet generals, flocked to the tennis courts, crowding up against the fence to watch him play. Karakhan had something of the beast about him when he leaped across the red clay, stretched out or flexed his arm, then with a swift stroke dealt a resounding blow to the ball. He would only play with tennis balls he'd had sent from London. He said with an apologetic smile that Soviet tennis balls were inelastic: "In Russia," he said, "whatever touches the ground doesn't bounce," by which I think he may have meant that things here weren't uplifting. Still smiling, he then turned to Lady Ovey, and with his good-natured insolence, with his haughty indifference, and with his perfect Oxford accent, said: "Marx did not foresee the superiority of the English tennis ball over the Soviet tennis ball. Marx lived in Soho and in the East End. In London's East End they don't play tennis, do they?"

To tell the truth, those little speeches, his *bon mots*, his impudent quips troubled me. I would have liked it if he, too, had nurtured a profound disdain for Europe. I came to Moscow convinced that it was an anti-Europe, or even just an alternative Europe, but had the painful realization that the whole Soviet nobility nurtured for Europe (*"pour n'importe quelle Europe*, for whatever Europe," as the French ambassador said) an unconditional admiration. Even in Moscow, as in every other provincial city throughout the world, no one could talk about anything else but Paris, London, New York, Berlin, Vienna, of the theaters, cinemas, restaurants, and nightclubs of Paris, London, etc. In Moscow, Madame Schiaparelli, Lelong, Paquin, Maggy, Rouff, and Molyneux were more famous than Giraudoux, Paul Valéry, or Claudel. In Moscow, one spoke far more frequently of Madame Schiaparelli than of Stalin—and it was no less dangerous to speak of Madame Schiaparelli than to speak of Stalin. In any case, what bothered me about Karakhan wasn't just his snobbishness, his admiration, his *engouement* for Europe, for the elegant life of Europe, but what I considered his cynical, insolent, overly ostentatious, and willful independence of spirit. I sensed in his independent spirit something deeper and more bitter than simple insolence. And it worried me.

Standing just behind Karakhan, observing his every gesture, his every move, coldly judging his every stroke with a light bat of his eyelashes, was the tennis trainer for the Spiridonovka Street mansion, the renowned Julianov, one of the most famous figures during those years in Soviet Moscow. He was tall, blond, and handsome, with blue eyes. All the Russian women of Moscow along with all the foreign diplomats' wives courted him openly in an effort to be favored with a few tennis lessons. Karakhan didn't condescend to acknowledge even with a glance the small chattering crowd of female admirers, and it seemed he didn't even have eyes for Semyonova, on the rare occasions that the famous prima ballerina of the Bolshoi Theater made one of her fleeting visits to the British Embassy or to the Spiridonovka Street mansion, yet it was said that Karakhan was insanely in love with Semyonova. I watched him while he played against Sir William Strang, an advisor to the British ambassador, or against some other embassy secretary. As I watched, I saw opening up behind him, as if Karakhan had been painted onto a canvas, that Novocherkassk landscape that Pushkin described in his *Journey to Erzurum*; a landscape where Europe gradually transforms into Asia, where the forests gradually cede into high grasses, into steppe, into arid windswept hills, and where eagles nest on the mounds of dirt marking the main road, as if guarding the doors to Asia. As I watched him, I also found myself, in that moment, reclining against the soft, lustrous leather seat of an English traveling coach like the young Pushkin who rode in the carriage of his friend —— on his way to Erzurum in Armenia to observe the war of Prince —— against the Turks. And in

Karakhan I saw Europe gradually transforming into Asia, the forests gradually ceding into steppe and arid windswept hills, the yellow horizon opening up under Asia's vast pale sky. Like everyone else, my curiousity about him was unquenchable and I sometimes asked myself whether Karakhan's essential character was determined by unbridled ambition, or by a supremely impudent and, at the same time, lazy disdain for humanity or, perhaps, only for Soviet humanity; and I wondered if beneath his sarcastic disdain he wasn't hiding a morbid passion, a painful longing for the free and individualistic life of the West. I asked myself if his personality hadn't been, in fact, determined by that typical Slavic narcissism that afflicts every character in Russian literature, especially in Dostoevsky, as well as every Russian hero, be he the most humble, the most deprived, the most ignoble, the most corrupt. I, like everyone else, had been struck by the mysterious force that emanated from that enigmatic man who was said to be extraordinarily cruel, and about whom the high-ranking Soviet dignitaries and his friends alike spoke as if he were a secret and mysterious being.

"He is the devil," said Madame Budyonny, wife of Marshal Budyonny, but her meaning of the word devil was not the same as Sollogub's, the author of *Wayward Devil*, nor was it that of Ilyusha in *The Brothers Karamozov*. Rather, she meant it in the Byronic sense of Pushkin, or in the Gogolian sense found in his more popular stories set in St. Petersburg. And I marveled that a communist society could produce such a rare man, so enigmatic, so magic, so, I must say, contrary to the ideal man that Marxism envisioned and produced. He was, this Karakhan, a romantic character. And, as I said, I was stupefied to find in a communist society that had from afar, from Paris, appeared to me to be a product of classicism, of rationalism as envisaged by Marxism, such a deeply romantic character, one Lord Byron or Pushkin would have claimed for his own.

In order to judge a man one must carefully observe his portraits. In a portrait, exposed and helpless, a man must trustingly abandon himself. I had long searched in vain for a portrait of Karakhan, for something other than the usual photograph found in a newspaper archive or in official publications. One evening, I wound up in Semyonova's dressing room at the Bolshoi among the posters for *The Red Poppy*, the great ballet about the Communist Revolution in China in which hundreds of dancers dressed in red—the poppies—at a certain point flood the stage and clash with the army of lotuses, dressed in yellow. I asked Semyonova if she would show me a portrait of Karakhan.

She turned to me, her eyes full of wonder: "Why?"

"I want to see how he wishes to appear to you," I responded.

"He never shows who he is," Semyonova said sadly, while looking at herself in the mirror.

"Not even to you?"

"Why are you asking me this?" Semyonova said. "He shows himself to me even less than to others."

As she spoke she opened a drawer in her dressing table and pulled out a large photograph in a silver frame and tossed it casually onto my lap.

"Take a good look," she said. "You might not recognize him."

It was a picture of Karakhan wearing a *tolstovka*, that *mujik* smock that buttons up the side, neck, and shoulders to which Leo Tolstoy gave his name. Wearing his *tolstovka* Karakhan looked humble, almost shabby; emerging from the gaping collar of the canvas smock his neck appeared thin, similar to Baudelaire's in his famous *toilette de guillotiné*. Karakhan was sitting at the edge of a lake, the lacustrine landscape pale and opaque under a gray sky that gleamed like porcelain and blended into a series of gray tones superposed one on top of the other like layers of skin (the Russian sky has the color, design, and porosity of human skin). It gave to Karakhan's face, to his gaze, to his demeanor, a slightly romantic melancholy completely at odds with the idea we had all formed of him based on his thin-flanked, broad-chested, small-waisted, tall stature, and the defiant, dignified, noble way he had of carrying his head with a relaxed pride, a calm contempt, almost with misgiving and caution, as if he were carrying someone else's head on his shoulders, someone he cared about, or, as Stanisław Patek, the Polish ambassador, said: "As if he were carrying a child on his shoulders." In that landscape, he appeared lost in an immense solitude, or better, he seemed to be imposing on that landscape his sense of solitude. He was the first "lonely" man that I had seen in Soviet Russia, where loneliness was considered a luxury, a form of bourgeois degeneracy, an intellectual condition that was incompatible with Marxism.

Although I am attempting to do so here, it is certainly beyond my station in life to paint a portrait of a man and a society—describe the passions to which the men of that society fall prey—without being one of their kind, without belonging to their society. In my opinion, one of Stendhal's characteristic traits is that he does not belong, feels he doesn't belong to the society or to any of the types of people in the society he describes. Perhaps Stendhal would have known how to draw a portrait of that corrupt, refined, fetid Soviet society that, like the Thermidor society, after having lead the proletarian revolution and founded communism, was fast becoming very comfortable with the privileges of power. He would have felt immediately and profoundly alien to that society: not like a Jacobin, but like, *déjà*, a Bonapartist.

The loneliness of that man, the sense of loneliness that he gave to the landscape, struck me in a strange way: I had expected to find in Russia the type of communist warmed by the embrace of the proletarian masses, a new type of intellectual, not estranged as in Europe from the more meaningful, animalistic life of the masses, but immersed in that life, and therefore at a great distance from the solitude of the European intellectual; at least as far away as the Western intellectual is distant from the life of the masses, from the life, I would say, of the species. And yet here I saw before me the type of man I already knew, that I had already encountered in Pushkin, in Gogol, and above all in Dostoevsky, the solitary man who welcomes his solitude like an addiction, totally dedicated to that particular Slavic narcissism in which a man is entirely pleased with himself, his degradation, his misery, his sins; it is the most typical characteristic of the decadent old Russian society overthrown by the Communist Revolution.

"He's handsome, don't you think?" Semyonova asked while looking at me in the mirror. Her arms were raised to straighten her hair and under the arch of her armpit I suddenly saw Karakhan reflected in the mirror, his watery image slowly emerging from the glass as if it were rising up from the depths of a pond. Startled, I quickly turned around. Hanging on the wall near the armoire was a portrait of Karakhan I hadn't previously noticed. Karakhan stared at me with a hard, hostile gaze. He was wearing a short leather jacket, the kind the communists wore at the time of the insurrection and civil war, earning them the label "leather jackets." A Persian sheepskin cap sank low over his forehead, on one side of his belt hung a holster containing a Mauser, and on the left side a curved dagger from the Caucasus with a silver handle. Behind him was a landscape of tall smoke-stacks, cranes, steel bridges, steel turbines, all in sharp relief against a horizon of black fog; a similar landscape to the Putilov Plant in Leningrad or the —— in Moscow. It was one of those official propaganda portraits in which the lead-ers of the October Revolution liked to appear prominently against a romanticized background of smokestacks and cranes and cogwheels as if to emphasize their participation in the proletarian revolution and their capability as leaders of the Communist Revolution.

I smiled and Semyonova's sharp, needle-like gaze fixed on my smile in the mirror's gleaming glass.

"No," I said, "he's not just handsome. He is beyond hand-some. I am afraid for him."

"You are very kind," Semyonova said, smiling ironically.

It was a view of Karakhan very unlike the one that Ma-dame Bubnova, manager of Torgsin, the store that catered exclusively to foreigners who could pay with valuable cur-rencies, showed me one day. That was a portrait of Karakhan painted by a Chinese artist during the time he and Borodin had set fire to China. All those Eastern traits secretly har-bored in every Russian—that light touch, that mysterious accent, something barely perceptible in certain gestures, and, more than the narrow and oblique cut of the eye, the par-ticular light that brightens their big, dull eyes—were to be found in that portrait of Karakhan, along with an unexpected insolence. The paintbrush of the unknown painter from Canton had depicted Karakhan in a Manchu outfit—a silk tunic with a wolf-fur collar—and he appeared more athletic, more fierce than he did in the portrait I'd seen in the depths of the mirror in Semyonova's dressing room. But it was clear from both those portraits that the revolutionary society that had risen to power through the violence of October 1917 was a hybrid society consisting more of adventurers than of Marxist purists, as they liked to call themselves. In those years the communist aristocracy was very different than the one that would appear a few years later, after the Great Purge, after the success of the First *Pyatiletka*. It was a society made up of members of the *ancien régime*—diplomats, intellectuals, officials who had quickly converted to communism—but also of adventurers who came from the Russian Empire's most distant Asian provinces. There were only a few workers among them and they rarely participated in the social life of the Soviet nobility. You never ran into them at the balls, the dinners, the parties, on the tennis courts, on the Nikolaiev hills, at Moscow's winter sports resort, or on the banks of the Moskva River, at —— where communism's *beau monde* liked to gather with their wives or their mistresses to paddle in canoes along the green riverbanks under Moscow's rose-and-green-tinted sky. I had arrived in Moscow full of enthusiasm, but now many of the heroes of the October Revolution seemed, ah, so different from those I had imagined from afar! They seemed corrupt, trivial, corroded by personal ambition, adventurers who had come from the Eurasian Steppe, or former czarist petty officers, full of the arrogance of a *sousoff,* or soured intellectuals, all of them prideful, their ambition unchecked, fighting amongst themselves to gain supreme power. I hadn't come to Moscow to enjoy myself. But what else could I do but enjoy myself? That society of corrupt and ambitious parvenus wanted to enjoy their power.

Let them dance, then, and have fun. But I was overcome by a profound feeling of sadness whenever I thought of Karakhan. I was afraid for him. And what else? At heart, I was embittered by the fact that he seemed to me to be just like the others—a corrupt and ambitious parvenu. It was as if he had betrayed me and I resented him for it.

The Viennese waltz the orchestra was playing just then wasn't by Strauss. It was one of those lean, arid, pinched waltzes that proclaimed the end of Dollfuss, Schuschnigg, and the Anschluss. All the fatty tissue of the Viennese Habsburg tradition, all the romantic pathos of Vienna between 1905 and 1914, had melted away to expose the smooth, white, naked bones of the waltz. Sir William Strang, advisor to the British ambassador, emerged in that instant from the buffet, Semyonova on his arm. Next to Sir William, tall as he was, Semyonova seemed tiny and very fragile.

"I learned today," began Madame Bubnova, who was standing at a corner of the buffet nearest the door opening onto the terrace, surrounded by actors and actresses from both Stanislavsky's and Meyerhold's theaters, "I learned today Semyonova was indeed invited to London by the people who run Covent Garden."

"Stalin," said Marshal Budyonny's wife, "will never permit her to leave Moscow."

"Semyonova in London! Ha! Ha! Ha!" exclaimed Madame Bubnova, lifting her hand to slap her own cheek. Her hair was thick and black, her forehead pinched and stony, her body athletic. She had big arms and a resonant voice, a bit low but not gruff, even rather pulpy and vibrant like the voice of an old and defunct contralto. Bubnova was the wife of Bubnov, a malicious and deceitful schemer who wished aloud every day for the death of Anatoly Lunacharsky, the Soviet People's Commissar of Education and Culture. And when Lunacharsky did, in fact, die of tuberculosis (of that Russian strain that doesn't outright kill the infected man but stays steadfastly with him far into old age and then follows the octogenarian into the grave), Bubnov took his job.

"And why not?" said Madame Yegorova, the wife of General Yegorov, Chief of Staff of the Red Army. Madame Yegorova was a petite brunette, very beautiful, clad in soft flab like a pearl in a velvet case, and, like a pearl, she had a damp, cold listlessness, a savage delicacy, a multishaded gray sheen of indifference, a distracted, distant callousness. "Why not? Semyonova is no better or worse than many others."

"Oh, yes, you're right. I do know much worse!" said Madame Bubnova.

"I find her charming," Madame Budyonnaya said innocently.

Madame Bubnova laughed and Madame Yegorova threw her a scornful glance. Madame Yegorova exhibited the most profound contempt for the "beauties" of Soviet society, especially for Madame Lunacharskaya, whose name appeared daily in the society newspapers and tabloids. At the same time, she displayed a conspicuous soft spot for Semyonova and Madame Budyonnaya, perhaps in order to lend greater significance and emphasis to her contempt for the others.

"She'll conquer London just as she has conquered Moscow," Yegorova said, her gaze tracking Semyonova and Sir William Strang as they glided across the marble floor to the slow rhythm of the waltz.

"My dear," said Bubnova, "she can have all the success she likes. I don't give a hoot. Since I don't dance, I can hardly be jealous."

"I don't dance either," said Madame Budyonnaya innocently, "and yet I still often feel jealous of Semyonova. She's so beautiful, so graceful, and she dances so well! She's a ... she's a ..."

"Butterfly," Madame Bubnova said laughing.

"That's it, a butterfly," said Madame Budyonnaya, blushing faintly.

Madame Budyonnaya was a small, busty, pleasantly cross brunette. Whenever Florinsky spoke of Madame Budyonnaya he laughed maliciously and stretched out his hand to show how short she was, then rounded his arms to show how rotund and fat she was. "Marshal Budyonny loves fillies," he would say, laughing and pulling his small red head down between his shoulders like a tortoise, "Neigh! Neigh! Neigh!" But there was nothing ridiculous about Madame Budyonnaya. She was a small woman, a little thing who'd come from nothing and had remained modest. Marshal Budyonny, during his vertiginous career, as he rose from noncommissioned officer in the czar's Dragoon Regiment to Marshal of the Red Army's cavalry, from *sousoff* to Murat, had not been able to raise his wife even one rung on the ladder of pride, arrogance, and vulgarity. Madame Budyonnaya had remained a simple woman, perhaps a little stunned by her husband's good fortune, a bit skeptical, and positively ebullient over the tacky jewelry she wore on her ears, neck, and fingers.

"That's it, a butterfly," said the faintly blushing Madame Budyonnaya, and she smiled.

"She won't have much success in London," Madame Bubnova said in her deep, sonorous voice. "The divine Pavlova is still immortal in London. Have you been to London?" she added, turning to me. "I remember seeing Pavlova's memorabilia on display in the Museum of London on St. James's Street. Semyonova can't compete with Pavlova's ghost."

"I also saw Pavlova's ballet slippers," I said, "the ones that divine ballerina wore in *The Dying Swan*. The entire Museum of London seems to revolve around that pair of white satin ballet slippers. But Pavlova's star sparkled in the shadow of a throne. She brought the wintry splendor of the czar's throne from white St. Petersburg to the throne of St. James's Palace in London. The splendor of her legend is immense, bold, and pure, but it cannot stand up to the red, ruby-blooded splendor that Semyonova would bring to London. Pavlova was the King's ballerina. Semyonova is the proletarian ballerina, the ballerina of the proletariat."

"Ha, ha!" said Madame Lunacharskaya, who had joined us amidst an entourage of young officers and Tairov's young actors. "Don't let Semyonova hear this unless you want her to poke your eyes out. The divine Semyonova a proletarian ballerina! Ha! Ha! Ha!"

"Forgive me," I said, "I didn't mean to ..."

"Don't apologize," Madame Yegorova said. "In Russia the word proletarian still hasn't acquired a negative connotation. But not everyone among us loves it, that's all."

"You're wrong, *daragaia*," Madame Lunacharskaya said. "My dear, I love to be called a proletarian. Ha! Ha! Ha!"

"Ha! Ha! Ha!" Bubnova laughed.

"Ha! Ha! Ha!" shouted the young officers and actors.

"But why shouldn't we like it?" said Madame Budyonnaya naively. "Thankfully, we are all proletarians! What is there to laugh about?"

"Ha! Ha! Ha!" Bubnova exclaimed, "What is there to laugh about? But my dear..."

"Are you finding this amusing, Signor Malaparte?" Yegorova suddenly asked me.

"Highly amusing," I said. "In Europe, too, when a woman has the good fortune to come into possession of a diamond ring she suddenly finds herself ashamed of her proletarian origins. Here, thank the Lord," I added, "not one of you is ashamed of your origins. It's proof of good taste, which pleases me."

"Look at that beautiful pearl necklace," Madame Bubnova said. "It's the first time she's worn it. And I can assure you she didn't buy it at Torgsin's."

"It comes from Paris," said Madame Lunacharskaya, "from Cartier."

"And you all call her a proletarian ballerina?" Bubnova said laughing, slapping herself lightly on the cheek with the palm of her hand, as she often did to show her amazement.

"Will you offer me a whiskey?" Yegorova asked me, leaning her hand on my arm. We moved off from the collection of "beauties," and discreetly slipped along the edge of the ballroom until we reached the buffet. I noticed that Litvinov, Lunacharsky, and Marshal Tukhachevsky were absent that evening. Sitting at a table in the bar were the Italian ambassador, Cerruti; the Polish ambassador, Patek; Steyer, an official from the Commissariat of Foreign Affairs; and the minister of Latvia, ———. Madame Yegorova and I sat down at a table and the barman brought us two Ancient Reserve whiskies.

"Didn't you know?" the minister of Latvia said, getting up from his table and going to the bar, "They've arrested Kamenev."

Madame Yegorova remained impassive. She was a little pale and I noticed that she carefully placed her glass on the marble bar.

"What's strange about that?" I asked.

"Nothing's strange about it," the minister of Latvia said, a little surprised, "but I think it's very significant. Do you know who Kamenev was?"

"He was one of Lenin's oldest friends," I said. "So what?"

"Well, it's terrifying!" exclaimed the minister of Latvia.

Looking around the room, I said, "All these men and women will end up in prison."

"And you think that's amusing?"

"They are a bunch of traitors," I said, "a bunch of careerists, parvenus, and profiteers of the Revolution. They had it coming."

"But Kamenev was one of the leaders of the Revolution!" exclaimed the minister of Latvia.

"Is that so? And now he can suck on it," I said, and laughed.

The minister of Latvia stared into my eyes for a few seconds, then turned to Yegorova and leaning over said in a whisper: "*C'est a vous que je donnais cette nouvelle.* This news was for you."

"I agree with Malaparte," Yegorova said indifferently, and coldly turned toward the ballroom.

At that moment, Sir Edmond Ovey approached Sir William Strang and whispered something in his ear. Sir William Strang abruptly pulled away from Semyonova, then spoke to her and bowed as if he were apologizing. He then offered her his arm and they headed through the dancing couples toward the bar. In the meantime, men and women had gathered at every door and were staring in with expressions of astonishment, even fear. Ambassador Cerruti, Ambassador

Patek, Steyer, Tairov, the minister of Latvia, the French ambassador, Herbette, the German ambassador, Baron von Dirksen, and the other members of the diplomatic corps had all risen from their tables and chairs, arriving from all over the place to peer in from the terrace door, from the door to the bar, from the door to the *fumoir*. Groups formed and then immediately disbanded, others separated off and whispered amongst themselves, and slowly everyone began to turn his or her gaze toward Florinsky, Chief of Protocol of the People's Commissariat for Foreign Affairs. He was standing in the middle of the room looking pale and smiling at Semyonova, who was resting against the bar, alone, occasionally bringing a glass to her lips, her gaze fixed on the door that led from the ballroom to the entrance hall. Slowly, instinctually, Lunacharskaya, Bubnova, Budyonnaya, all the "beauties" of the Soviet world, came together and were gradually joined by the crowd of young officers and actors. The ballroom was empty, the orchestra continued to play quietly, a tepid wind carrying the scent of leaves and grass came in through the open windows. Moscow's spring entered the room with its dulcet violence, its dulcet smell of a pregnant woman. Through the trees in the park, damp and swollen with indistinct sounds and vague aromas, one could see the church domes and the Kremlin towers lit up with electric lights, and red flags waving from the Armory Tower. The vast sky, pink and green, was inundated by the moon's antique silver glow. The Moscow spring was entering through the windows with the dulcet, tepid violence of a pregnant woman. Kamenev, Lenin's friend, one of the triumvirate Lenin had brought to power along with Zinoviev and Bukharin, had been arrested. The Great Purge had begun. The terror commenced with the arrest of the peaceful Kamenev with his gray goatee, his myopic eyes behind the glistening glass of his spectacles. After Trotsky, Kamenev. The orchestra softly played the melody from a Viennese waltz. Jewels sparkled on the necks and plump fingers of the Soviet "beauties."

Suddenly the door opened and Karakhan stood on the threshold. He was paler than usual. His tall figure stopped for a moment, then he slowly made his way to Semyonova, still leaning on the bar. He bowed, kissed her hand, pulled her toward him, and gradually abandoned himself to the music of the waltz. They were alone in the vast ballroom. Smiling, Yegorova put her hand on my arm and whispered, "*Qu'ils sont beaux!* How beautiful they are!"

In that moment Florinsky, also smiling, came up to me: "*Vous ne trouvez pas,*" he said, "*qu'il ressemble* ... Don't you think he looks like ..."

Gradually other couples began to dance. Madame Lunacharskaya abandoned herself in the arms of a young officer from the Proletarsky Division, laughed carelessly, her beautiful face raised, her nostrils dilated. Sir Edmond Ovey bowed before Madame Yegorova and led her onto the ballroom floor. Steyer came over and offered me a cigarette.

"I need a breath of fresh air. May I accompany you to your hotel?"

"It's a beautiful evening," I said. And I headed toward the door, Steyer next to me, a veil of sweat pearling over his pale face.

2

IT WAS nearly dawn, spring having cut short the nights, and already a diffuse white light was spreading to the east behind the Kremlin's towers. Walking next to Steyer, I watched that distant patch of white sky while the first birds flew through the dawn's murky air. They were quiet birds and seemed almost afraid of chirping as they darted among the rooftops, clustering together and then dispersing again. Meanwhile, as happens at dawn, I saw the sky lift slowly above the rooftops, as if a giant piece of paper were glued to them and was unrolling, rising, and receding into the distance, like in certain films when the movie camera raises up, the rooftops recede, and the sky's edges roll into a river of light, of time, of sounds, flowing and gradually expanding between the rooftops and the camera lens. It was as if a knife blade were slicing down between the buildings, separating and distancing them from one another, creating a gap full of light, and the city began to wake up, and waking up it took shape and became aware of itself, of its true form, and over there a chimney emerged, there a tree, there a dome, there a tower, until slowly an immense population of rooftops, windows, towers, and domes gathered under a vast, remote white sky and I heard, almost suddenly, the birds chirping, the river flowing slowly between its banks green with trees and black with coal.

We were in front of the Cathedral of Christ the Savior. From our elevated position Moscow appeared enormous and smoldering under the white sky. The Kremlin, spread out before us, was a little lower than we were, and the screech of a tram laboriously climbing toward us on the wide street rather disturbed the serenity and stillness of the landscape; it seemed almost as if a metal saw were cutting down the towers and the domes, each one toppling into the bluish mist rising from the river amidst a whirl of crocuses illuminated by the first rays of the rising sun. Seen from that elevated place, the Moskva River tended to appear much wider than it actually was; and the Kremlin, with its crenellated walls of red brick, its towers rising above the gates, its green, yellow, red, and turquoise church domes, was not reflected in the river, as if the Moskva were a sheet of opaque metal, of zinc. And this gave the view a harsh quality, like in an old German print where the castles, villages, cities, and mountains are never reflected in the rivers; as if among humans, manmade things, and nature there was an ancient hatred, an inability to coexist; as if humans, the river, the towers, and the water were made of different material in the eye of the engraver.

The hills rising on the far side of the river—the Sparrow Hills and the Hill of Bows—slowly disentangled themselves from the night's undertow, and those hills, resembling a set of hard black gums, blocked the horizon to the south and west, then slowly softened, changing from black to pink— Manet's black, Manet's pink—until a gentle tremor of green penetrated that pink and that black, and forests of acacia and birch trees appeared, expanding across the sky. On the far bank, in the Dorogomilovo District, the first trams began running along the Moskva River, and the rumble of the first trucks crossing the bridges resounded in the distance, stirring up tiny green and rose flakes from the gray stone quays along the river, from the red bricks of the buildings, from the glistening asphalt of the roads. A car passed near us, a particularly shrill laugh reached our ears, and I had just enough time to catch a glimpse of Madame Lunacharskaya amidst some officers as they drove quickly by.

"Did you know Kamenev?" Steyer suddenly asked me.

A great breath exhaled from the city as if from a sick cow; a hot, thick breath that smelled of grass and wet leaves. It was the sleep of an immense proletarian city, the sleep of workers. A worker gives off a certain odor when he sleeps, which is not the odor of filth, promiscuity, or poverty. It is the odor of dreams. A dream has a smell, just as wakefulness does. A man who sleeps has a different smell than a man who is awake. Workers' dreams are different than those of the bourgeoisie. A worker doesn't dream about machines or bread or a life of luxury. This is the petit-bourgeois meaning of "dream." Those who truly desire luxury and an easy life are the petit bourgeois. A poor man who works, toils, suffers, and struggles doesn't dream about American films or a luxurious life; he dreams of grass, the countryside, fields, and simple human things. Or he dreams of machines. He dreams of a poverty that is different from his own, a poverty he knows, but as master not slave. He dreams of a poor world, not a rich world. Poor, but where justice reigns. The worker does not know what to do with liberty. It is not a necessity for him. Liberty for the worker doesn't make sense; justice makes sense. The worker wants power, not liberty. He dreams of power, justice, and a poverty that is simple, childish, familiar, a poverty that is his legacy and with which he can organize his own culture, his own society, his own way of life. The Western worker dreams of riches. His revolution is personal. The Russian worker doesn't include personality in his dreams. His is a collective dream, a dream of the masses. All workers dream the same things at the same time. The workers on a *kolkhoz* dream about life on the *kolkhoz*, but elevated to a higher level. In his sleep, a worker is more conscious than when he is awake. His sleep resembles a soldier's sleep. A soldier dreams of war. In his dreams he has a greater sense of responsibility than when he is awake. I felt solidarity with the dreams of this immense proletarian city. Like the fluff on a wool carder, the dawn emerged from behind the wall of the horizon, and the city slowly awoke. What did it matter to me that her awakening was cruel, violent, and a terrible struggle? I was looking for sincerity and coherence in the lives of the people, in their awakened existence. The worker is tormented by the horror of betrayal. We men of the West can't understand the unconscious accords that have formed between the working masses and their revolutionary leaders. The torment that oppresses the masses in a revolution is their obsession with betrayal. The revolutionary masses are like soldiers who are always afraid of their leaders' betrayal. The first cry of soldiers when the enemy looms over them is: "Treachery!" They don't feel so much vanquished by the enemy as betrayed by their leaders. This rapport of mistrust is unilateral. Leaders are never afraid of being betrayed. But the masses are. The people have an acute, sensitive, ineluctable instinct. They feel betrayal as soon as it arrives. The Russian people felt their betrayal by the ruling class. The corruption of that revolutionary class was evident. When Lunacharsky's wife passed by in a car, then descended from the car in front of the Bolshoi Theater covered in expensive furs and jewels, the people felt and saw their betrayal sparkling in those glittering jewels, in those precious stones. I felt it was all doomed—all that rot, that corrupt class, that great jumble of prostitutes, pederasts, actors, actresses, libertines, and profiteers, of Nepmen and kulaks, of black-market merchants, of Soviet functionaries who bought their clothes in London and Paris, and imitated the fashions in New York and Berlin (a recent fad was for thick cigars, the kind that dangled from the plump lips of capitalists in Hamburg and on Wall Street as seen in the drawings of Grosz). I knew democratic, intellectual, bourgeois Europe would cry crocodile tears for the fate of that corrupt class. I laughed to myself while imagining that class up against the wall, Madame Lunacharskaya stripped of her jewels and furs, sent to perform in the theaters of the *rabotniki* clubs in some distant region of Asia. I laughed to myself thinking about the exiled Trotsky. Why should I have cried? What did Trotsky think would happen if he lost? The hateful thing, in my opinion, about Trotsky wasn't that he killed thousands upon thousands of the bourgeoisie, of counter-revolutionaries, of czarist officers, nor that he killed them with bad feelings—good feelings do not make for a good revolution—but I reproached him for having placed himself at the head of a political faction that identified itself for some strange reason with the corrupt Soviet ruling class of the years 1929–30. Behind his rhetoric lurked the pederast, the prostitute, the enriched bourgeoisie, the petty officers, all those who exploited the October Revolution. Trotsky's sin was not that he had placed himself at the head of a proleteriat faction, but at the head of the most corrupt faction comprised of the revolutionary proletarian's exploiters. Yes, of course, Kamenev was a harmless man, but one doesn't have the right to be a harmless man when among the leaders of a revolution. Kamenev, like Trotsky, wanted to prevent the emergence of a new proletarian class, a puritan class, and instead to preserve in power the corrupt class who wallowed in luxury and pleasures. The sum total of Trotskyism is found in its strange, painful, paradoxical connection with the corrupt ruling class. A few years on, twelve years later, when on a warm, fragrant morning in June we entered Russia with submachine guns in hand, I felt that the only circumstance in which Soviet Russia might have lost the war was if Trotsky had led on horseback the German armed forces followed by a retinue of priests waving sacred flags, bearing sacred icons and crucifixes, and it wouldn't have mattered if the priests were real or fake. The people were expecting something different from the communists, a solemn and spectacular return of the old Russia, but an old Russia represented by new men, Marxists, communists, revolutionaries, and not that thing similar to communism presenting itself as Nazism. Stalin won the war against Hitler the day Jacques Mornard killed Trotsky with a blow of an ice axe to the skull. That day Hitler lost the war. It was Mornard who won the war, not Marshal Zhukov. If Trotsky had entered Russia in June 1941 during those beautiful warm Ukrainian days at the head of an army of priests in sacred vestments intoning ancient litanies, accompanied by a crowd of soldiers and officers, the entire Ukrainian population would have come out to greet him, since Trotsky was the counterrevolution, and only a counterrevolution could overthrow communist Russia—or could have. Moscow's entire ruling class would have joined Trotsky's cause since the bureaucracy in a communist regime is and always will be

Trotskyite. We would have seen a truly formidable upset, the people would have followed Trotsky, and Russia would have become, under the name of communism, a fascist Russia led by a kind of Jewish Mussolini who was pompous, bombastic, a speechifier, polemicist, thunderer, militarist, and hedonist surrounded by a small court of the decorated and bejeweled. Since Trotskyism is fascism—and that is mostly because communism can't emerge in a country, as in Europe, where the cities are ancient—it isn't able to centralize itself around a city. In the same way the ultimate goal of communism is to be a society without a state, it also aims to be a nation without cities. Wherever there is a city, communism rapidly expires. If you were to make Paris, London, or Rome communist capitals, communism would rapidly degenerate into fascism, into Trotskyism.

This was what I was thinking as I walked along next to Steicher. And I didn't give a damn about his present concerns, I didn't give a damn that Kamenev had been exiled, I didn't give a damn that all those corrupt people would one day be sent into exile or buried in a mass grave. What mattered to me was the manifest emergence of a new revolutionary class and I was astonished by the Trotskyites who had deluded themselves into believing they could *entraver*, or impede, the rise of that new puritanical, cruel, hard, inflexible, monstrous class.

3

STILL the Holy City of Russia then, the ancient and noble Threshold to the Orient, the Third Rome, Moscow was the capital of an immense "continent" of peasants, soldiers, clerks, students, Cossacks, Jews, and Tatars controlled by a small army of pale and reticent communist workers. In the Kremlin, on the ancient throne of orthodox czars, sat a small man with short arms and shiny black eyes. His name was Stalin. Stalin's throne was surrounded by the new Marxist nobility— a greedy, vicious, dissolute clan of communist boyars, parvenus, profiteers of the Revolution, ballerinas, actresses, and *merveilleuses* proletarians who had replaced the *ancien régime* and who, just a short time later, following horrendous and mystifying trials, would succumb to the lead of firing squads in the courtyard of the Lubyanka.

At the base of the Kremlin wall in Red Square, inside the great wooden mausoleum designed by Shchusev, Lenin's mummy, small and shrunken like the mummy of a child, was slowly rotting. Periodically, German specialists showed up from Berlin to empty, scrape out, and disinfect the shell of that precious crustacean, that sacred mummy, the porcelain white face lit up by red freckles veiled by a greenish mold-like sweat. "Lenin's skull has the same shape as Balfour's," H. G. Wells once wrote. In the crystal coffin (in which he had been enclosed to protect him from mice who had already nibbled on his ear and on the toes of one foot), Lenin slept smiling in the cold, brutal glow of the electric spotlights, his left hand gently raised to his chest, the palm of his right hand lightly resting on his hip. Amidst the red flags of the Communist International and the Paris Commune of 1871, he slept with half-closed eyes, an ironic smile on his lipstick-dabbed lips. As they filed past the glass coffin day and night, the Russian people wept.

Moscow, in these years, was still the old orthodox city of a thousand churches, and still hiding in the damp green shadows of the thousand green, yellow, red, and turquoise majolica-clad domes were the old wooden houses spared from the fire of 1812. The new gigantic cement, steel, and glass buildings, the pride of Soviet architecture, hadn't yet replaced those houses once owned by the old boyars and rich Muscovite merchants. Near the Arbat, around the *Sobachaya Ploschad*, or Canine Square, the imaginary houses of the characters from *War and Peace*—Count Bezukhov, Prince Bolkonsky, Prince Kuragin, Marya Dimitrievna—were still standing. Still visible at no. 52 Povarskya Street, today called Vorovsky Street, was the Dolgorukov Princes' mansion, described by Tolstoy as Count Rostov's home. Squads of workers, however, had already begun to demolish church domes and dilapidated convent walls with the indifferent, dogged haste of their pickaxes. Only a few days earlier the construction laid out in the First Five-Year Plan had been solemnly launched and in the green air the smell of coal and iron from the first *Pyatiletka* was already mixing with the warm smell of spring.

I often wandered the streets of Moscow in search of the imaginary houses of Andrei Bolkonsky, Pierre Bezukhov, and Marya Dimitrievna (Marya Dimitrievna lived on Old Stables Street near Podnovinsky Square), or I would go say hello to Scriabin's pale ghost at no. 11 Nikolopeskovsky Lane, or converse with Gogol's melancholic shadow in the house at no. 7 Prechistensky Boulevard, today called Gogolevsky Boulevard, or leave my calling card for the elegant ghost of Princess Gagarin at her beautiful mansion designed by Bovet near Novinsky Boulevard. Sometimes I went to the Tolstoy Museum on Krapotkin Street and sat for hours on end in the seventh room; a little room called the "Astapovo room," an exact replica of the small waiting room in the tiny Astapovo Station where Tolstoy, realizing death was upon him, had fled from his home, Yasnaya Polyana, and where he'd spent long agonizing hours waiting, as Gorky put it, for the final train. I liked to wait long hours in that small room where Tolstoy had died, in that tiny station without stationmaster or train tracks, waiting for a train, for that same final train, the exact time of arrival unknown even to the museum guard. And some evenings I would go and sit on the edge of the fountain in the middle of Sobachaya Ploschad in front of no. 12, where Pushkin had lived for a long time after returning from exile in Bessarabia. Staring at his closed window, I would see the thin, transparent hand of his pale ghost pull back the curtains.

At that time, thick white clouds of dust hung heavily over the streets of Moscow, which had been smashed up by pickax blows and were loud with the cranes' screeching iron chains and the hoarse wheezing of cars. I walked through those dust clouds and repeated to myself a Russian word that I had learned in those days, an old Russian word that I heard ring across everyone's lips. I said to myself, "*Naplivaiu,*" meaning, "I spit on it." It was a dear old Russian word expressing an ancient and noble national Russian tradition. "*Naplivaiu*," I said to myself and smiled. "*Naplivaiu*," everyone around me said, smiling sadly.

One could feel in the appearance of both the city and its inhabitants the grandiose and heroic push toward modernity that so profoundly transformed the Russian spirit from that moment on. The entire Russian population slowly turned its face—a pale, gaunt face bathed in sweat—toward the West. Hanging across the streets were immense red canvas banners on which were written in large white letters: LONG LIVE LENIN. LONG LIVE COMMUNISM. LONG LIVE THE PYATILETKA. Still visible on the soft gray octopus-like flesh of people's faces were signs of terrible suffering from the past years, from the "naked years" as Boris Pilnyak called them, the years of civil war, hunger, epidemics, massacres, when there appeared in the people's eyes the first glimmer of fear that the *Pyatiletka* and the triumph of communism promised to the Russian population would cause terrible suffering. On the red canvas banners that hung across Petrovka Street, Tverskaya Street, Bolshaya Dimitrovka Street, and Arbat Street I read, LONG LIVE LENIN. LONG LIVE COMMUNISM. LONG LIVE THE PYATILETKA. And I said to myself, "*Naplivaiu*." Everyone around me said, "*Naplivaiu*," and smiled sadly, spitting on the ground.

The thought that the Russian people suffered additionally for me was repugnant to my conscience. I said, "*Naplivaiu*" and spit on the ground because my dignity as a human, as a civilized man, as a European was offended at the thought that perhaps the Russian people were also suffering for me, endured hunger, fear, slavery, and death also for me, for my freedom, for my future, for my health. I could never bear the thought that another suffered for me. This thought had always profoundly humiliated me. I am a Christian because I accept that Christ suffered for me, but no one else except him. I allow only Christ to suffer for me. That a Christian must accept that others suffer for him, this is what repulses me about Christianity. It was during that time in Moscow that I began to reflect upon my Christianity. I couldn't bear the thought that the Russian people, Russian children, men and women all over Russia were suffering for me. Like an intolerable privilege, the enormous pride of the Russian people profoundly humiliated me. For the first time in my life, I welcomed as natural and definite the idea, absurd to the Christian conscience, that suffering was noble, pure, and *useful* only if it is gratuitous, only if it serves no purpose, helps no one, not even he who suffers, only if it is an end in itself, only if it is absolutely *useless*. Sometimes, when I was not able to distance myself from the necessity of suffering the Russian Revolution as a fact of my conscience, as my own personal experience, I had the suspicion that communism perhaps contained an element of Christian truth. But each time I was, as usual, overcome with repugnance at the idea that Christ hides in every man who suffers for others. And a strange question arose in my mind: "What is Christ called in Soviet Russia? In the USSR where is Christ hiding? What is the name of the Russian Christ, the communist Christ?" I told myself, "*Naplivaiu*" and spit on the ground. Among all the problems facing the Christian conscience in Soviet Russia, the most constant, the most difficult is under what likeness, under what name Christ hides. It is the problem that both Patriarch Tikhon, in his spiritual testament, and Metropolitan Sergius of Nizhny Novgorod, in his famous declaration professing the Russian Orthodox Church's absolute loyalty to the Soviet Union, tried to resolve a short time earlier. The name of the Russian Christ, of the communist Christ is *Naplivaiu*.

Thanks to the courtesy of Lunacharsky, the Soviet People's Commissar of Education and Culture, I spent the better part of my days in the Lenin Institute library, not yet open to the public. My young secretary, Marika S., a Georgian girl from Tiflis, who was recommended to me by Madame Kameneva, the director of Intourist and Trotsky's sister, considerably lightened and facilitated my work, translating for me Lenin's unpublished writings and letters, consulting the official documents related to the days of the October Revolution and the role played by Lenin and Trotsky in those memorable events, helping me to collect the invaluable material I relied on to write *Technique du coup d'état* and *Le bonhomme Lénine.* At the time, I did not foresee that those two books would, in Italy, condemn me to many months in the Regina Coeli prison in Rome, and to five years of exile on the island of Lipari. If I had foreseen such a thing, I certainly wouldn't have renounced writing them. It is right for men to pay for what they do and for what they think, for all the good or ill they do, even if their suffering does no one any good, not even themselves. No man is immune to this law: suffering is absolutely useless and is precisely why it is necessary for men to suffer.

"It's useless to be Christians. And yet it is necessary to be Christians," I would say now and again to the writer Mikhail Afanasyevich Bulgakov, the celebrated author of the play *Days of the Turbins*, who often accompanied me during my wanderings across the city.

"*Pas la peine*," Bulgakov responded, "Not worth it."

"Humans need to suffer," I said. "Christianity is suffering."

"One is not a Christian only because he suffers," Bulgakov

responded. "One is a Christian precisely because he refuses to suffer uselessly. One must suffer for something. For others, above all."

"Do you think then that the communists are also Christians? That in order to be a Christian all one needs to do is suffer for others?"

"Yes of course they are Christians. They are *also* Christians, those bastards," Bulgakov responded.

"One is a Christian because he accepts suffering uselessly," I said. "Didn't mankind, perhaps, wish for their Christ, didn't they summon him here on earth? So they should suffer for it! But they must suffer uselessly if they want to be true Christians."

"*Pas la peine*," Bulgakov responded, wiping a hand across his swollen, pale face.

Herein lies the problem: Did the people invoke Christ, summon him to earth? Or did Christ descend to earth without being summoned by mankind? The entire question of communism consists of this: Did mankind summon him, did they really want him to come? Or not? How much more just and meaningful it would be if mankind hadn't wanted him to come, if communism had arrived on earth against the will of man. An undesired suffering, an ordeal dreaded, not asked for. Necessary, but not desired. A fatality.

"*Pas le peine*," said Bulgakov.

At that same time, at the Stanislavsky Theater in Moscow, Bulgakov's play *Days of the Turbins*, based on his famous novel *The White Guard*, was playing, having recently been put on in Berlin by Piscator with immense success. The last act takes place in Kiev in Turbin's house where Turbin's brothers and their friends, all officials faithful to the czar, gather for the last time before going to their deaths. In the last scene, as the measured tread of the Bolshevik troops entering the city is heard from afar, then nearing, the song of "The Internationale" growing ever louder, ever stronger, the Turbin brothers and their friends sing the anthem "God Save the Czar." Every evening, when the Turbin brothers and their companions sang on stage "God Save the Czar," an extended shudder spread throughout the audience, and barely stifled sobs arose intermittently in the darkened room. As the curtain fell and the lights suddenly went up, the proletarian crowd packed into the orchestra seats quickly turned to scrutinize the eyes of the spectators. Many eyes were red, many faces lined with tears. Shrill cries of scorn and threats arose from the orchestra: "So you're crying, eh? Are you crying for the czar? Ha! Ha! Ha!" and an evil chuckle spread throughout the theater.

"In which of your play's characters is Christ hiding?" I asked Bulgakov. "Which character is called Christ?"

"Christ has no name in my play," Bulgakov responded with a tremor of fear in his voice. "Christ is by now a useless character in Russia. It's useless to be Christians in Russia. We don't need Christ anymore."

"You're afraid of saying his name," I said. "You are afraid of Christ."

"Yes, I am afraid of Christ," Bulgakov responded in a whisper, staring at me with fear all over his face.

"You are all afraid of Christ," I said to Bulgakov, giving his arm a strong squeeze. "Why are you afraid of Christ?"

I loved Bulgakov. I had loved him ever since the day I saw him crying silently while sitting on a bench in Revolution Square watching Moscow's throngs pass before him, that pathetic, meager crowd of pale, dirty faces bathed in sweat, their flesh moist and soft like that of an octopus. High above the rooftops, in an antique silver sky, rose a pale, lifeless moon resembling the face of a drowned man emerging from clear, deep water. The crowd that passed before Bulgakov had the same gray, inchoate face, the same extinguished watery eyes of the monks, hermits, and beggars who swarm behind the Virgin in icons. The sky shone like an icon's silver encasement, and the moon's glow was just like the pale glow of the Virgin's face on an ancient icon rising from the clear deep water of a spring sky.

"Christ hates us," Bulgakov said in a whisper, staring at me with a terrified expression.

It was, at the time, Easter week in Russia. But the bells were silent. At the tops of the bell towers of Moscow's thousands of churches, the church bells hung silently, their thick clappers dangling like tongues from the heads of cows hung out to dry in the sun. In the greenish-blue tinged white sky, already beginning to crack like a sheet of ice with the first warm breath of spring, the great green eye of spring was slowly opening. I walked next to Bulgakov and felt someone watching me, felt the stare of that great green eye slowly opening in the sky, felt the gaze of spring blowing on my neck, warm like the breath of a cow.

Moscow's sky is not like the one in the old paintings by Simon Ushakov in the Church of Our Lady of Georgia in Kitay-gorod, crammed with wrinkled and decrepit cherubs, with Christs whose faces are emaciated and wooden, like those Spanish Christs with hair and beards made with real hair and real skin, with human teeth, and real human fingernails embedded into the ends of wooden fingers, their glass eyes shining like human eyes. This wasn't like the green sky of the popular ancient icons scattered with red and yellow angels, fluttering around a yellow sun fringed with eyelashes like a human eye. It was more like a spring sky by Chagall, when the warm spring breeze begins to melt the glassy, icy winter air encircling the houses, the trees, the animals. Above the Moskva, above the *Poklonnaya Gory* or Hill of Bows, above the *Vorobyovy Gory* or Sparrow Hills the sky was a landscape of white clouds and green grass, crowded with turquoise cows, donkeys playing the violin, horses with great slanting eyes gaping at the horizon; and the warm breath of the cow-spring was already liberating from their glass prison the houses, the trees, the hills, the animals, immured in the cold, glistening air like fish caught in ice.

High on the dome of St. Basil's Cathedral, that pale glow the color of shrimp in clear spring streams diffusing around him, a naked Christ rose slowly into the sky, his pale gills fluttering like a shrimp in love. And this was the Russian Christ of Easter, sweet and tender, with a delicate carapace, who in the painting of Metropolitan Alexius in the Church of St. Nicholas the Wonderworker in Hamovniky rises slowly from the green waters of the sky above the Kremlin towers. He was the shrimp-Christ, surrounded by green fish with human faces, by ancient icons from the Preobrazhenie Gospodne Church, or the Church of the Holy Transfiguration in the Novodevichy Convent. A scent of water, grass, and fish, which is the scent of the Russian spring, sweetened the air in the squares and streets of the Krasnaya Presnya, Hamovniky, Dorogomilovo, and Zamoskvoretsky districts.

The trees were already thick with new, shyly rustling soft-green leaves that were laughing and chatting amongst themselves in the warm wind that blew off the river. Passing through the sweet air were high-pitched fragile sounds, female laughter, long laments, the buzz of bees, a shrill sigh of violins, the swishing of bare feet on the grass, an exchange of shouts in the lazy and musical accent of the Muscovite. Every once in a while, the sudden, violent sound of an accordion interfered, accompanied by a flash of red lips that were like a slice of watermelon, as in that painting by Picasso or Braque of a funeral procession where a young Jewish girl pours her laughter into the arms of her fiancé lying in a coffin painted black. On rooftops and balconies, or sitting on windowsills with their legs dangling in the air, pairs of lovers with red hair laughed while eating sunflower seeds, spitting the black shells into air the color of watermelon pulp. The blaze of a wedding party erupted at the end of the street and open carriages drawn by white, green, yellow, and red horses went galloping past with a furious clatter of bells. Flocks of doves flew with a great roar of their wings around the domes of St. Basil's Cathedral and of the Cathedral of Christ the Savior, around Sukharevskaya Bashnya and the Kremlin's crenellated walls.

From the loudspeakers hanging on the electric lampposts in front of the church doors came the thick voice of Demyan Bedny, head of the League of Atheists, of the *Bezbozhniks* (the Godless), and author of *The New Testament Without Shortcomings of the Evangelist Demyan*, which recounts the story of a certain Christ born in a brothel to a young prostitute named Maria. Bedny shouted: "Comrades! Christ is a counterrevolutionary, an enemy of the proletarian, a saboteur, a dirty Trotskyite who sold out to global capitalism! Ha! Ha! Ha!" From the wall next to the Iberian Chapel at the gate to the Red Square and under a large banner reading RELIGION IS THE OPIUM OF THE PEOPLE swung a hanged puppet wearing a crown of thorns, an effigy of Christ, with a sign on his chest reading: "Spy and traitor of the people."

From the loudspeaker attached to a column of the Bolshoi Theater in Sverdlov Square, Demyan Bedny's thick voice shouted: "Christ was not resurrected! Christ was not resurrected! When Christ tried to go up to heaven he was shot down by the glorious Red Army Air Force. Ha! Ha! Ha!" Demyan Bedny's raucous laughter echoed off the walls of Kitay-gorod, the Tatar City, like the snap of a whip. On the trams, bands of young workers sneered and pointed to the sky shouting: "There he is, there he is, look at how he flies!" People raised their eyes searching the sky and many said, "*Naplivaiu.*"

In the shops of Univermag, smells of resin and sludge, the smells of Russian rivers, wafted off enormous trays covered with mounds of fresh caviar surrounded by blocks of ice. The fresh caviar was gray and pink in color, like a cream made of butter and blood, like a pile of tiny slimy and bleeding pearls. The young salesgirls in the Univermag dipped their large wooden spoons into the caviar and a sweet smell of blood filled the room. "Comrades!" Demyan Bedny's voice shouted out of the loudspeaker attached to the facade of the Palace of the Moscow City Soviet in Sovietskya Square, "Comrades! This morning in an alley near Bolotnaya Square, in the Zamoskvoretsky District, the corpse of a six-year-old girl was found raped and strangled. The killer, who claims he is Christ, was arrested while trying to escape to heaven. Ha! Ha! Ha!" I thought of the fresh caviar, of that butter and blood cream, of that pile of slimy, bleeding pearls, and the Univermag salesgirls dressed in white aprons resembling those worn by children's nannies. As they passed by, groups of girls said: "*Christos voskres!* Christ is risen!" and they laughed while brazenly staring me in the eye. Demyan Bedny was also laughing: "Ha! Ha! Ha!" and his thick and raucous laugh echoed from one loudspeaker to another, from street to street, from square to square, throughout the city.

The women on the sidewalks of Tverskaya and Petrovka streets appeared to be dressed in that same "tunic, so soft that it fitted him like the skin of an onion" like the one Odysseus wears in Homer's poem when he leaves behind the bloody amphitheaters of Troy. The smell of onions, sweet and strong, drifted about their naked arms and legs which made the slight rustle of silk, like the rustle made by the skin of an onion. I walked alongside Bulgakov and felt the green eye of spring open upon me, I felt the warm breath of a spring cow blow across my neck, and every once in a while I turned to look behind me.

"Why do you turn around like that?" Bulgakov asked me. "Are you perhaps looking to see if someone is weeping behind you?"

The sky shone green like a lawn. From hour to hour the grass grew in the curved lawn of the sky, and the soft glow of the grass reflected off the walls, off the glass in the windows, off the pavement of the roads, off the faces of the people. Moscow was slowly awash in that beautiful green color of antique copper, of moldy wood, which is the color of the Russian spring, the color of the icons in the crypts of the old monasteries, of the silver samovars in dimly lit rooms, of the horseshoes along the banks of the Moskva River, of the ponds on the outskirts of the Presnensky District; that beautiful green color that is the color of the sound of the bells during the Russian Easter. But the bells were silent. Instead, skimming through the air were clear, bright glances, feminine laughter, and the rustle of onion skin, and that long lament similar to the lively hiss of a reed in the wind which is the secret voice of the Russian spring. "*Naplivaiu*," I said to myself, spitting on the ground.

"Why are you turning around?" Bulgakov asked me.

I turned around every once in a while and gazed at the crowd's red eyes, the red eyes, moist and soft, of an octopus.

4

ONE SUNDAY morning I went to the flea market on Smolensky Boulevard with Bulgakov. Every Sunday morning all those who were left of Moscow's former nobility, all the well-bred, miserable ghosts of the czarist aristocracy, gathered on the sidewalks of Smolensky Boulevard to sell their meager treasures to foreign diplomats, to those enriched by the Revolution, to the Nepmen, to communist profiteers, to the new Marxist nobility, to the wives, daughters, and lovers of the new Red boyars. They gathered to sell their last snuffbox, their last ring, their last icon, their last silver medallions, toothless combs, torn and faded silk scarves, used gloves, Cossack daggers, old shoes, silver bracelets, German and Russian porcelain, ancient Tatar scimitars, their last tattered French books, their last old and dramatic women's hats from the Anna Karenina era, all puffed up with feathers, clownish, naive, and befuddling. Sitting on canvas chairs along the tree-lined avenue running up the middle of Smolensky Boulevard, or standing along the edge of the sidewalk under the green trees, those sad phantoms of the *ancien régime*'s nobility chatted amongst themselves for hours about all the daily events in their lives—weddings, funerals, divorces, engagements, suicides, intrigues, scandals, gossip—as if they were sitting in the drawing room of a neoclassical mansion in Bely Gorod, the "White Town," designed by Bovet in the fabulous era of their glory, of their joyful, happy youth. They chatted amongst themselves, in the French of Madame du Deffand adapted to the slight Muscovite accent of the Countess of Ségur, born Rostopchine, bowing to one another continuously, turning to one and then the other with graceful gestures of the head and hands like a ballet of dolls in a theater at court, interrupting themselves every so often to attend to passersby, their voices piercing and plaintive: "Look at this trinket, Monsieur. A souvenir of Moscow, Monsieur. A pretty Russian souvenir, Monsieur."

On Arbat Street we met an old, short man, at once stocky and fragile, with bushy white muttonchops, who walked hunched over while balancing on his head an enormous gilded armchair. It was a Louis-Philippe chair covered in red damask, resting on top of an old black English hat in the shape prescribed by Edward VII—that narrow, curled-up brim in the baroque fashion—the Edwardian style perpetuating, both in hats and literature, the Bath style. Precisely and only in its faithfulness to the hats of Edward VII's era, czarist Russia revealed the dark presentiment of its approaching doom. That man carrying the armchair on his head seemed to be one of those old women in Goya's *Caprichos* who wore a chair on her head. Bulgakov went up to him, greeting him cordially and without familiarity.

"*Bonjour, bonjour,*" the old man said, his voice shrill and vicious. He was Prince Lvov, who in 1917 was the last President of the Duma. The old man's face was shiny with sweat and he appeared exhausted by his hard work. He put the chair down on the sidewalk, plopped himself into it, then used a dirty handkerchief to wipe his forehead. He said he'd come to Smolensky Boulevard convinced that he would finally be able to sell his armchair. "Gilded armchairs are back in fashion," he said. He had five more at home, a treasure trove, he added, that would allow him to keep going for a couple more years. "Then we'll see. Ha! Ha! Ha!" he exclaimed, laughing. He laughed while closing his eyes and shrugging his shoulders, all hunched over as if he had been stricken by a fit of coughing.

Suddenly, he opened his eyes and turning to me asked if I knew X who, before the Revolution, was the Italian ambassador in St. Petersburg. He smiled as he spoke, calling me "*jeune homme*" and every so often marveling at my shoes, my suit, and my hat. "Do they all dress as you do in Europe? It's a strange way to dress. The tailors over there must have lost their minds. In my day..." And he started to count the buttons on my jacket, amazed that there were only three. He counted the buttons on his own jacket and said, "Four! That's the cardinal rule, *jeune homme*! Not even the Communist Revolution was able to rip the fourth button off my jacket." He shook his head with disgust at my shoes with their thick soles and low heels, fastened with thin leather shoelaces, and after a while he said triumphantly that he wouldn't exchange his shoes for mine for all the gold in the world. He wore black ankle boots, scuffed and torn, that buttoned on the side.

"Do you know Colonel Marsengo?" he asked me.

Colonel Marsengo was, just before the Revolution, military attaché in St. Petersburg. Prince Lvov seemed astonished that I didn't know him. "He sang so well," he said, "and played the guitar like a true gypsy. *C'etait un homme délicieux*, he was a delightful man, an utterly charming man." Passersby glanced distractedly at the old man reclining in a Louis-Philippe gilded armchair in the middle of the sidewalk on the Arbat, one of the busiest streets in Moscow. An old woman wearing a faded, torn green blouse and a long white petticoat with a frayed hemline, her forehead in the shadow of a large ribbonless Marie Antionette–style hat made of Florentine straw, with the brim chafed like a gardener's hat, stopped on the sidewalk directly in front of him and called him by his name, familiarly, waving a hand covered by an elbow-length black glove. "*Bonjour, bonjour, bonjour!*" Prince Lvov cried out jumping to his feet with youthful force, then taking off his hat and folding himself into a low bow. "Poor woman!" he said with pity and contempt when the old woman had left, disappearing into the crowd. "Poor woman! *Elle est un peu toquée*, she's a little touched in the head. She insists the czar is still alive!" And he began to laugh, flashing his long, yellow teeth. "Don't you know her?" he added. "She's Princess Galizin. She sells cigarettes outside the Hô- tel Métropole." He sighed, then sat back down on his arm- chair, crossing his legs, and asked me if it was true that Cerruti, the Italian ambassador in Moscow, was a very intel- ligent man. I told him that Cerruti was without a doubt the best of our ambassadors. "That makes me happy," he said, "the foreign ambassadors in my day…" But he interrupted himself, looked around, and shaking his head said that he was very disappointed that he wasn't able to meet him per- sonally but that it was quite dangerous for Soviet citizens to approach foreign diplomats. "*Oui, jeune homme,*" he added, lowering his voice, "in Russia we're afraid. We are all afraid." He looked over his shoulder with a worried air, took off his hat and, turning it in his hands, stared at it intently, then put it back on his head and asked me the time. It was ten o'clock. "*Jolie montre*, nice watch," he said, grabbing my arm and examining my wristwatch intently. He touched it with his finger, tapped his nail against the glass, then stuck out his lips and held his breath as a child might. Under his knitted eyebrows his eyes had become lucid, almost as if swollen with tears. I was tempted to ask him if he wanted to exchange his armchair for my watch; I would have liked to humiliate him and I was sure that it would have been for him a great and painful humiliation if I had offered him my watch in exchange for his armchair.

"Would you like..." I said, but I stopped myself, biting my lip in order not to humiliate him with my stupid and contemptible proposal. I turned my head away so as not to look at him, so as not to see old Prince Lvov, the last President of the Duma, sitting on his gilded armchair in the great gilded and stuccoed room of the Duma, lifting his white, soft, decrepit hand to smooth out his bushy muttonchops while Lenin from the balcony of the building where the ballerina Kschessinskaya lived incited the crowds to execute all of the gilded armchairs from the Duma, the Senate, the Admiralty, and the Winter Palace, to destroy all the gilded armchairs in Russia, all the gilded armchairs throughout Europe and the world.

Suddenly Prince Lvov burst out laughing, throwing himself against the back of the armchair. "*Ridicule*, utterly ridiculous!" he said, his voice strangled with laughter. "Could you see me with that? With that watch on my wrist? Ha! Ha! Ha! Ridiculous! A sign of the times. They've really lost their minds in Europe. Could you possibly imagine anything of the sort here in Soviet Russia?" He then became quiet, looking around him with a frightened air, and for a long while with his eyes he followed first the back of a passerby, then a tram (it was the no. 4 tram which went to the Dorogomilovo District) that ran screeching along on its wheels down the opposite side of the Arbat, then a youth who ran across the street; he then stared with alarm at a worker who was approaching us at a swift pace. "Ten o'clock!" he said, as if he had remembered something that distressed him. "Ten o'clock!" And he jumped up, still hunched, and grabbed the armchair with both hands. I offered to help him, and without waiting for his answer, I lifted up the armchair and put it on my head. *"Doucement, jeune homme,* gently," said Prince Lvov, looking at me oddly. And with his head down he set off toward Smolensky Boulevard.

I was a little ways behind him, and while walking I observed the hunched old man with the bushy white mutton-chops and the hat pushed back onto the nape of his neck who went forth with his hands clasped behind his back, hopping to one side the way the lame do. Every so often he turned around, telling me in French: *"Doucement, jeune homme, doucement!"* And he would shake his head crossly. That man hopping along in front of me irritated me. I felt resentment toward him (it was a vile and unfair sentiment and I was the first to admit it, a feeling that made me blush inside with shame); I harbored resentment for the subtle, spiteful complicity that I obscurely felt existed in his intimate relationship with that armchair. The era of the gilded armchair was returning in Russia and Prince Lvov was certainly not to blame. In the panorama of the proletarian Revolution, gilded armchairs were becoming newly necessary, an element that wasn't just decorative but also moral, as necessary for the dignity of the communist landscape as it was for the dignity of the *ancien régime*'s landscape. The time in which gilded armchairs elicited contempt, hatred, and rage in the Soviet people was over: an age of respect, admiration, and national pride in regard to gilded armchairs was returning. The workshops, machines, blast furnaces, mills, and power plants of the *Pyatiletka* had started to lose their worth in comparison to the gilded armchairs of the *ancien régime*. I harbored resentment for Prince Lvov because I sensed in his Louis-Philippe armchair a sly solicitation, an evil temptation, a cruel trap. All of Soviet Russia seemed to me to have by now become the phantom of an enormous gilded armchair, a gigantic Louis-Philippe armchair alone at the edge of the horizon of the squalid landscape of cogged wheels and smoke-stacks of the Communist Revolution. And out there, seated upon that gigantic armchair, I saw a child-size mummy with a shiny porcelain face, its left ear gnawed by mice.

At a certain point, Prince Lvov turned to me and asked if in Rome I had known the old Princess D. I told him that naturally I knew her. "Why *naturally*?" Prince Lvov asked indignantly. "Princess D is not a woman one knows naturally."

"Princess D is a delightful woman," I said, smiling.

"*Vous voulez dire un vieux chameau,*" Prince Lvov said. "You mean an old swine."

"Yes, naturally an old swine."

"Ha! Ha! Ha!" Prince Lvov cried out in a triumphant voice while clapping his hands and jumping up and down on his short legs. "*Un vieux chameau! Voilà! Voilà!* So that's what one becomes now even in Europe! Not only here! Not only in Russia!" And thrusting upon my face two eyes lit with wicked joy, he added: "Everyone is an old swine in Russia. Everyone is an old swine in Europe. Everywhere! What do you think will become of Semyonova, Yegorova, Budyonnaya, Bubnova, Lunacharskaya, all the beauties of Soviet Russia? They will become old swine like Princess D, they too will be old swine like everyone in the whole world! Ha! Ha! Ha! And Stalin? He too will become an old swine like me, an old swine like everyone in the world. Ha! Ha!

Ha!" He laughed while stamping his feet and rolling his head and hissing like a cat. "Why are you looking at me like that?" he asked suddenly, ceasing his laughter. I told him that I was trying to remember who he reminded me of, that I thought he looked like Prince Adam Czartorisky.

"That old buffoon? Strange," Prince Lvov said, as if he found my comparison singular and sad. "Very strange ... It's the first time I've ever heard such a thing." And he looked at me with a melancholic hatred while shaking his head.

To console him Bulgakov said, "*On ressemble toujours à quelqu'un.* We all look like someone else."

"Not here, not in Russia," Prince Lvov said turning angrily to Bulgakov. "Not here." And he started walking again, repeating every so often: "Poor Adam! *Quelle idée.* What a thought."

When we turned onto Smolensky Boulevard, I felt as if we were entering the Paris drawing room of Princess Maria Dimitrievna T—— during a czarist colony reception. Along the central avenue lined with green trees running down Smolensky Boulevard were assembled all the items that still survived in Moscow belonging to the *ancien régime*'s nobility who were sitting on canvas chairs and, without reverence or shame and with a puerile and insolent pride, displayed their miserable treasures on threadbare towels spread out on the ground at their feet. Old ladies wearing worn and faded outfits, white or green or yellow blouses with puffed sleeves, high-necked lace collars held up by short whalebone sticks, their foreheads shaded by sad hats decked with feathers and fake flowers, chatted in French among themselves with a sweet tone of reciprocal disdain, their accents, gestures, and smiles replete with reciprocal resentment. Dressed in very long, wide skirts, they wore boas, matted and plucked, around their necks, and badly mended thick veils over their faces behind which, as behind a fogged window, one could see lips opening and closing, restless eyes moving about suspiciously. On their lips, on that street, under those green trees, under Moscow's high white sky strewn with red freckles like the skin of a blond woman, against the background of that landscape of ancient monasteries and gigantic cement and glass buildings, the French language sounded both old and foreign, having the same sound as a dead language, the sound the ear of a modern reader could hear in the French accents of the characters in *War and Peace*. With a kind of dark fear, one suddenly understood that Marx could never have written *Das Kapital* in that tired precious language full of grammatical errors and obsolete words. All the malice, suspicion, resentment, misgivings, envy, senile cruelty expressed by that language across those lips lent to that particular French an accent of poignant and beautiful senescence, the dignity of an inhuman, incorporeal, impartial language of an abstract and marvelously transparent nature, full of that tired and sweet quality of the Alexandrian Greeks, as heard on the lips of André Chénier in the verses of *The Young Captive*, or on the lips of Chateaubriand, or on those of Proust in *The Guermantes Way*, whose graceful melancholy preserved, like a final memory, the proud taste of death. Groups of mostly elderly men—who by their gestures and the proud way they moved their heads and shoulders revealed themselves to be former officials or high-level functionaries of the czarist regime—stood under the trees with large cardboard boxes hanging around their necks and resting against their stomachs, in which they had carefully displayed little objects: pipes, ivory snuffboxes, razors, rings, faded silk neckties. Dressed in uniforms without epaulettes, Cossack kaftans

with very large sleeves, white linen jackets, these men addressed themselves to the elderly women with exaggerated
bows, using refined and courteous language to call out to
them by name with obsequious familiarity, and with a respect
dulcified by a feeling of communal misery and suffering. A
light breeze, clear and warm, in which the houses, the trees,
and the people were reflected as if in a clear stream, flowed
down the middle of the boulevard, sweeping along in its
current the images and sounds, the rustling and murmuring
of the green leaves, the human voices, the swallow cry of the
tram wheels on their tracks, the birds chirping amidst the
tree foliage. At the beginning of Smolensky Boulevard, Prince
Lvov took off his hat, gesturing grandly with his arm, and
bowed low, saying in a loud voice, "*Bonjour, bonjour,*" his
eyes darting this way and that, almost as if he were looking
for the mistress of the house. The old ladies responded to
him, smiling and lowering their heads, with a gracious gesture of their hands, shouting with shrill voices, "Here you
are finally, *cher Prince,*" and the men bowed in turn, answer-
ing his greeting with their own, "*Bonjour, bonjour.*" I too
bowed, using both hands to keep the gilded armchair bal-
anced on my head. I bowed and smiled, saying loudly in
Italian (not out of caution because no one could understand
what I said, but because those words came to my lips in my
language), "*Andate al diavolo, andate tutti al diavolo,* Go to
the devil, all of you go to the devil!" I was ashamed of those
words but I couldn't stop myself from saying them. I was
ashamed more by their sound than by their sense, as they
seemed to me to be words full of compassion and respect.
One is not responsible for the sounds of one's words, but one
is responsible for the sense. I wasn't able, in that moment,
to find words that better expressed my compassion and

sympathy. "Go to the devil, all of you!" I repeated loudly, and I stopped in the middle of the street, both of my arms lifted to steady the armchair on my head.

Suddenly, at the corner of the sidewalk, under an enormous green tree, I saw a woman, still young and beautiful, dressed in a faded and wrinkled women's Red Cross uniform. She stood in front of me, stern and unmoving: she held on open display, with her two hands extended like Saint Veronica with her shroud, a pair of women's white silk underwear trimmed with lace and yellowed ribbon. I saw her there alone and I blushed. All I could see was that dreadful Veronica and I couldn't take my eyes off that silk underwear hanging from those two bony, dark hands like iron hooks. "Go to the devil, you too, go to the devil!" I said loudly in Italian, and I shook with shame and indignation, because it seemed to me to be the height of dishonor for a woman to have to prostitute her own underwear. It seemed to me to be the height of cowardice (not her cowardice but everyone's cowardice, all of ours, mine too, also Bulgakov's, and Prince Lvov's, the cowardice of all Russia, all Europe) to reduce a woman who was still young, still beautiful, to prostitute her own underwear on a public street. "*Naplivaiu*," I said to myself, and I turned my back on Veronica and put the armchair down on the sidewalk.

"*Merci*, thank you, you are very kind," Prince Lvov said to me, easing himself down into the gilded chair. He had taken off his hat and was using the palm of his hand to dry the interior leather strip. Suddenly he lifted up his head and looked at me, his eyes furious. "Why are you laughing?" he asked me. "Perhaps you find me ridiculous? Perhaps you think that an armchair in Soviet Russia is a useless and ridiculous object? Lenin actually died in an armchair."

I started to laugh. "You're right," I said, "Lenin did die in an armchair."

"Have you been to Gorky?" Prince Lvov asked me. "Have you seen the armchair in which Lenin died?"

"Yes, I've been to Gorky and seen the armchair," I told him.

"Do you remember what it was like?" asked Prince Lvov. "It's an old bedroom armchair like the ones that were in every bourgeois home in Russia. It was covered in faded and torn fabric with oily stains on the backrest and armrest. It certainly wasn't an armchair like this one here. Lenin died too soon. He died in a bourgeois armchair, like a character from Zola. If he'd waited a few more years to die, he would have died like a character from Balzac in a Louis-Philippe armchair."

"I like it better," I said, "that Lenin died in an old, faded, and worn bourgeois armchair."

"Not everyone knows how to die in a gilded armchair," Prince Lvov said, wiping his brow with a dirty handkerchief. "Eh! Eh, *jeune homme*! I'm telling you that the Louis-Philippe armchair is coming back in fashion. In a little while, all the heroes of the Revolution will want to sit in an armchair like this one. It's always the same story!" His hand was terribly old, older than his forehead, his mouth, his nose, older than his pale and gaunt cheeks covered in a web of violet veins and wrinkles. His small decrepit hand, dark and hairy, moved across his face like a large spider on its web.

I was annoyed that he couldn't speak about anything besides his armchair. I turned my back on him in order to hide from him how much his words irritated me, as well as his air of evil triumph, and I saw in front of me, standing at the edge of the sidewalk, the statuesque woman with her hands extended like Saint Veronica.

The woman looked at me and smiled. I blushed and lowered my eyes to remove my gaze from her underwear.

"Fifty rubles, Monsieur," said the woman in a soft voice.

I said: "*Trop cher*, fifty rubles is too expensive."

"It's not too expensive," Veronica said, taking a step forward. "They're not new, but they're still in good condition. It's a bargain. For this price, you wouldn't find another pair like them in all of Moscow. Look at them closely, Monsieur."

"I'm a foreigner," I said. "I'm sorry that I'm a foreigner in Moscow."

"They're not expensive, sir," said the woman, taking another step closer. "Fifty rubles is nothing with the exchange rate. For a foreigner, they're not expensive. Look at them closely, Monsieur," and as she spoke she brought the underwear up near to my face.

It gave off a smell of old dusty linen. I stepped back a pace and, smiling, said: "It's a noble city, Moscow. Everything is noble in Moscow. It's a shame that I am a foreigner in this marvelous city."

"Touch the material, Monsieur. It's real silk," Veronica insisted. "It's not at all expensive for fifty rubles."

The fact that she could speak of nothing else besides her underwear pained and humiliated me. I would have liked to change the subject, to have encouraged her, without her even knowing it, to speak of something else, but I didn't know how to do it and I wasn't able to take her attention off that underwear of hers, even if I was fascinated with the underwear and could think of nothing else. I felt myself blush with shame and humiliation, thinking that the woman was reduced to prostituting her own underwear on a public street and I was also to blame, or perhaps the only one to blame. She had a withered face, black circles under her eyes, but she was still beautiful, still young. Her beauty, tired and faded as it was, making it all the more precious, offended me as if it were a shamelessness on her part, a lack of delicacy.

"Buy them, Monsieur," said the woman with a humble smile.

"No," I said. "I will not buy your underwear."

I turned my back on her and moved off toward the gilded armchair.

After only about three steps my knees were touching the armchair in which Prince Lvov was sitting. My legs were heavy and it took a great effort to lift my feet. I felt like I was walking with a pair of underwear carved out of very heavy stone on my back.

I suddenly whirled back around to her and said, "Not even for thirty rubles."

"*Trente roubles*," the woman said, "buy them for thirty rubles."

She came off the sidewalk and up to me with her arms outstretched, smiling, and put into my hands her poor underwear. I felt myself turn pale, I felt I had become as white as a corpse. I stood there with that underwear in my hands before a woman who was staring at me, smiling, and I shivered.

Through clenched teeth, I said, "*Allez-vous en*, go away." I was trembling with shame. The woman seemed to be standing naked before me, entirely nude from head to toe. I could give her neither fifty, nor thirty rubles, nor could I give her even a kopek. I didn't have the right to give her even a kopek. I didn't have the right to give money to the naked woman there in the middle of the street.

"*Prenez vos culottes*," I said, through clenched teeth, "Take your underwear and go away, do you understand? *Allez-vous en!*" I shouted, my voice trembling with shame.

The woman took the underwear I held out to her. "Forgive me, Monsieur," she said.

Now she was standing in front of me, smiling humbly, and she wasn't naked anymore. She appeared once again dressed in her women's Red Cross uniform: on her chest, near her heart, a safety pin was fastened. Smiling, I pulled from my pocket a hundred-ruble banknote and, handing it to her, I asked, "Will you give me that pin you have on your chest? Will you give it to me for a hundred rubles?"

"No, Monsieur," said the woman, "that's not even worth a kopek. I wouldn't give it to you even for a thousand rubles. I'm sorry. You understand, Monsieur?" She smiled at me, her smile humble and sweet.

So I turned and left without even saying goodbye to her or to Prince Lvov. I walked slowly away, my legs trembling.

Bulgakov joined me at the corner of Smolensky Boulevard and Arbat Street.

"*Pas la peine*," Bulgakov said. "Not worth it."

"Why isn't it worth it? What's not worth it?"

"It is not worth getting upset over so little," Bulgakov said. "Pride isn't involved in these things."

"It wasn't pride," I said. "It was modesty."

"It's the same," Bulgakov said. "It's not worth being modest over so little."

"She was naked," I said.

"Yes, she was naked," Bulgakov said, "but she knew she was naked."

"No, she didn't know she was naked," I said. "She was dressed only in that pin. Without that pin she would have felt naked."

"When we are hungry we feel clothed," Bulgakov said. "Hunger is the cloak of the poor. We never feel naked when we are hungry."

5

THAT SAME night I went to a banquet given in my honor by the Union of Soviet Writers in Moscow. Assuming the demeanor of judges, my fellow diners interrogated me across the table during the meal. Like someone accused of a crime, I sat there, my plate and glass before me, as the judges shouted across the table at me: "What are the writers up to in your damned Europe?"

I responded: "They're eating Midas's gold, rolling in capitalist manna."

"Ha! Ha! Ha!" they shouted, laughing.

"Pardon us, *daragoi* Malaparte, but is it true that the writers in Europe are corrupt right through to the marrow?"

I responded: "It's true, those sacred sons of noble prostitutes are rotten to the core and stink!"

"Ha! Ha! Ha!" shouted everyone around the long table, laughing heartily and staring at me with blazing eyes.

Demyan Bedny, head of the League of Militant Atheists and the *Bezbozhnik*, Demyan Bedny, the enemy of God, author of *The Gospel According to Saint Demyan*, leader of the league crusading against religion, clasped his fat, flaccid stomach with both hands and across the table asked me: "How do the poets live in Europe? Is it true that they live hidden away in capitalist prisons?"

I responded: "Which poets?"

"The true poets," shouted Demyan Bedny, "the proletarian poets, those who sing of the poor, the miserable, the outcasts."

I responded: "In Europe the poets don't sing of the poor, the miserable, the outcasts; they sing of what all poets, from Homer onwards, have always sung of: they sing of the clouds, the flowers, the eyes of women, of nightingales, of Helen's fatal beauty, and of Achilles's gleaming weaponry."

"Ah, the damned!" shouted Demyan Bedny.

"The damned, the damned!" shouted everyone around the table.

And I said: "Yes, the damned; damned are the bourgeois poets who sing of Alexander and Caesar and Augustus, who sing of Lesbia and Laura, of Doric columns and Corinthian capitals, of Venuses and Cupids, of jewels and perfumes, of French and Spanish wines, of corpses painted gold and the crimson of kings and queens, of the tender leaves on trees, and of God's radiant face."

Everyone was laughing raucously, slapping each other on the back. And I stared at the pale sad face of the poet Mayakovsky who sat at the far end of the table.

"What do poets sing about in Russia?" I asked in a raised voice.

Everyone fell silent and a young man, tall and thin, stood up. He had very black curly hair, a broad white forehead, and a wide mouth with thin red lips. "We sing of the smell of iron filings," he said, "of the smell of human sweat in Soviet workshops full of men drunk on weariness, we sing of calloused hands, unkempt beards, of the flaming eyes of naked men before the mouths of blast furnaces. We sing of the Five-Year Plan, of tractors, of mechanical plows, anvils, hammers and trip hammers, of Stalin's genius and of the red flags fluttering on factory chimneys."

"Ha! Ha! Ha!" I shouted, laughing raucously. "And what else? What else do the poets in Russia sing about?"

Mayakovsky stood up and said: "We sing of Lenin's radiant face; we sing of the men of fire William Blake saw rise on the waves of the Atlantic."

"Ha! Ha! Ha!" shouted Demyan Bedny, reaching his arm toward Mayakovsky."What did you sing of during your visit to America? You sang of New York's skyscrapers, the pigs of Chicago, the Hudson River tugboats, the negroes of Harlem! Ha! Ha! Ha!"

"I sang of Lenin's skyscrapers. He drew them with a trembling hand on great sheets of paper just before he died," said Mayakovsky.

"You're wrong," I cried, "Lenin drew enormous Eiffel Towers!"

"No, no," everyone cried, "Lenin drew skyscrapers."

"Ha! Ha! Ha!" I cried. "So Lenin also sang of America's glory? So this is what the poets in Russia sing about: America's glory?"

"No!" cried Demyan Bedny standing up. "In Soviet Russia the poets sing of workers, cogged wheels, transmission belts, pistons, red-hot cast iron, hardened steel, cities without God, men without God, the death of God, the damnation of God!"

I laughed, threw myself back in my chair, and cried: "Ah, damned are the poets, all poets, bourgeois or proletarian, Homer and Virgil, Dante and Petrarch, Shakespeare and Racine, Blok and Sergei Yesenin, and you too, Demyan Bedny, you too, Mayakovsky, you too..." and I turned to a young poet who was sitting opposite me, "you too...what's your name?"

The young man looked at me and said: "Ivan Karovy."

And laughing, I shouted: "You too are damned, Ivan

Karovy, all poets are damned, damned are all bourgeois poets who don't sing of the Five-Year Plan, of men naked before the mouths of blast furnaces, of red flags fluttering on factory chimneys, and damned are the proletarian poets, you too are damned, poets of Lenin's Russia, who don't sing of clouds, flowers, nightingales, jewels, of Helen's fatal beauty and Achilles's spear, of luxury cars, and the vermilion lips of Barbara Hutton. Damned poets!"

Everyone around me was laughing, staring at me with blazing eyes, and Demyan Bedny lifted his glass and said: "To the health of a putrid Europe, to the prostitute Europe!"

I too lifted my glass and said: "To the health of a putrid Europe!" Everyone laughed, and Mayakovsky stared at me across the table with his sad eyes.

By the time we left it was dawn. We went in silence, Mayakovsky and I, the sky white and crinkly, like tissue paper, especially in the distance over the domes of St. Basil's Cathedral. The red flags on the Kremlin towers paled in the weary glow of electric spotlights, themselves fading in the soft pink light of dawn. The dew on the shiny leaves of the green trees reflected the white sky and birds sang amidst the virgin spring foliage. I said to Mayakovsky: "Listen, the poets are singing amidst the foliage."

"William Blake saw angels perched on tree branches," Mayakovsky said.

"Hush, it's forbidden to speak of angels in Russia."

"Is it forbidden to speak of angels in Europe too?" Mayakovsky asked me.

"Yes, in Europe too," I responded.

Our footsteps echoed forlornly on the deserted pavement as we traversed Kitay-gorod, the Tatar City. On Nikolskaya Street, passing the little church dedicated to Saint Nicholas,

Patron Saint of Holy Russia, I said: "Saint Nicholas was from Bari, in Puglia. He was an Italian saint."

"The saints have no country," Mayakovsky said.

"The country of the saints is the proletariat," I said. "Isn't it true that the country of the saints is the proletariat?"

"Yes," said Mayakovsky, "their country is slavery, misery, hunger, filth, the sufferings of the proletariat," and he began to laugh, spitting on the ground.

"The other day," I said, "I went into the little church on Nikolskaya Street. Look what the poor little curate gave me." And I showed him a small medal with the image of Saint Nicholas on it. "When I told him I was Italian, he started to cry. I promised him I would go to Bari and light a candle for him on the tomb of the Patron Saint of Holy Russia."

"And will you go do it?" Mayakovsky asked me, smiling ironically.

"I will. I promised him I would."

"I hope you won't also light a candle for me on the tomb of your Saint Nicholas," Mayakovsky said. "I don't believe the saints can help us. No one can help anyone else. Praying for others, suffering for others, dying for your neighbor, all of it is futile, all of it useless." He stopped and stared at my face with his luminous eyes. "Don't you think that I too am tired of suffering for others, for humanity? Do you think humanity would gain a thing if I died for it? Do you think I would like to die for humanity? And you, would you like to die for others?" he cried, grabbing me by the arm.

"No, I wouldn't like to die for others," I responded.

"You would instead like to die for you, for yourself?"

"No, I wouldn't like to die for myself, not even for myself. I would accept dying for nothing, that's all. For nothing, yes. But for others, on behalf of others, or for myself, no.

That's it, no, I really wouldn't. I wouldn't like to die for someone, for something."

"Ah ha! You don't want to die for someone or something either, eh?" cried Mayakovsky, while forcibly squeezing my arm.

"Do you think that in Europe," I said, "men don't also ask themselves if it's right to die for others?"

"*Tas d'ignobles chrétiens!*" cried Mayakovsky. "A heap of vile Christians!"

"We, too," I said, "we're tired of being a heap of vile Christians. We too are tired of suffering for others, of dying for others, for humanity, for our country, for the Revolution, for the proletariat, for democracy, for liberty, of suffering and dying for a heap of noble and sacred causes."

"You too, eh?" cried Mayakovsky. "And so why don't you try dying for nothing? You are afraid of dying for nothing, that's the truth, you are afraid, *tas d'ignobles chrétiens!*"

He stared at me with his luminous eyes, then turned and began walking again in silence, a little hunched, his arms dangling by his sides. We emerged onto Red Square, directly in front of Lenin's tomb. On the far side of the square, the domes of St. Basil's Cathedral slowly emerged out of the green mists languishing on the banks of the Moskva. Near the Iversky Gate, we met the first groups of workers heading for work, others running behind the trams screeching their way across Revolution Square. The tiled rooftops, the yellow, green, red, turquoise tiles of the church domes, the walls that encircled the Tatar city, the tall towers of the Kremlin, the brass door handles of the Hotel Savoy all shimmered in the rose-colored morning light.

On the hotel's doorstep, Mayakovsky extended his hand to me and, laughing, said in a whisper: "Everyone be damned."

I said: "Everyone be damned."

Tall, elegant, a little hunched, his arms dangling by his sides, he slowly walked away and I followed him for a long while with my eyes, whispering through my clenched teeth: "Damn you too." I watched him make his way down Pushechnaya Street, clenching my jaw hard to keep myself from calling after him, to keep myself from shouting at him to stop, to stay. I wanted to run after him, put a hand on his shoulder, and tell him in an affectionate whisper: "Damn you too, Mayakovsky."

A few days later, Marika opened the door and announced that Mayakovsky had killed himself in his bedroom at dawn. He'd put a pistol in his mouth and shot himself.

I said: "He was tired of being obligated to suffer for others."

"No," Marika said, "he killed himself because he didn't feel worthy of suffering for the triumph of communism."

I said: "Marika, don't be silly."

"Mayakovsky was nothing but a dirty bourgeois."

"Don't be silly, Marika."

"You pig," Marika said. "Mayakovsky didn't have the right to kill himself."

"You're right, Marika," I said. "In Russia, it is forbidden to kill oneself *for nothing*."

"The word *nothing*," Marika said, "doesn't exist in Lenin's Russia."

"Maybe he killed himself," I said, "precisely because in Russia the word *nothing* doesn't exist."

"You pig. You dirty pig," Marika said.

In the afternoon, we took the no. 9 tram to where Mayakovsky had lived on a cross street of Sukharevsky Pereùlok.

"Do you have a permit?" asked the custodian, observing us suspiciously. "In order to enter Mayakovsky's apartment you need a special permit from the police."

That evening I went to Lunacharsky, the Soviet People's Commissar of Education and Culture, to plead with him for a police permit to visit the room where Mayakovsky committed suicide.

"Why do you want to see the room where Mayakovsky died?" Lunacharsky asked. "Are you by chance a bourgeois romantic? That would surprise me." He spoke slowly, in a cold, hard Italian.

"I was in Mayakovsky's apartment only once," I said. "His bedroom was simple, bright, neat. I want to ask his papers, his personal belongings, the appearance of his room if his death was serene, happy; if he was compelled to commit suicide out of fear or hope; if he killed himself because he didn't believe in God or because he believed in God."

Stroking his goatee, Lunacharsky gave me an odd look. His age was somewhere between fifty and seventy, his thick mop of black hair beginning, here and there, to thin and turn white. Purplish spots had appeared among the hairs on the backs of his hands, and his forehead, chunky and twisted like wool, resembled a goat's fleece with mangy patches. His rosy cheeks, like those of a consumptive, made his pale face even paler. A broad, floppy collar attempted to conceal the withered skin punctuated with large gray hairs on his white neck. While he spoke both hands clutched his chair's armrests, and every so often, with a sudden jerk, he threw himself against the backrest, causing his fat belly to shake beneath his waistcoat. Senior Soviet officials have a morbid passion for waistcoats, perhaps even stronger than their by-now famous passion for leather briefcases. At the time, in fact, a play entitled *Portfolio* ridiculing the Soviet obsession with briefcases was having a huge success at a theater in Moscow. In the USSR, a waistcoat and a briefcase under your arm were signs of power. In the satirical magazine *Krokodil*, the Soviet bureaucracy is symbolized by the waistcoat and the leather briefcase. Protruding from the little pockets of Lunacharsky's waistcoat (a Louis-Philippe bottle-green velvet *gilet* with large mother-of-pearl buttons that would have made both Théophile Gautier and Balzac envious) were five or six varicolored pencils, two fountain pens, a comb, a toothbrush, a notebook, and a pack of *Herzegovina Flor*, the favorite cigarettes of Moscow's Marxist nobility, of the Kremlin's "Upper Ten."

I had a great deal of sympathy for Lunacharsky. He was the only one among the communist "highbrows" who didn't judge the bourgeois, the counterrevolutionaries, the enemies of the people, the writers and the artists, and he wasn't afraid that the freedom of art was a grave danger for the State. During the October 1917 Revolution, he saved a large proportion of Russia's artistic treasures by placing detachments of Red Guards not only outside the doors of museums, but also in front of buildings housing private art collections. Even though he had a weak character and feared, above all, compromising himself, exposing himself to the criticism of the Jacobin communists, he never refused Soviet artists his utmost protection as the Soviet People's Commissar of Education and Culture. The malicious insinuated that he granted his protection exclusively to those artists that his wife—one of the most elegant women in Moscow, an actress at the Meyerhold Theater, and the most famous *cuisse légère* in the USSR —deigned to take to her heart. This was, perhaps, nothing more than a naive maliciousness, just as, without a doubt, it was with innocent malice that Lunacharsky was labeled *Sov-cocu* in Moscow's *Blue Book*, "a red-covered Blue Book," as Sir Esmond Ovey, the British ambassador, called it.

But Lunacharsky was too afraid of injury to worry about maliciousness, too afraid of being stabbed in the back to worry about pinpricks. And in this he proved to possess that which a parvenu rarely possesses: a very acute sense of what distinguishes an aristocracy of parvenus, i.e., Moscow's Marxist high nobility in which only one's head is at stake, as opposed to the authentic blood nobility in which everything else but the head is at stake. (The Chief of Protocol of the People's Commissariat for Foreign Affairs, the blond and ruddy Florinsky, the most famous homosexual in Moscow, expressed this same idea in a very seventeenth-century French manner, saying that in an authentic nobility, "*Il y a parfois des morts, mais jamais des cadavres,* occasionally there are deaths, but never corpses.")

In a certain sense, for Lunacharsky, Mayakovsky's suicide was a stab in the back. In recent times, and especially after his trip to the United States, Mayakovsky had become the target of the acerbic criticism of young communist writers who not only accused him of being corrupted by capitalism, aestheticism, and bourgeois narcissism, but publicly denounced his poetic opus as an act of counterrevolutionary "sabotage." The only person to come to his defense was Lunacharsky, and that was certainly not due to the fact that Mayakovsky was considered by Moscow's communist "smart set" to be one of Madame Lunacharskaya's lovers. By defending Mayakovsky's poetic opus, the Soviet People's Commissar Lunacharsky had made himself in some ways the guarantor of Mayakovsky's attitude toward communism in the Soviet State. Suicide in the USSR was a typical counterrevolutionary act, an act of "sabotage" against Soviet morals that didn't have serious political consequences for the one who committed the act, but did implicate his family and friends. Furthermore, if the suicide was a writer or artist, his admirers and those critics who favored his literary opus or art were also implicated since his was not a spontaneous, solitary act but a product of the environment in which the suicide had lived, the fruit of a tree, the suicide being merely a branch.

The tragic end of Mayakovsky had followed much too closely upon the clamorous suicide of the poet Sergei Yesenin (who, after his marriage to Isadora Duncan, his "escape" from Moscow, and the extravagances to which he abandoned himself during his long exile in Europe and America, "one beautiful day climbed up to the top of the highest skyscraper in New York, onto the highest balcony in the West," as Mayakovsky told it one evening just a few days before his own death, "and threw himself headfirst into the abyss, crashing onto the pavement of Moscow's streets"). Mayakovsky had repeated the determinant motivation—disgust for a godless country—with too much impudence to not put the Soviet People's Commissar Lunacharsky, one of Lenin's oldest friends, one of Lenin's "twelve," in a very delicate position. Lunacharsky was certainly not responsible for the poet Mayakovsky's suicide, but he was, in the Party's eyes, guilty of having granted his official protection to a man who had for some time been considering and planning such a grave act of counterrevolutionary "sabotage."

Lunacharsky stared at me, the dull glow of his myopic eyes oddly reflected by the glass in his spectacles. "By now in Mayakovsky's room," he said, "you won't find even a bloodstain. The police have long since removed all trace of the crime."

"The crime?"

"In the room where Mayakovsky died a crime was committed," Lunacharsky said.

I looked at him and laughed.

"No one in Soviet Russia," Lunacharsky said, "has the right to remove himself from communal work, from communal sacrifice, to desert his post of labor, struggle, and suffering, no one has the right to betray the cause of the Revolution. Mayakovsky has betrayed the Revolution."

"Mayakovsky was tired of suffering for others."

"He was tired of being *obligated* to suffer," Lunacharsky said. "Is that what you mean?"

"Of being obligated to suffer for others."

"Do you believe that being obligated to suffer for others is what makes men so disgusted with suffering?" Lunacharsky asked. "You're not suggesting that in Europe things are so very different from here."

"In Europe, too," I said, "we are tired of suffering for others."

"In Europe you, too, are *obligated* to suffer?" Lunacharsky asked, leaning forward on the table and peering at me over his spectacles.

"No, we're not obligated," I responded, "and this is why we suffer without rebelling against suffering. But we are tired of suffering for others."

"I hope you're not now going to talk about God," Lunacharsky said, lowering his voice.

"Mayakovsky believed in God," I said.

"Why are you talking to me about God?" Lunacharsky said, running a hand over his face.

"He killed himself because he believed in God. It's certainly not a good reason to kill yourself. But in Soviet Russia, a country without God, what better way is there for a believer to give decisive proof of his faith in God?"

"You speak," Lunacharsky said, laughing, "like a man who would never choose to kill himself, not even in Russia, to prove his faith in God. But are you sure you believe in God? All foreigners, as soon as they've set foot in Soviet Russia, suddenly realize they believe in God!"

"What you are saying is rather dire for Soviet Russia."

"Perhaps," Lunacharsky said, "but in any case, I don't know if Mayakovsky believed in God and I don't care to know either. What is certain is that he no longer believed in communism. When he returned from America, he was profoundly changed. I must confess that I never put much stock in what he said about his crisis of conscience, full of bourgeois ideas and ridiculous individualistic sentimentality. People said he had been converted while in America. To what, I asked myself, could an intelligent man ever be converted to in America? I never took seriously his supposed crisis of conscience. I was mistaken. I was mistaken to pity him. His act had nothing to do with his faith in God. It was not an act of Christian faith, but a banal example of bourgeois pessimism. It was a bourgeois act, that's all."

"In Soviet Russia," I said, "suicide has the explosive power of a miracle."

"But it's not a miracle. I understand what you're getting at, but no, suicide for us is not a miracle, it is not evidence of the existence of God. In the USSR, miracles don't happen. God doesn't count for anything here and has nothing to do with what happens in Soviet Russia."

"Everything that happens in Soviet Russia," I said, "is the work of God. Poverty, hunger, tears, blood, all that which the Russian people suffered for the triumph of communism was not the consequence of the material difficulties that must be overcome for the creation of a communist state, but rather the consequence of the moral difficulties God has with the creation of a human society founded on the negation of God. You must acknowledge that God doesn't care at all about capitalism or communism. God is exclusively concerned with affirming His presence in all things human, between humans, in the hearts of humans. God does not shun a crime, even the worst of crimes, if the crime is necessary to prove His presence. God doesn't always fight evil with good: often He fights evil with evil, a crime with a crime. Sometimes He fights good with evil, when the good is not done in His name. God is certainly not ashamed to have His hands drenched in blood. Everything is exploited to His purpose. Even out of the humblest of men, the most banal fact, the vilest thing, even a man with the barrel of a gun in his mouth, even a can of sardines, God knows how to make Christ out of it, how to make it an instrument of redemption, evidence of His presence."

"So the only one truly responsible for Mayakovsky's death is God? Mayakovsky's blood is on God's hands?" Lunacharsky asked, his voice shrill. "Is that what you're saying?"

"No," I said, "that's not what I'm saying."

"God killed him: that's what you mean."

"You shouldn't say that. It's useless to say that God is an assassin," I said, lowering my voice.

"Yes," whispered Lunacharsky, running a hand over his face. "God is an assassin."

Having said this he relaxed back in his chair, crossed his hands over his velvet waistcoat with large mother-of-pearl buttons, closed his eyes behind his thick glasses and fell silent. He seemed to be sleeping. A huge fly buzzed around the room, crashing now and then into the windowpane. Seeing him there as he was, Lunacharsky appeared to be an old man, tired and sick (he was gravely ill with a chest ailment), a humiliated man whom I'd seen many times sitting alone during receptions at foreign embassies, or during galas thrown by the People's Commissariat for Foreign Affairs in the rooms of the Spiridonovka Street mansion. Moscow's communist high nobility didn't like to show off in public places. In the bar at the Hôtel Métropole, in the Scala *tabarin*, the Bolshoi's *fumoirs*, in the theaters of Meyerhold, Tairov, and Stanislavsky, it was rare to meet the Soviet aristocracy, who feared publicly revealing themselves as they basked in the louche splendor of their power and riches, in their at once vulgar and sophisticated luxury. Only at dinners given by the foreign diplomatic corps, or at the People's Commissariat for Foreign Affairs, also known as the Narkomindel, or at the tennis courts of the Spiridonovka Street mansion and the British Embassy, or on the ski slopes of Nikolskoye, at the British Embassy's skating rink, or at the Kolomenskoye and Nikolaevsky Bridge rowing clubs was one guaranteed to glimpse a gathering of the communist high nobility.

Lunacharsky had a morbid conjugal passion for Madame Lunacharskaya, who usually attended the dinners and balls at her husband's side. He appeared oppressed by a resentful modesty, by a sad jealousy, but at the same time intoxicated by the deep gratification of his own public humiliation, which is characteristic of Russians and left him naked and helpless. At the diplomatic corps balls it was not at all rare to find Lunacharsky sitting in a corner, his eyes half-closed, his hands clasped over his white piqué cotton waistcoat, half-listening in his troubled and untrusting sleep to Madame Lunacharskaya's husky sweet voice, her acerbic laugh, the rustle of her silk clothing (original pieces by Schiaparelli, ordered in Paris at the State's expense, which she and all the Soviet actresses were permitted to wear only while on stage and which they removed from the Meyerhold Theater's wardrobe to wear to dinners and balls, causing a great scandal among the innumerable Cato-like petit bourgeois of the Communist Party). He followed the shimmering soft tones of her voice with his eyes closed, turning his tired face, as if attracted against his will by an affectionate and painful enticement, in the direction of the provocative movements of Madame Lunacharskaya's beautiful limbs, the playacting motions of her eyes, mouth, hands as she laughed surrounded by her court of young foreign diplomats, actors, officers, and Party officials. Every so often some of them threw an ironic glance in the direction of the *Sov-cocu*, and laughed. Sir William Strang, advisor to the British ambassador, who displayed a contemptuous pity for the Soviet aristocracy, didn't hide his sympathy for Lunacharsky. "Only a blind man," he said, "could laugh at Lunacharsky. Of all the communist high nobility in Moscow, he is the only one who has a presentiment of death."

"God is an assassin," Lunacharsky repeated. His hands, covered with black hair, were slightly trembling and clasped over his green velvet waistcoat with large mother-of-pearl buttons.

Suddenly the door opened and two young men entered the room. I had met them at the banquet given in my honor by the Union of Soviet Writers in Moscow. One of them was the Union's secretary Demyan Bedny, head of the League of Atheists: it was said that he was a dangerous fanatic and enjoyed a dubious authority among young writers of the avant-garde. The other was a *bezbozhnik* poet, an atheist poet who wore the cold stare of a gossip. Lunacharsky shook himself awake, opened his eyes, stared with a stunned look at the new arrivals, and then, his face brightening, stood up, pushed back the chair angrily, turned to me and, as if continuing with the conversation that had been interrupted by the unexpected appearance of the two intruders, said to me in a ridiculing voice: "Why don't you repeat in front of my friends what you've been saying to me about Mayakovsky. I have no personal reason to esteem Christ more than Mayakovsky, but it seems ridiculous to me to compare Mayakovsky to Christ! Ha! Ha! Ha!" He then turned to the new arrivals: "It's true, all the same, that for Malaparte, Christ is nothing more than a tin of sardines! Ha! Ha! Ha! A tin of sardines!" Lunacharsky's tone, emphasis, and gestures had all suddenly changed—he had become pale and his lips trembled.

"A tin of sardines? Ha! Ha! Ha!" cried the new arrivals, slapping their knees.

"And why exactly a tin of sardines?" cried Lunacharsky. "Why not a pair of old shoes or an old top hat? Haven't you noticed how an old top hat resembles Christ?"

"Ha! Ha! Ha! An old top hat!" cried the new arrivals, staring at me with violent contempt.

"Even from the vilest of men," I said, "even from the most superfluous object, God can make a Christ."

"Even from a mangy dog?" cried the atheist poet.

"Even from a mangy dog," I responded.

"Mayakovsky was a mangy dog: Is this why you compared him to Christ?" cried Lunacharsky, laughing, and he pressed his hands against his green velvet waistcoat.

"I came here to request permission to visit the room where Mayakovsky died," I said, staring at Lunacharsky's face.

"Mayakovsky was a traitor," the new arrivals cried, "a dirty saboteur of the Revolution!" And they stared at me with anger and contempt.

"Mayakovsky was a poet," I said.

"He was a traitor!" Lunacharsky cried, "and it astonishes me that you ..."

"He was a great poet," I said.

"A great poet?" Lunacharsky cried with a tone of profound astonishment. "A great poet? Ha! Ha! Ha!" and he erupted into convulsive laughter not unlike a violent coughing fit. He was very pale and he stared at me with glassy eyes.

"A great poet? Ha! Ha! Ha!" cried the new arrivals, writhing with laughter.

"Why don't you repeat to my friends what you said about Mayakovsky?" cried Lunacharsky, resting both his hands on the table and staring at me with a look full of anger and fear. "Didn't you tell me that it was God who killed him? That God is an assassin?"

"God is an assassin? Ha! Ha! Ha!" cried the new arrivals.

I remained silent, staring at Lunacharsky's face.

"I'll get you the permit," Lunacharsky suddenly said in a husky voice. "Did you think I wouldn't get you the permit? It will be waiting for you at your hotel. This very evening. When do you want to go visit Mayakovsky's room?"

"Tomorrow," I said.

"At what time?"

"At dawn."

"At dawn?" Lunacharsky said, profoundly astonished.

The morning after, at dawn, I went with Marika to visit the room in which Mayakovsky committed suicide. Marika was irritated with me. "*Toujours tes idées ridicules*, you always have the most ridiculous ideas," she said while we were on the tram heading in the direction of Sukharevskaya Bashnya. The apartment where Mayakovsky had lived after returning from America until his death was in one of those enormous, bleak, miserable buildings that arose in great numbers in Moscow and St. Petersburg during the second half of the last century and were filled with a crowd of minor types, mostly civil servants and workers. The cold light of a June night, that spectral light of Moscow's "white nights," gradually gave way to the delicate pink fire of day. I showed my permit to the porter and he accompanied us silently up the stairs. On the third floor he stopped and opened the door with his key. We entered into a hallway.

"Thank you, I won't be needing you further," I told the custodian.

People—the inhabitants of that enormous apartment building, every room occupied by a family—could be heard moving about behind the doors that opened onto the long hallway immersed in drab and dirty shadows. Mayakovsky's room was the last one at the end of the hallway, on the right. I pushed the door open and entered.

It was a small, bright room covered in a faded pale green French wallpaper which had been patched up here and there with newspaper. A bookshelf stood between the door and window. Against the opposite wall there was a daybed, a discolored and torn yellow cotton blanket tossed on top. Tacked to the wall were panoramas of New York and Chicago, a sea view of Manhattan skyscrapers, portraits of Pushkin and Baudelaire, photographs of a few young actresses from Sovkino. Beneath the window there was a table and on the table there were a bronze inkwell and a stack of papers on top of which sat a heavy bronze ashtray. The room contained only one chair. Marika sat on the bed and lit a cigarette. I sat in front of the window with my elbows resting on the table and I stared at the sky.

It was dawn, the hour at which Mayakovsky had killed himself. The pink light of day flowed into the white night of summer like a river into the sea. The delicate morning waves gently sauntered toward the sky's distant shores, rippling across rooftops with a long algae-green throb. Sitting right there in that same seat, before that open window, at that same hour, Mayakovsky had killed himself. It was dawn. He had laid down his head, resting his cheek on the table. Only a few drops of blood had flowed from the wound at the back of his mouth. Birds on rooftop gutters chirped and the sharp cries of swallows streaked across the pale sky. He smiled with his bloody lips. Far away at the edge of the city against the eastern sky (the sky had the round pink face of a baby), the Kremlin's red towers rose out of the river mists. A church dome, so close it almost seemed like I could reach out and touch it, dangled in the crystal-clear air, its green and azure ceramic tiles glittering in the first rays of sunlight. Suddenly, I saw in the middle of the courtyard a large tree.

It seemed to be an oak, but it couldn't be an oak. The leaves were a dark, dense, and shiny green, and amidst the somber foliage fluttered small new leaves, sheer and silvery like the surfaces of certain seashells. "Perhaps it's a laurel," I said to myself. No, laurels don't grow in northern Russia. And besides, Mayakovsky never would have killed himself in front of a laurel, looking out his window at a laurel tree. As the clear night was absorbed into the delicate light of day, as the delicate waves of the morning penetrated deeply into the sky's white shells, a shimmering of green and gold, like the soft glow of amber, melted in the high and remote sky where white clouds drifted here and there, forlorn and bemused. The rooftops and the church domes were bathed in a golden patina, the distant river glistened a deep honey color. Even the leaves on the large tree in the middle of the courtyard turned gold in the morning's warm triumph, and little by little that soft amber glow penetrated the dense, deep green of the foliage, slowly becoming paler, as if a silver moon were hiding in the sky.

"That's not an oak," I told myself, "neither is it a laurel. Perhaps it's an olive tree." And I was moved and frightened as if by a miracle, as if by something marvelous, since I knew that olive trees didn't grow under those cruel skies, and I shook my head, saying to myself: "No, it's not an olive tree." Still, as I stared at the great tree, alone in the sad courtyard, it appeared to gradually transform into a great, leafy olive tree and I thought of Mayakovsky, of his deliberate act, of the cold weight of the gun in his warm hand, and I wanted to pray, I wanted to pray for him, to look up at the sky and pray. But the words that came to my lips weren't those of a prayer, they were the words of the Sophoclean chorus in *Oedipus at Colonus* which Mayakovsky had recited for me one evening on the riverbank, before the Sparrow Hills: "It is a tree, self-born, self-grown, unaided by men's hands, a tree of terror to our enemies and their spears, a tree that grows best upon this very land!" I repeated two or three times to myself: "*A tree of terror to our enemies ...*" As my eyes roamed the room I saw the photographs of the young Sovkino actresses tacked to the wall, and the portraits of Pushkin and Baudelaire, the Manhattan skyscrapers, the books on the shelves, Marika sitting on the bed, and the color of dawn slowly filling up the room with the warmth of honey. Hearing in the hallway the neighbors' voices and footsteps, I clenched my mouth shut; I clenched my mouth shut so that I wouldn't shout out Mayakovsky's name at the top of my lungs and tell him to stop, to turn back. I had to force myself not to run to him, to take his hand and tell him in an affectionate whisper: "Damned. You, too, are damned."

Just then I heard the door open and someone enter the room. I forced myself not to turn to see who it was. I heard footsteps move about the room, the thud of a large, heavy object being placed on the floor, and someone take off his jacket and throw it on the bed: I glimpsed a fat hand with patches of blond hair approach the table and drop a yellow leather bag on it. I turned. The man was tall, strong, and in shirtsleeves. On the edge of the bed next to Marika sat a pale, disheveled woman whose face was shiny with sweat.

The man looked at me, and showing me a piece of paper, said: "I'm sorry, Comrade. You have to leave. My papers are in order. This room is mine now."

"Yes, it's yours," I said.

"So then get out," the man said. "What are you waiting for?"

"Let's go, Marika," I said.

"*Toujours tes idées ridicules*," Marika said, as we were descending the staircase.

I didn't answer her. I whispered affectionately, "You, too, are damned, Mayakovsky."

6

WE TOOK the no. 32 tram from Sverdlov Square to the Novodevichy Convent located at the tip of a long peninsula formed by the Moskva River as it snaked through the valley. The tram traveled lazily along for a while before plunging into the city's suburbs. In the Khamovniki District, a district of hospitals, the smell of carbolic acid wafted through the air as we passed a long succession of modern clinics constructed out of concrete and glass. Marika was happy. She liked these long tram rides across the city; or the bus trips with a *rabotniki* club to visit historic palaces on the outskirts of Moscow; or picnics in the Sparrow Hills (*Vorobyovy Gory*) where she would admire the vastness of the city with its thousands of golden domes covered in red, yellow, green, and turquoise ceramic tiles, and red flags waving atop the crenellated towers of the Kremlin. She admired that sprawling city rising out of a golden haze, emerging from that golden dust, the gold dust of Asia, the dust cloud of dusty Asia.

We got off the tram at the end of the line and headed on foot toward the Novodevichy Convent, a convent established for the nobility's virgins. It was renowned as the place where Peter the Great had locked up his sister and where he'd had the Streltsy rebels hanged from the windows' iron railings. It was here on the threshold of forest and field where Moscow became the provinces, a village. Surrounding the

Novodevichy Convent was a scattering of houses, poor dwellings on the edges of swamps and marshes extending along the Moskva's banks. The stale odor of hay and wet grass mingled in the air with the sweet dry smell of the smoke from burning birchwood. Small yellow dogs with scab-covered muzzles and red, human-like eyes (the provocative, embittered eyes of certain men between the ages of forty and fifty), stared as we passed by, then followed us at a distance, stopping only when Marika and I stopped. Next to the Novodevichy Convent was a small cemetery surrounded by a wall. We entered the enclosure and Marika led me through the graves to the tomb of the great Russian musician Scriabin. We sat down on a bench next to the tomb, one of those wooden benches in Russian cemeteries located near the graves so that relatives have a place to sit, pray, drink tea, and chat amongst themselves, displaying that loving familiarity with the dead unique to the Russian people.

"I wish someone from my family was buried in this cemetery," Marika said. "I would come here every day and spend a few hours. My dead are far away in the Caucasus. My family is from Tiflis."

Marika was a girl of sixteen, really still a child; she was a brunette with a dash of that fiery red in her dark hair that Gordon Setters have. The color was a kind of burned black repeated in her eyes, dark yet burning with a red flame, the whites—tiny glossy blots—only visible at the outer corners of her eyes. She had wide shoulders and small pert breasts, and her extensive training as a tennis player was demonstrated by the way she moved, how she gesticulated, how she walked with her left shoulder jutting slightly forward. Every time she moved her right arm, it seemed as if she were swinging a racket and hitting a ball. She wore her hair in plaits and the long, soft, heavy braids fell over her shoulders with a somewhat surly grace.

"Oh Marika," I said to her, "if I were to love you and you were to love me, wouldn't you come to Italy with me?"

Marika looked at me and laughed, her foot resting on the small iron fence around Scriabin's grave. "Italy?" she responded. "I don't like oranges."

"There aren't any oranges in Italy," I said.

"Ah, so there aren't even any oranges in Italy?" she said, smiling her mischievous smile.

I stroked her braids and, tossing her head, Marika said in English: "*You pig.*"

"Come with me to Italy, Marika," I said, stroking her hair.

Marika stood up and hurried away through the tombs as if she wanted to escape. I ran after her and, catching up to her, I put a hand on her shoulder.

"See there? That's the great Russian writer Chekhov's grave," Marika said.

"I don't give a damn about Chekhov," I said.

"And that's the grave of the historian Solovyov, and that one over there is Krapotkin's grave."

"I don't give a damn about Solovyov and Krapotkin," I told her, stroking her hair.

"*You dirty pig,*" Marika said, and she looked at me through her large black eyes with those white blots at the outer corners near her temples.

"Come with me to Italy, Marika."

Marika stared at me and said suddenly, "Oh, Italy!" Then she added, "Where in Italy is Mussolini's tomb?"

"In Italy, we don't bury men alive," I responded.

"I'd like to see Mussolini's tomb in Italy," Marika said, looking at me with her mischievous, sad eyes.

"All of Italy is a tomb," I replied. "All of Italy is Mussolini's tomb."

Marika stared at me contemptuously and, pulling away, suddenly said: "*You pig, you dirty pig.*"

She always called me this when she wanted to show her contempt for me and every so often she used another English word, which by now had found its way into the Soviet dictionary: "*Hooligan,*" which she pronounced "*huligan,*" in the Russian fashion.

I laughed and said: "All of Russia is also a tomb. All of Russia is Stalin's tomb."

"*Huligan,*" Marika said.

We had stopped near a fresh grave, the earth still moist, the mound strewn with large bouquets of still-fresh flowers. They appeared to have been recently picked and the sky was reflected in their petals, its pale silvery blue mingling with the pinkish-green ivory of the large delicate petals. These bouquets of flowers, gently deposited on a mound of fresh earth, or against a gray stone slab on which only a name and date were written, seemed detached from everything, inert and alive in a vast desert, abandoned in a profound solitude with their absolute significance as still-life events unto themselves, an accident, in no way tied to the history of the world, the history of living men.

Some of the petals had fallen off of their buds and were spread over the mound of fresh earth in an extraordinary solitude, sad, desperate, an abstract, remote solitude, the petals very far away from the bouquets like events themselves, detached from the main event without ties to the history of the world, to the history of dead men. And they seemed to be made of a hard, shiny, shell-like material that was abandoned on the seashore; and like the shells, their very form, their concave appearance, their curved world apart, exhibited signs of abandonment and solitude, a detachment from the history of the world, from nature, from the life of nature; and yet it was designed to gather the surrounding universe into itself, to enclose the universe within its concave world, inside its secret architecture.

Suddenly, I lifted my eyes to the gray gravestone and read the name: von Meck. I remembered having read the name in the newspapers. It was the name of the Director General of the Soviet Railways, executed by firing squad two days earlier for sabotage. Von Meck had been an old functionary, an honest functionary of the Russian railways since the prehistoric times of the czarist regime. He had been shot because the old locomotives and the antiquated railway apparatus, worn out from the war, could no longer bear the enormous load put upon them. The locomotive boilers, the newspapers reported, had been blowing up with suspicious frequency for some time. Von Meck had been shot for presenting Soviet public opinion with a political explanation for the technical reasons the Soviet railways were malfunctioning. He was a man without guilt, an innocent man, finding himself at a particular moment in the middle of railway tracks, and the locomotive that was the Soviet Revolution had run him down. He was not guilty in the least, he had no personal responsibility for his own death. The newspapers had announced that, exceptionally, von Meck's corpse had been given to his family so that he could be buried. It was, after all, an unimportant story, an episode like many others, by now detached from the story of the living. So what if an innocent man was shot due to the greater needs of the Revolution? He was not the first, nor would he be the last. It's what always happens. There is always someone, some innocent person, who dies for the others. And even if he dies alone, whether by killing himself or by being shot, he always dies for others. One cannot pretend that in a revolution only the guilty die. Imagine such a thing! Someone has to die. In fact, the death of someone innocent is always much more useful than the death of someone guilty. *On est toujours le jacobin de quelqu'un.* We are always someone's Jacobin. It's a great honor to be even a little bit of someone's Christ. A great honor to be a Jacobin to a Jacobin. A great sin that no one can be Christ to Christ.

"Von Meck was an enemy of the Revolution," Marika said. "A bad guy, *un sale type.*"

"He was an innocent man," I said. "Do you know what an innocent man is?"

"He blew up the locomotive boilers," Marika said.

"It's no longer *à la mode* to be innocent," I said.

"It was his fault the trains didn't work," Marika said.

"The trains still don't work," I said. "It's very dangerous to be the Director General of the Railways when the trains don't work. One must never be the *chef de gare* when there is *une révolution.*"

"*Tu dis toujours des bêtises*, you always speak such nonsense," Marika said.

"*Naturellement*," I said. "*Je dis toujours des bêtises.*"

I was beginning to get irritated with poor von Meck. It irritated me to think that he had found himself in the middle of the train tracks of the Revolution. It wasn't his fault if the trains didn't run, if the boilers blew up. *Mais tout de même!* But still! What presumption, what insolence, what a lack of tact to be stationmaster during a revolution. He deserved what he got. It's a luxury to be innocent when the world is blowing up like an old locomotive boiler. And after all, *de quoi se plaignait-il?* What was he complaining about? Wasn't he a Christian, a good Christian? He had become a martyr.

"They must be crushed without pity, all of them. There can be no pity for the enemies of the Revolution," Marika said.

That poor von Meck was really irritating me. It was a bourgeois presumption to believe oneself innocent, always innocent. Christ hadn't possessed that stupid bourgeois presumption. He was not bourgeois, Christ. He knew that he wasn't innocent. He knew that he deserved to die even if it wasn't his fault that the locomotive boilers blew up. Naturally, there was an enormous difference between Christ and von Meck. Christ wasn't the Director General of the Railways. For Christ, that was an extenuating circumstance. But even if he had been the Director General of the Railways, he would have died on the cross at Golgotha just the same. Von Meck, even if he had been Christ, would have been shot all the same for sabotage. I was beginning to get irritated with that poor von Meck. It irritated me to think that I was mixing Christ up with the stupidest things, with the most banal incidents, and even that, on my part, was a bourgeois presumption. One can't just suddenly liberate oneself from his bourgeois upbringing, traditions, and prejudices. Always Christ, *toujours le Christ*, and Christianity, and Christian morality, and the Christian idea of justice. To hell with all of it. One can't judge everything under the guise of Christian morality. At a certain point, one must have the courage to liberate oneself from Christian morality. I was irritated with von Meck above all because it was precisely his death that proved Christ's innocence. It was proof of the existence of God. Von Meck didn't have the right, with his stupid death, to provide the proof of the existence of God, of the superiority of Christian morality.

I leaned over von Meck's grave, picked up a flower, and offered it to Marika. I offered it to her without asking myself if poor von Meck would have been pleased by my offering his flower to Marika. But why shouldn't he have been pleased that I offered one of his flowers to such a beautiful girl, so young and pure? Marika, however, brusquely pushed my hand away and said, "*You dirty pig.*"

"He's dead," I said. "The flower belongs to a poor dead fellow, a flower I picked from the grave of a poor dead man."

I was standing before Marika with that dead flower clutched between my fingers, that poor flower shot for sabotage, thinking that the Russian Revolution is merciless, with no pity for treacherous flowers that blow up locomotive boilers in order to sabotage Soviet Russia. Standing before Marika, I smiled as I stared at her while she blushed, perhaps from modesty, or perhaps from shame, or anger. At a certain point, Marika extended her hand, brushing it against mine, and caressed that poor flower, touching its petals crushed by the lead of the firing squad, and I stared at her long white fingers, expecting them to be stained with the innocent blood of my poor flower.

Behind Marika's back stretched the landscape of *Voroby-ovy Gory*, delineated on one side by the white crenellated wall of the convent, and on the other by a green wall of wooded hills. In the distance, beyond the expanse of marshy meadows thick with reeds, a freight train was performing a maneuver on the railway embankment, puffing away as it went back and forth. The locomotive's whistle cracked the clear pinkish-green tinged air like a piece of glass. I saw the river glistening at the foot of the hills and the air over the trees and river trembling with the white flight of doves. The sky just above the convent wall was splotched with gray, suggesting finger smudges on the corner of an old print. Bushes thick with little yellow flowers similar to wild hyacinths grew next to the lane that curved along the marsh bank. The whole landscape was perforated by bullet holes, and the sky, the green hills, the white wall of the convent riddled with firing-squad bullets, also resembled an old, dusty, fragile, worn-out print. The objects strewn across that landscape—the freight train, the rocks, the cemetery crucifixes, the yellow dogs with the eyes of grown men—had a clear, precise significance as events outside of the history of the world, detached from the history of men, dead and alive.

Marika took the flower in her hand, squeezing and crushing it between her white fingers in a sad gesture that blended into the landscape with the slowness of a piece of paper blown by the wind out an open window; with the persistence of the river flowing along the foot of the distant hills.

I said to Marika in a quiet voice: "It's a dead flower, a flower shot for high treason. It betrayed the Revolution and the People and so was shot. It's still bleeding; look, your fingers are stained with blood."

Marika let the crushed flower fall and I noticed she had become slightly pale. But she laughed and said: "*Ne dis pas des bêtises*. Don't say such nonsense. Do you think you're scaring me? Such miracles don't happen in Russia. Flowers in my country don't bleed."

"I know, Marika," I whispered. "In Russia, all the flowers are made of paper."

We alighted from the no. 34 tram in Sverdlov Square before the two open archways—still there at the time—dividing Red Square from Sverdlov Square. Also still there was the tiny chapel dedicated to the Iberian Virgin, renowned throughout all of Russia, and so revered by the people that even Napoleon, out of respect, had placed a guard of honor, two grenadiers, by the door.

I said to Marika: "I'd like to see the Iberian icon of Our Lady."

The Iberian icon of Our Lady was from the Caucasus, and Marika's compatriot. Marika said, "Come on," and seemed happy to go greet her Virgin of the Caucasus. We crossed the threshold into the chapel. It was quite cold and at first we couldn't see a thing, it was so dark, but slowly from the shadows emerged the image of the Madonna on an altar adorned with candleless candelabras. Marika stopped before the icon, threw her lit cigarette onto the ground, crushed it under the tip of her shoe, and remained there unmoving and silent as if she were praying.

I said: "Marika, I'm happy to see you pray."

"*You pig,*" Marika answered in a slightly hoarse whisper.

I laughed and said: "You're praying for Stalin, aren't you, Marika?"

"*Taisez-vous,*" Marika said, turning toward me. "Be quiet," and suddenly she ran out into the square where she stopped at a cigarette vendor who wore a poster board around her neck that read MOSSELPROM.

Marika was angry with me because I had been alluding to a joke that was going around Moscow at the time. The joke was this: a *mujik* walks into the Chapel of the Iberian Icon of Our Lady and throws himself down on his knees before the miraculous icon and immerses himself in prayer.

"You're praying for Stalin, aren't you, Comrade *mujik*?" asks the Red Guard who was stationed at the chapel entrance.

"Naturally," responds the *mujik*.

"But before the Revolution you prayed for the czar, didn't you?" the Red Guard says, laughing.

"Naturally, I used to pray for the czar. What's wrong with that?" the *mujik* responds.

"Eh, but what good have your prayers done for him? You saw what a bad end your czar came to, didn't you?" the Red Guard asks him.

"That is precisely why I pray for Stalin," the *mujik* responds.

It was a Soviet joke, one of the many going around Moscow at the time, whispered with a laugh by everyone. There wasn't anything harmful in telling it, but Marika took offense at my laughter. She had also become angry with me a few days earlier for telling a funny story about Lunacharsky and the curate. There wasn't anything nasty about the story and I didn't understand why Marika had taken it so personally, as if the joke threatened to bring down the Kremlin. And even so, if the Kremlin was so unstable that a joke could cause it to fall apart, too bad for the Kremlin.

The joke was this: The anti-religion campaign had been launched and the Kremlin's official poet, Demyan Bedny—head of the League of Atheists, of the Godless, author of pamphlets against God—spoke on the radio against Jesus Christ and gave lectures decrying religion (and who could blame him? Jesus Christ was a notorious instrument of global capitalism, a dangerous Trotskyite). Out of loudspeakers attached to utility poles in front of church doors, the voices of the anti-theist propagandists were incessantly squawking, morning to night, vomiting insults and injuries against orthodox religion, against Christ's faithful. The Soviet People's Commissar of Education and Culture, Lunacharsky, was invited by the League of Atheists to give an anti-theist lecture in a Moscow theater. It was Easter Day and the theater was packed. For almost two hours, Lunacharsky spoke in his proud, eloquent manner, scientifically proving that Jesus Christ was dead and buried and had never been resurrected. The crowd had wildly applauded, and afterwards, as is the custom in Soviet Russia, Lunacharsky asked the public if someone would like to present an opposing viewpoint. An old, scruffy curate with a long unkempt beard and dressed in rags, a poor curate like so many thousands of others who still existed in Soviet Russia then, stood up and announced that he would utter only three words.

"Go ahead and speak, Comrade curate," Lunacharsky said.

Everyone stared at the curate, laughing, and many shouted at him: "You'd be better off keeping your mouth shut, Comrade curate. You don't want to contradict Comrade Lunacharsky, do you?"

But the curate turned to the crowd, raised a hand, and clearly pronounced the words of the greeting ritual said by every Christian in old Russia whenever encountering a friend on Easter morning: "*Christos voskres*, Christ is risen."

And the crowd responded in a chorus: "*Voistinu voskres*, He is risen indeed!" And everyone hugged one another.

"Forgive me, Marika," I told her. "I didn't mean to offend you. I only wanted to..."

"I know you were just having fun," Marika said, "but I don't like it when you make fun of certain things."

"I didn't mean to make fun of the Iberian icon of Our Lady," I said.

"I know," Marika said. "I know you didn't mean to make fun of the Iberian icon." She looked at me and smiled. "*Huligan!*" she said, and smiled. It was a sad smile, the corners of her mouth creasing in such a way that a childish bemusement took over her serious face.

"I am sorry that you can't love me in the way I would like, in the way you too would like, Marika," I said. "I am sorry that between us there are many things that are alive, and many things that are dead, and that you can't figure out which ones are alive and which are dead. Why don't you come to Italy with me, Marika? Would you like to come to Italy with me?"

"*J'aime bien vivre en Russie*," Marika said. "I quite like living in Russia."

She spoke French with an accent that was a bit sing-songy, like the Swiss governesses who before the Revolution taught French to the rich bourgeois families and the lower Russian nobility. Her upbringing had been the same as that of all the young girls from noble or wealthy bourgeois families before the Revolution, but a bit weak and vague due to the advent of the Revolution. Marika had been three years old in 1914 when the war broke out, and she was six in 1917 when Lenin came to power and took over Peter the Great's throne by seating himself on Czar Nicholas's lap. Her upbringing was the one inflicted by Swiss governesses on their wards, and it was more faddish than properly educational. Marika still had the dulcet hallmarks of the *Bibliothèque Rose* in her accent which echoed the dulcet accent of the Countess of Ségur, born Rostopchine, whose accent would become the accent of the rich bourgeoisie and of the nobility of Russia, overpowering the Pushkinian accent of Eugene Onegin and the cadences of Lermontov. With me, Marika liked to act the part of the "*jeune fille bien élevée*." It was like a game for her, a kind of innocent and childish show she put on in which she played the well-brought-up young lady, a

European girl who had lived through the atrocious years of the Revolution preserving intact the moral principles she had learned in her family, and hadn't let herself be disheartened or corrupted or degraded by the events, anguish, or misery of those atrocious years. But something hard had been born in her, something that perhaps she wasn't even aware of, something that didn't belong to her, that wasn't hers, that belonged to her generation, to the previous ten years of Russian history, not to her, Marika. Her knowledge of the French language, however, along with the shortcomings and uncertainty of her upbringing, even her coquetry, so unusual in a Soviet girl, betrayed her social origin, denounced what was in her both authentic and false, what was hers and what was imposed or acquired. In the brief hours Marika spent with me every day, she blindly trusted her instinct, her feelings for her origins and upbringing, her pride and pleasure at being able to show to a foreigner, to a European, to a "*sale bourgeois,*" that in the Russian proletariat in which the Revolution had overthrown all traditional social and moral values, all principles of the traditional family, it was still possible to meet "*une jeune fille bien élevée,*" "*une parisienne russe,*" a Russian-Parisian girl, who wasn't ashamed to be a "Red girl," to be "Lenin's daughter." I instinctively felt, however, that there was a kind of bitterness, a contempt in everything Marika said. I heard a sadness in her voice when she called me "*huligan,*" when she said to me "*you pig, you dirty pig,*" when she addressed me as a "*sale bourgeois.*" Marika, like all the young people of her generation, was sick with the anxiety that always accompanies an acquired faith, an external faith, an overly absolute certainty, an overly rigid, overly restricted moral system. All of that which in Karl Marx, even if rarely, is a concession to hope, to peace, to a reciprocal indulgence, to love, became in Marika, and in all of the young people of her generation, of her origins, a stolen tenderness, a weakness enjoyed only in secret, a bitter doubt. And every so often, in certain of her behaviors, in certain things she said, this anxiety of hers surfaced so suddenly and unexpectedly that Marika blushed as if she had demonstrated with an involuntary and instinctual gesture her secret wound.

"I feel dead in Russia," I told her.

"More of your nonsense," Marika said.

"Since living in Russia, I've realized that one has to learn how to live, that I have to learn how to live. I felt more alive in Europe. Europe is a dead place."

"*Les Russes* are very much alive," Marika said.

"Here I feel dead and rotting because this place is alive."

"It is a country of living men," Marika said.

"We're also alive, we feel alive over there; perhaps because Europe is a dead place, a putrid continent. It is a dead life, ours, over there. The Germans say *totes Leben*, living dead."

"In Russian we say *miòrtvaia jisn,*" Marika said.

"If you really think about it," I said, "it makes you want to laugh, really laugh. They torture us, make us suffer, bury us in prisons, take away our freedom to think, to be happy, to live, and all this for what? In order to teach us how to save our own skin! If they were to torture and kill us in order to teach us how to save our souls, I might understand. But our skin! Our human skin! That's how it is all over Europe. There's more hypocrisy in Europe than in Russia regarding skin. In Europe, everyone works toward the same goal. In Europe, human skin isn't worth anything anymore, and is worth much less than the soul, and yet all they can think about is teaching men how to save their own skin."

"Just think how Christ is laughing up there," Marika said. "If God exists, just think of the laugh he must be having."

"Don't say such things. You shouldn't say those things, Marika. What do you know about God?""

"What do you want me to know?" Marika said. "*Ici*, here, actually, we are less sure than you are *chez vous*, I think. But they teach us to be sure of everything, even what we don't know. There's nothing here we are more sure about than that which we doubt. We enjoy devising *les statistiques*."

"It's the same all over Europe."

"They want to substitute faith with statistics," Marika said. "The other day, our physics professor at the university claimed that if Christ had truly ascended into heaven, you should be able to calculate the speed at which he got there. He told us that airplane engines had made enormous progress from Christ onwards."

"Enormous progress for sure," I said.

"But one must believe in something, don't you think?" Marika asked.

"Certainly, one must believe in something," I said, and whispered the lines from Apollinaire's "Zone":

"C'est le Christ qui monte au ciel mieux que les aviateurs
Il détient le record du monde pour la hauteur."

(Christ soars higher in the skies than all aviators
He holds the world record for altitude.)

"*C'est jolie*," Marika said, "very pretty."

"It's at least as pretty as statistics. And far more reliable . . ."

"*Les statistiques*," Marika said, "are as reliable as poetry. Statistics don't deceive us."

"No, they don't deceive us," I said. "Even now we're able to calculate how many times in thirty seconds two plus two makes four."

"You shouldn't make fun of statistics," Marika said.

"Oh, no, we shouldn't make fun of statistics," I said. "It's all we have left that's certain in Europe today."

"So it's the same thing for you in Europe?" Marika asked.

"Naturally," I said, "it's the same thing. It's the same morality, the same philosophy, the same religion, the same science. Morality, philosophy, science, religion, all of these things that in Europe have no other aim than to teach men how to save their own skin. We'll all end up killing one another under the pretext of saving our own skin. Human skin has become the European flag. Each country has its own colors and design, but the fabric is made of human skin. Aren't you afraid of death, Marika?"

"Naplivaiu, j'y crache dessus," Marika said, spitting on the ground in that vulgar Russian manner.

"Don't say *j'y crache dessus*, Marika. It's better if you only say it in Russian, *naplivaiu*. In France you don't say *j'y crache dessus*. It isn't proper."

"Naplivaiu," Marika repeated, and spit on the ground.

"That's right, like that, in Russian, *naplivaiu*, that's better. In France you don't say '*j'y crache dessus*.' The French are polite. They know that you can spit on everything, even in France, but that it doesn't get you anywhere. And then, you know, it's depressing in the end to spit on everything. The French don't like to be sad."

"Are the French really happy? In Russia there is a saying—'happy as a Frenchman.'"

"Oh, no," I said, "*les Français ne sont pas gais*. No, they are not happy. They see very clearly. They see terribly clearly.

How could one be happy if he sees things terribly clearly? All the same, the French don't like to be sad."

"We don't see clearly," Marika said. "Russians don't see clearly."

"No," I said, "they don't see clearly, but they see far."

"Do the Russians see very far?" Marika asked.

"*Oh, oui, très loin*," I said, "very, very far. Even too far. But they don't see clearly. There's a better way to see far: presentiment. But Russians don't have presentiment."

"*Tais-toi*, be quiet, you're starting again with your nonsense," Marika said, placing her hand on my arm.

I could feel her hand trembling and I said: "*Il ne faut pas voir trop loin*, Marika. One mustn't look too far ahead."

"*You pig*," Marika said, "*you dirty pig*," and I felt her hand trembling softly on my arm.

The next day I went to visit Madame Kameneva. Everyone in Moscow's diplomatic world called her Madame Kameneva and I think it was a sign of respect, or perhaps of pity. Madame Kameneva was Leon Trotsky's sister. Only a few weeks earlier her husband, Kamenev, had disappeared from public life, exiled, it was said, to the Volga Delta, and Trotsky had been deported to the Caucasus. Everyone knew that exile was a prelude to death. Madame Kameneva remained sitting behind her desk at her job as the Director of Intourist, raising her eyes every time the door opened. She had been living like this for a few weeks, waiting. At the time, to be Trotsky's sister and Kamenev's wife was sad. When I opened the door, Madame Kameneva looked up at me and smiled. She was about forty years old, of medium height, pale, already gray, listless, and hunched—no, she wasn't exactly hunched, she appeared so because of the way she looked up to see who was coming into her office, the way she scrutinized the face of her interlocutor, the way she took a defensive stance, almost as if in ambush, bent over as if afraid of being struck from behind. She had blondish hair streaked with gray, but the hair near her temples was white. Her blue eyes, encased in a thick web of tiny wrinkles, squinted like a cat's whenever she spoke. She had little hands, a bit swollen, and so white that her veins looked like tattoos. She spoke French with a correct accent but seemed unsure about her choice of words. She appeared distracted while she spoke, as if thinking of other things. Whenever speaking with a Russian, one almost always had this impression. While he or she appeared to be thinking about something in particular, one never knew what he or she was actually thinking about; one might even say they were all thinking about the same thing, something that had absolutely nothing to do with the topic of conversation; they were all thinking of something from the distant past.

One always felt that the characters in Dostoevsky, Tolstoy, Gogol, Goncharov, and Chekhov, despite the passion with which they spoke, were actually thinking of something else, but always the same something else, everyone thinking about the same thing: Death, and the best way to become Christ. They thought of death in a precise way, as if it were an isolated object, illuminated by an overhead light and casting no shadow; they thought of death as a solitary object in a vast and desolate world, an object that filled the entire world. One felt that they were tormented by the thought of death as one is tormented by regret, rancor, and resentment, or by fear, by some ancient and savage fear. They never thought about life, about the mysteries of life; and that was a sure sign that they were alive in a world inhabited by death.

In today's Soviet Russia, however, one always had the suspicion that people were thinking about something else, that they were dominated by a lofty and fixed idea from which their attention never strayed. And they were tied to that idea like a man condemned to death is tied to the stake, his eyes blindfolded, his hands bound behind his back. No, certainly, oh, no, certainly not, they were not thinking about death; they were not thinking about death as an abandoned object, solitary in a solitary world; they thought, perhaps, about the emptiness left in the world by that object, the emptiness left by death. They thought of the emptiness left by sin, by Christ. But no, actually, they did not think of sin, of Christ, of the emptiness left by sin, by Christ, by death. They explored with their thought, their intense, fixed, pointed, sad, sharp thought, with it they explored an empty world, an empty hell, an utterly barren world without even a green leaf, where not even an insect would live, where any being, plant or animal, would die unable to breathe.

Madame Kameneva smiled, entirely absorbed by her pointed and sad idea. And that medieval German university joke came to my mind: "What is it that the dead don't eat? What is the thing that if eaten by the living would cause their death? That thing is: *nichts*, nothing." And I felt uneasy sitting there before Madame Kameneva thinking about that *nichts* of ancient German philosophy.

"So is that it? You're still ill?" Madame Kameneva asked me.

I wasn't ill. Madame Kameneva used the word "ill" in an attempt to express how ill at ease I had felt since coming to Russia. But I hadn't come to the USSR in order to flee Europe, to climb over "*ses anciens parapets*," to escape Western civilization, to find in Soviet Russia the revelation of freedom and human happiness. I had come to the USSR simply to collect documentary and bibliographical material in order to write *Technique du coup d'état* and *Le bonhomme Lénine*. When crossing the Russian border, I didn't think I had climbed over Europe's "*anciens parapets*"; instead I was crossing just another threshold of the many administrative kinds that divide our various European nations. In handing over the keys to my suitcases and my passport with all of its visas in order, I was in no way upset, rather I was irritated, like any traveler woken up in the middle of the night at a border station. But a few days after my arrival in Moscow, I began to feel uneasy. Not quite because I was in a country extraneous to Europe, in a country outside of European or Christian morality; not quite because I felt that having crossed the border into the USSR I had crossed the border out of Christianity; I felt uneasy because of something deeper, hidden, because of something absolutely "mine," and I couldn't express it or communicate it to others. In the crowds of Moscow, Leningrad, Kiev, Smolensk, Nizhniy Novgorod, Ivanovo-Voznesensk, Kazan, Samara, I didn't feel the kind of uneasiness one feels when one is lost in a crowd of strangers. I felt as if I was amidst a throng of workers on the periphery of some large European city. In Moscow, the hotel where I was staying—the Hotel Savoy, right in front of the walls of Kitay-gorod, the Tatar City, and the crenellated towers of the Kremlin—could very easily have been found in a working-class neighborhood of some European metropolis, or on the main street of some working-class city such as Essen, Manchester, Lodz, or Spandau. I didn't feel at all like a foreigner, I didn't feel at all uncomfortable among that crowd of young women and workers of every age, but above all young, who, toward evening when the offices and factories closed, flocked to the trams and filed down the sidewalks,

hurrying toward theaters, cinemas, gyms, pools, playing
fields, tennis courts, and *rabotniki* clubs. It was the same
crowd one sees on the outskirts of London, in Paris's Red
Belt, or in East Berlin, right after the workday is over. Tens
and tens of thousands, legions of bare-legged young women
wearing cotton skirts and canvas shirts, scarves over their
heads and tied beneath their chins, strolled jauntily along
swinging their tennis rackets like weapons. And the young
male workers were dressed in light blue overalls, or wore a
blue, white, red, or tan *tolstovka*, shiny black leather visored
caps, and galoshes. Those youths didn't look any different
from the crowds of young women and workers from the
suburbs of all the big European cities. Their way of laughing,
speaking, walking, of looking around themselves, was the
same as the crowds of Western workers at the end of a hard
day's work. That type of modern humanity had been achieved
at immense cost to the Russian people. It was painful to
think of how many victims, how many sacrifices, how much
struggle, how much hunger, how much blood had been
spilled in order to produce *l'enfantement*, the birth of those
exemplars of modern working humanity. All of it was, without a doubt, the magnificent result of a Marxist education.
"*Tout ça nous a coûté horriblement cher*, all of that cost us
very dearly," Madame Kameneva said proudly. It didn't disturb
me to think about all that blood, all those sacrifices that
were the price of such an extraordinary outcome, but instead
it filled me with a savage pride, a brutish satisfaction, and
envy, to think that all of that was the fruit of the Russian
people's labor and sacrifice rather than due to the easy heredity of Western civilization, as was the case for Europeans. I
was tired of that heredity that weighed on the conscience
and well-being of Western people. I was extraordinarily

moved to the point of trembling by the sad, gray splendor I saw in the eyes of young workers sitting in trams and on park benches in the evening, immersed in literature, or whom I saw talking amongst themselves while leaning against the bulwark at the far side of the Islands, the Leningrad park across the Neva, as pale amber waves from the Gulf of Finland beat gently against it, waves arriving from the distant misty horizon the silver color of cast iron. Already I was under the sad, cold spell of Leningrad's white summer nights, the "*bielaie noci*"; under the spell of the lazy silver-green water of the Fontanka River reflecting off the white and gold stucco walls of buildings by now empty and dead, their windows broken and, at best, covered with cardboard; under the spell of the vast deserted squares, their perimeters lined with ancient elderly people sitting along the sidewalks shaking their heads. I had not, however, let myself be overcome by the anguish emanating off the enormous buildings of Gogol's St. Petersburg, those immense gray structures from Hay Square where the student Raskolnikov, the murderer from *Crime and Punishment*, had lived and where today, on the sidewalk, in the drab, ghostly, cold night light, you ran into thin, pale young workers with bright eyes, their cheeks sunken by the ardor of the first *Pyatiletka*. Nor was I overcome by the dusty sadness of the workers' districts in Moscow; nor by the peaceful greenery of Sverdlov Square; nor by those Moscow streets where rich merchants lived behind window curtains, and where it still seemed possible to glimpse the pale and sweating face of Rogozhin, and to hear the buzz in the turbid air of the blowfly that emerged from the bedroom when Rogozhin showed Nastasya Filippovna's naked foot to Prince Myshkin. Every day I went to a *stolovaya*, a cafeteria where for forty or fifty kopeks I was offered the luxury of borscht, a soup of cabbage and sour beets, and *stakan chai*, a cup of tea, in the company of students from Sverdlov University or from Sun Yat-Sen, the Chinese university, and with workers from the chemical or electrical industries. I didn't feel uneasy when they looked at me strangely, often with hostility, staring at my suit and tie, my well-combed hair and manicured hands. They regarded me with a contempt that offended me, that I deemed unfair, but which I sensitively deflected without resentment because I understood their contempt wasn't personal to me, and that I had no reason to be ashamed or to feel uneasy in their regard. I was not, however, indulging them either. Their contempt was rightfully aimed at a society, a class, a civilization, not at me as a man, so my pride shielded me from feeling wounded by it. There was also perhaps an unconscious envy in their contempt, a repressed desire for a world they hated without knowing. Perhaps I also felt in their contempt something that was coming from somewhere far away, from distant resentments and suffering, from a hatred so repressed that it came to me as a caress and, like a bitter smile, barely touched me.

No, my discomfort was something else, somewhere else, located in the feeling that in Europe we had lost the ability to suffer for others, that each one of us in Europe suffered for himself and only for himself, that no one in Europe believed anymore in the necessity of a morality of suffering. We had lost that love of suffering, that taste for suffering so apparent in the Soviets and so immodestly on display for us foreigners to observe. My unease was located in the feeling that those young people, each and every one of them in that throng of workers, suffered for everyone, suffered for others, and no one suffered for himself alone; it was the feeling that each one of them was ready to sacrifice himself for others so that the people in Russia could have a better life; that each person in Russia, each man, woman, and child, everyone was ready to sacrifice his own happiness, his own life for the good of others, for the happiness of others. I was uneasy because I felt that in Russia where God was denied, and often rudely and loudly insulted with a kind of savage fury, here one was able to feel the presence of God more than in Europe, where by now even the energy needed to deny God was lost, his denial being a way of affirming him, of invoking him, of loving him. I felt Christ was here in Russia where everyone suffered for everyone else, because that was Christ's revenge, to be present as a living being, present in the love of sacrifice and suffering precisely in the places where he was denied and repudiated. I finally understood that the liberation of man was the liberation of God, that the brutality of man, of the Soviet life, of the fanatic thirst for suffering, the brutality that inflamed and skinned to the bones the Soviet young people was the greatest proof of the presence of God that an atheist people could possibly produce. I was uneasy because I felt Christ was there in those shiny gray eyes, and he was staring at me.

"*Le Christ est aveugle*," Madame Kameneva said.

"Christ doesn't have eyes, but he's not blind," I said. "He needs our eyes to see. *Il se cache en nous*, he hides in us, and he looks at the world through our eyes. He hides inside of us, in the deepest part of ourselves."

"*Dieu méprise les hommes*," Madame Kameneva said. "God despises humans. He abandons them to themselves. God couldn't care less about us."

"*Oui, Dieu méprise les hommes*," I said. "The Russian people are conscious of this abandonment, this solitude.

Man's greatest strength is precisely his consciousness of his abandonment, of his solitude. A man who doesn't feel God's contempt, his abandonment, is not a free man, but a miserable slave. In fact, the enslavement of the European people consists precisely in their conviction that God watches them, helps them, takes care of them, protects them, guides them, worries about them like a father worries about his children. Their glory and misery are caused by their belief that God forgives them and inspires them. They mix God into all their smallest matters, their business affairs, their passions, their daily well-being, their happiness and unhappiness. Without their conviction that God helps them, they wouldn't know how to live, struggle, suffer, build, hope, be happy, despair. The decline of Europe consists precisely in the inability of the people to accept the idea that God doesn't help or oppose them, that God is removed from their petty matters, that God is waiting for them at the gate, like an enormous spider. Humans don't know how to be alone. They don't know how to be human. They don't know how to be happy without God. They have a perpetual need for new proof, new signs, new miracles. They want God to reveal himself through these things; they want him to show his face in miracles. The modern world is thirsty for miracles. They don't know humans can be happy without proof, happy without believing in God, happy by themselves."

Madame Kameneva listened to me while staring at her small, slightly swollen hands, her pale, opaque nails too big for her tiny hands. She was a fat woman who was slowly beginning to let herself go, to sag, and the pallor of her face, the deformed swelling of her hands, legs, and face were not only signs of an incipient exhaustion of the flesh, but indicated the revelation of something even more horrible and inscrutable. She was a woman who was already dead. A subtle odor of dead flesh spread through the room. The soft fat encasing her had a dull amber glow, a yellow hue with long, deep, greenish reflections. Hers was not the corpulence that comes with age, that precious, soft, delicate, and smooth fattiness of tired flesh common in women over forty: it was the sweet adiposity of death, that sad embonpoint or swelling of corpses. There was something lugubrious in her slow movements, in her fixed stare, in her way of speaking in a low, deep voice. While she spoke, gently lifting her face, slowly moving her lips upon which a dead, bloodless smile trembled, something alive briefly shone on her brow and in her eyes, something that was almost immediately extinguished, and silencing herself she lowered her head while composing her face into the attentive immobility that awaits the dead. Her entire way of moving, her slow, almost lazy vivacity, her fearful and suspicious way of leaning forward, peering at the door as soon as she heard the vaguest sound of footsteps, the turn of the handle alerting her to someone's arrival, all were things done by those who believed themselves to be gravely at risk, who lived with the terror of an ambush, endured the nightmare of being under constant—as horrible as it was unidentifiable—threat. This is precisely how a painter would depict those condemned to hell, as a soul not yet dead, and no longer alive, teetering on the edge of hell's abyss where one finds the powerful secrets of life and death. This is how Sophocles depicted Alcestis as she was vied over by Hercules and Thanatos. All the perfumes in Admetus's kingdom could not extinguish that smell of lifeless, tired flesh, the smell of death's sweet fat that Alcestis left behind her when she set off toward Hades, Thanatos leading her there by the hand.

I looked at Madame Kameneva and a profound pity arose from deep in my heart. She was a woman who had already begun to die, who was already in agony from the day her husband, Kamenev, and her brother, Leon Trotsky, were led away by the "leather jackets" of the GPU. And though embarrassed for her, I felt it an insult to have pity on that poor, lost, aggrieved woman oppressed by the nightmare of death. All my Italian and German blood, that entire combination of Italian kindness and German brutality (no, not brutality, but a Faustian envy of death, *der Todesneid*, complacency at the thought of death, complacency in the face of suffering, and severe brutality toward oneself, a brutal examination of oneself and others), forbade me from insulting her by having pity on her. That poor woman was oppressed by the shame of mixing her own suffering, her own weakness, with suffering for others, with her thirst and her "duty" to suffer for everyone else. She shuddered at the idea that someone would realize that she suffered herself and for herself. She was ashamed of being afraid and perhaps she shuddered because I had noticed that she had already begun to die, and it wasn't the tired corpulence of her years, but the horrible embonpoint of death that had already invaded her body, already swollen her legs, arms, hands, her pale and desperate face. For the first time, I saw in her that happy anguish of Soviet life, that fear of not being worthy of suffering for others, that shame of suffering oneself, for oneself, that marvelous, if cold and brutal, tendency of the soul to sacrifice itself for others, to give life to the Revolution, to communism, to bringing about a better world in which *others* would live free and happy. It was that envy of death, that *der Todesneid*, which always made me feel like a foreigner in my own country, among my own people, so servile in the face of death; it was that envy of death, almost a secret envy, that made me realize to my horror that the woman was happy, that already dead woman was happy to sacrifice herself for the cause, to die, even if innocent, by the hands of her people.

"*Les Russes sont heureux*," said Madame Kameneva in a whisper, "the Russians are happy even if in Russia it's not easy to get used to happiness. It's not a question of habit. This idea of a happiness that is difficult to get used to is a sentiment particular to the Soviet Union. In Europe, one gets used to everything. *Tout y devient habitude*, everything becomes habit. Our happiness is changeable, unstable, so full of moral and intellectual adventures. Marxism is not a rigid prison, a world of cement and steel, a flat, immense plane; it is a marvelous world, full of marvelous inventions, discoveries, revelations. It is like that enchanted forest found in German fairy tales. In Russia no one ever thinks about death. Lenin truly killed death. You were Mayakovsky's friend, weren't you? Do you remember what Mayakovsky said about Lenin? 'The most earthly of men.' Lenin truly struggled against death his whole life and he won. Today in Russia, Soviet life is restricted to the essential themes of life. We think of nothing else but life. This is the true way toward human freedom. Don't you think that it could lead humanity toward something higher, purer, and new, this death of death?"

"Do you think it's possible to be happy," I asked, "without continually thinking about death?"

"No, that is not what you mean," Madame Kameneva said. "That is surely not what you mean. You mean that one cannot live without the thought of death." She straightened her hair with a slow stroke of her hand, then lifted up her face and stared at me a while. Finally, she said, "By now, it's over for me. I don't regret having sacrificed my life for a better future for humankind. I gave all of myself to the communist revolutionary cause. If in Russia death still existed, I might wish to die. But death no longer exists in Russia. Do you understand what I'm saying?"

She got up and returned to the window. She pressed her forehead against the glass. "In Russia, death is a closed door," she said, "you knock and knock and no one answers. It ends like this, like a sick dog before a closed door. It ends: yes, this is the expression. One doesn't die: it ends. The rest, the physical death, is no more than an administrative formality. But death, that safe refuge, that high hope, that forbidden world, doesn't exist anymore in Russia."

I said in a whisper: "You all believe in God."

Madame Kameneva turned and silently stared at me for a long time, while in her cold gray eyes something gently died: "*Ne soyez pas ridicule*," she said, "don't be ridiculous."

We were in Theater Square, in the middle of a small crowd intent on observing a few workers who were, with the help of ropes and pulleys, unloading onto a pedestal from the platform of an enormous truck the enormous statue of the playwright Ostrovsky, when to my great surprise, I saw a carriage coming slowly toward us across Sverdlov Square. I hadn't yet seen a carriage in Russia. The Revolution had blasted them into a hell of rusty junk with that fanatic and rather ridiculously juvenile hatred the Communist Revolution had for all that represented aristocratic privilege, all instruments of individualism. It was an old "landau," its wood worm-eaten, its original pink paint by now blackened by weather and wear. An old coachman wrapped in a faded green cloak, a true *isvocnik*, was seated on the box. A thread-bare and grease-stained brown top hat sat upon his ruffled white hair. The *isvocnik* had an unkempt beard, dark liquidy eyes, and a toothless mouth.

"A carriage," I shouted. Curious, the small crowd turned and stared with me as the old landau approached, pulled at a slow trot by an ancient and emaciated horse.

"*Ne criez pas si fort,*" Marika said, staring at the landau with deep disdain, "don't shout so loudly."

The carriage passed in front of us and I shouted: "There's a ghost inside, Marika!"

"*Toujours des bêtises,*" Marika said, "your incessant non-sense."

"The czar's corpse is inside," I said.

"You pig."

"The czar's corpse is in there, I tell you, there's a ghost, a corpse in there. I saw him sitting in the corner. I tell you, a corpse is in there, Marika."

"You pig."

"Perhaps it's Lenin's mummy, Lenin's embalmed corpse. I saw him with my own eyes, I tell you. What's so strange about that? Can't he go for a ride in his carriage to get a bit of air? Oh, Marika, why don't you run over to the *isvocnik* and ask him to stop and let us get in? I would love to go for a ride around Moscow in a landau with Lenin's mummy."

"You dirty pig," Marika said.

And just at that moment, the landau did stop and a pale face peered out of the door. In French, a voice said: "*Bonjour, bonjour, Malaparte, est-ce que je peux vous offrir une place dans ma voiture?* Hello there, Malaparte, may I offer you a ride in my carriage?"

Inside the carriage sat Florinsky, Chief of Protocol of the

People's Commissariat for Foreign Affairs of the Soviet Republic, all rouged and powdered, his little yellow eyes rimmed with black, his eyelashes hardened with mascara. Red hair stuck out from under the yellow leather visor of an odd hat made of white canvas which he wore at an angle. He was dressed entirely in white linen and wore white tennis shoes and white silk socks. He was seated in a corner of the carriage, sitting up straight, his white-gloved hands resting on the ivory pommel of a Malacca cane, the sort once carried by the *beaux*, the beautiful people of 1905, and similar to the one in the famous portrait by Boldini of Robert de Montesquiou, and in his hands Florinsky held a bouquet of flowers. A former functionary in the Ministry of Foreign Affairs under the czar, he was the most famous man among the entire world of foreign diplomats in Moscow. When the ambassadors and diplomatic representatives of foreign states initially arrived in Moscow, the first official person they glimpsed was a tall and willowy man who was at the same time plump and ruddy, dressed entirely in white linen and wearing an odd white canvas cap with a yellow leather visor, hopping about on the station platform. He was the Chief of Protocol of the People's Commissariat for Foreign Affairs. Flushed and smiling, Florinsky would wave his arms and lean in while saying in his sharp, high-pitched voice, like an anemic woman, *"Mon cher Ambassadeur, mon cher Ministre,"* as if he weren't welcoming to the Soviet Republic a representative of His Majesty's Britain or someone from the Republic of Guatemala, but rather a personal friend whom he hadn't seen for many years.

In winter, Florinsky wrapped himself in the folds of a huge overcoat lined with wolf fur and sported a tall fur hat, his red hair framing his forehead. When he took off his coat, he resembled a sea urchin emerging from its spiny shell, his red crustacean flesh coming out of its wolf-fur carapace. "*Vous connaissez mes habitudes*, you know my habits" wrote Jean Cocteau modestly, soberly in his letter to Jacques Maritain. Everyone in Moscow knew Florinsky's habits, and they smiled at them indulgently. He was sophisticated, spirited, gossipy, grudge-holding, nasty, and mean. Outlandish stories were told about him in the world of foreign diplomats, and it was good practice to be prudent when speaking in his presence. Everyone believed he was a coward and they attributed his cowardice to his suspicious character and shady dealings. Even Florinsky disappeared from one day to the next during the Great Purge of 1936. But at that time, in 1929, he was a man *à la mode* in Moscow, and if there was a bridge table adorned by an ambassador or the wife of an ambassador, it was inevitably also ornamented by Florinsky's presence. I always wondered if he truly was a coward. At the time, it took some courage in Soviet Russia to show off certain "habits." Revolutions always had their puritanical side—of which one needed to be wary. Much more than ugly people, beautiful women and handsome men, the clever and witty, but especially handsome men, were in constant danger during a revolution. Revolutions despised physical beauty under the pretext of moral beauty. One could be beautiful and virtuous, but not in revolutionary times. Physical beauty for Jacobin or communist fanatics was always reactionary and counterrevolutionary. Only at a later time, when the passions of the uprising, revenge, and murder had been placated, did the historians of revolution discover that Louis XVI was ugly, that Marie Antoinette wasn't beautiful, that Czar Nicholas was short. But revolutions vaunt a hatred for sexual perversion, an incredible intolerance. Patek, the

Polish ambassador, who knew Florinsky for twenty years, said, "He was so afraid of giving himself away, he slept with women." And raising his eyes to the heavens, he added: "Poor Florinsky! What self-abnegation! What proof of his communist faith!" When Moscow was invaded by bands of hungry *bezprizorni*, homeless boys who, armed to their teeth, attacked pedestrians and homes, committing all manner of theft and murder, their juvenile association one in which cocaine, syphilis, prostitution—in sum, debauchery—reigned, it was said that Florinsky took to wandering the streets at night in search of one of these *bezprizorni* whom he then brought home, fed, and housed, making of him his *mignon*, his pretty boy, for a few days.

Florinsky's black carriage was legendary. It was the only one left in all of Russia. It was an expression of his supreme decadent elegance, that landau painted black with its worm-eaten wood and torn upholstered seats protruding with tufts of oakum and horsehair. It was similar to Oscar Wilde's green carnation or to Montesquiou's tie and goatee. Like certain decadent types, certain perverts who dress in an eccentric fashion, abandon themselves to singular habits, indulge in extraordinary luxuries and liberties, so it was with Florinsky who abandoned himself to his singular, precious, and decadent tastes in that old landau. That landau was his love nest, in the same way that for certain Proustian characters their carriages had been their stage. And if in a man like Florinsky, who was always joyful, smiling, mannered, light-hearted, and *spirituel*, his somewhat lugubrious taste was marveled at by some, he wasn't a marvel to me since it seemed evident that Florinsky's smiling way of doing things concealed a particularly lugubrious sensibility, a suspicious compliance with dead things. In a certain sense, this way of his was even more his secret chamber, his *boudoir*, and also the old-world window through which he contemplated the new world, and one was never sure if he did so more with love or regret.

Florinsky was sitting up straight in a corner, resting his hands on the pommel of his cane, the bouquet of flowers in his hands making his face by contrast appear even more crimson and pasty, made up as it was with rouge, eyeliner, eyebrows elongated with pencil, eyelashes thickened with mascara, a red fringe of hair cascading over his forehead. All of it gave an impression of a wax mask. He laughed, and laughing showed off teeth that were too white, so white they seemed false. He looked at Marika with suspicion and obvious vexation, as if she were an intruder. I sat in front of him and Marika to his side. On his lap was a box of chocolates into which every so often he sank his long fingers with their shiny pink nails.

"I like to go out every day in my carriage. Moscow is very pretty when one sees it from the window of a carriage such as this." And with a grimace he added: "I despise automobiles."

Contemplating that surprising character, I stared at him with sadness and a hint of disgust. Florinsky was not a recently converted communist. He had joined the Bolshevik party some years before the Revolution. He sucked on a chocolate for a moment, then spat it out into a handkerchief, wrapping it up carefully in the soft folds of fine linen batiste. He was a *"vieux bolchevik,"* one of Lenin's old guard. He had been attracted by the morbid, decadent, prankish aspects of the Communist Revolution, along with its secret conspiracies, clandestine operations, and danger. His Marxism wasn't, however, that of a dilettante. He found himself on this side of things for the same reasons the Goncourt brothers were on the other side; not due to snobbery, which might have been one's snap judgment, but rather due to his taste for the precious, the rare, and the unusual. For Florinsky, Marxism was a kind of complement to his perverted nature.

"*Voulez-vous un chocolat*?" he asked me. They were chocolates from the famous Fuchs of Warsaw. Florinsky—his name revealed his distant Polish origins—did not like the Polish.

"Ah, chocolates from Fuchs," I exclaimed. "There is nothing more exquisite in the world."

Florinsky laughed heartily, opening his mouth wide and twisting in his seat while making exaggerated womanish gestures. "Do you remember Skirmunt?" he asked me. "Where might he be now, poor old Skirmunt?"

"I think he's dead," I said.

A few days earlier I had run into Florinsky at the Scala, an upscale *tabarin* in Moscow reserved for foreigners and he had spoken to me at length about Warsaw, where I had been the junior attaché with Minister Tommasini's Legation for nearly two years (the Italian Legation in Warsaw was at the time in the Potocki Palace on Krakowskie Przedmieście Street). We spoke about Maurice Potocki and the beautiful Countess Potocka. Florinsky asked me if I knew Skirmunt, who had been the Polish Ambassador to Rome in 1921. Indeed I did. One evening, Skirmunt invited me to lunch at the Excelsior Hotel. I was then frequenting Rome's Polish society circles and had many friends among them. I didn't know the "*habitudes*" of Skirmunt, and so was surprised when Ambassador Skirmunt received me in his dressing gown. Skirmunt was already an old man, thin, with that false embonpoint that certain thin men have who are too flushed, too pasty, too primped. I didn't know if I should stay or leave, in no way relishing that tête-à-tête lunch in a hotel room with an old man who drank one shot of vodka after the other. The drinking animated him, made him laugh and flit about the room while waving about a shaker and offering *zakuski* (hors d'oeuvres) from a large tray of solid silver. He caressed the liquor bottles with his fingers, grazed with his fingertips the slices of smoked salmon that lay on top of toasted bread, and with the tip of a silver fork picked at the caviar, the butter, the pickles, the sardines, the anchovies, and the Greek olives, which were distributed around the room in silver dishes. The waiters looked at me out of the corners of their eyes with imperceptible smiles on their lips, and I wasn't quite sure what to do, whether to stay or go. In the end, I decided to stay, reassured by the presence of the domestic staff. They were also Polish and had huge drooping mustaches like those still worn by the Zakopane mountaineers of the Tatra Mountains, and they were dressed in strange red uniforms with delicate gold embroidery on the sleeves and around the buttons. We began to eat and Skirmunt, ignited by alcohol and the anticipation of prey, pushed the *zakuski* on me followed by shots of vodka and, while gesticulating, let fall open his dressing gown to expose his chest, revealing sagging pinkish breasts covered with curly white chest hair like the soft curls draped over the ears of Greek statues of Apollo. As the lunch went from *zakuski* to *zakuski* according to the Polish ritual, and from vodka to vodka, and from the *zakuski* moved on to the *barszcz*, which is the Polish version of Russian borscht, and from *barszcz* to goose and on to traditional game hens swimming in a purple puddle of blueberries, and from game hens to a veal pot roast wrapped in pungent bay leaves, "the laurel of the Capitol,"

Skirmunt said, grazing with his fingers a piece of roast and trying to flick it into my mouth across the table with a gesture that, who knows why, made me think of Marie Antoinette and her amiable follies at Trianon (and this was without a doubt not very respectful of the memory of poor Marie Antoinette), I slowly began to detect a mysterious atmosphere of complicity between my Amphitryon and his Polish servants who had moved to surround my seat and were pouring in my glass every kind of wine with an attention too exquisite not to be suspicious. I had the impression that I was a prisoner in some perfumed Bastille caught in the coils of one of those dangerous conspiracies of which the Polish are masters. Any minute I expected someone to bite my neck. Skirmunt sent the two Italian servants away from the hotel room and in that instant I felt I was lost. Even though I had drunk quite a bit myself, forced as I had been to imbibe, I was still in control of my actions, if not entirely of my thoughts, and I perceived the dangers arising before me. Already once, when I had tried to stand up, I had felt a heavy hand rest on my shoulder and push me back down into my chair. I was preparing myself for a fight when Skirmunt stood up and wanted to teach me to dance the Polish mazurka, *la polonaise*. I had learned that elegant and bellicose dance in Warsaw, taught to me by rather different teachers, where it had been a pleasure for me to dance in the halls of Princess ———'s beautiful home, visited regularly by the officers of the Third Guards Uhlan Regiment. While the Polish servants beat time with their hands, I tried to dodge Skirmunt but he had already forced me into the first steps when the door opened and, *en coup de vent*, the Countess Potocka breezed into the room shouting, *"Ah, mon cher!"* She was living in Rome at the time in her beautiful Trinità dei Monti apartment. She was accompanied, if I remember well, by Count Pálffy of Hungary. At the sight of them, Skirmunt became red with fury, wrapped his dressing gown around him like a toga, and advanced threateningly toward the Countess Potocka. *"Ah, malheureuse!"* he cried, and waved his arms about like a banshee. I got ready to flee, taking advantage of that happy, unexpected circumstance, when I heard a shout and turned around just in time to see the Countess Potocka lift a hand to her face and for Skirmunt to withdraw his hand while the air resounded with that sacrilegious slap—which was the first but not the last. Count Pálffy moved forward and with a grace that certain gentlemen impose on all their actions planted a strong backhanded slap on Skirmunt's cheek before the widened eyes of the Polish servants. I don't know what happened next because I slipped out the door and ran down the stairs, and was no longer witness to that ancient Italian comedy in which at a certain point all the characters start beating and slapping one another. The uproar that slap caused all over Rome was tremendous, even if slaps in Rome weren't a rarity. My story pleased Florinsky no end, and I owed to that adventure, I think, the kindness and sympathy poor Florinsky always showed me thereafter.

Sitting in the corner of his lugubrious carriage, Florinsky munched his Fuchs chocolates and laughed heartily, his head bobbing on his shoulders in the manner, I believe, of certain Gogol characters. *"Ah, ce pauvre Skirmunt!"* he said laughing. "I can just see him now in his dressing gown, hee, hee, hee!" After that, every time he ran into me in the *fumoir* at the theater, at a diplomatic reception, or at a concert hall, he would ask me to tell him about my adventure with Skirmunt, and about the slap Skirmunt gave the Princess Betka

Radziwill, and finally, after having laughed for a good while, he would say to me: "Why don't you write a story about Rome's most famous slaps?" He proposed, naturally, that I begin with the slap Sciarra Colonna gave to Pope Boniface VIII in the Anagni Cathedral.

"No, let's leave the past alone," I said. "Modern slaps are much more entertaining." And I told him the story of the most infamous slaps given or received in Rome over the last several years. I had calculated that by just remaining within the realm of the foreign diplomatic corps in an embassy or foreign legation posted to the Quirinale or the Vatican, during the past ten years a great number of slaps had flown through the air, and as many scandals had ensued. Florinsky, as he put it, "*adorait*" these gossipy stories. "You tell them so well!" he said. "*C'est un art.*" And he added: "Even at the British Embassy?"

"Naturally," I said. "But one mustn't mention it."

"*Pourquoi pas?*" Florinsky cried, grabbing my knees with both of his hands. "If you tell me what went on at the British Embassy, I'll tell you Moscow's gossip. There is a long history of slaps in Moscow too!"

"I would think so!"

"Tell me about the scandal at the British Embassy and I will tell you about the wife of our *Commissaire...*"

So I told him the story of the British ambassador in Rome, which I can't repeat here. Florinsky squeezed my knees with trembling hands, leaned forward, his lips parted, his tongue between his teeth, hissing with pleasure, joy, and wonder while stamping his feet and shivering with pleasure. "*Et alors, Son Excellence l'Ambassadeur d'Angleterre...* tell me, tell me again... your Minister of Foreign Affairs, Monsieur Grandi... tell me, tell me again, I beg you... the police...

Ha, ha, ha! An entire night of violin … Ha, ha, ha!" and he hissed with his tongue between his teeth, as if the chocolates from Fuchs were searing his tongue.

"*Tovarisch* Florinsky," Marika said, sternly, "Comrade Florinsky."

"*Oh, je le sais*, I know, all of this isn't worthy of the Revolution, etc., etc., but you are only a little girl who knows nothing of life …" Florinsky said, staring at Marika with impatient resentment. Turning to me, he said: "*Oui, naturellement*, but do you think we don't hear similar stories in Moscow?" And he began to tell me all the gossip and scandals of the communist nobility regarding high-level functionaries of the Party and State, high-level officers of the Red Army, Soviet diplomats, of everyone, in sum, who belonged to Soviet high society and who today, looking back after almost twenty years and across three Five-Year Plans and the war, seem akin to the *ancien régime* of the Communist Revolution. Florinsky was a typical product of those years, a leading representative to the highest degree of that communist *ancien régime*. Combined in him, with a particular acidity, were all the moral, aesthetic, social, and intellectual elements of the communist period during the war, fermenting variously with the politics of NEP and Trotskyism still lingering in Soviet life at the time—such things as a sense of the provisional; regret over the underground struggle; the survival of desires, habits, prejudices, and the sophisticated high life under the czar; the moral detachment from the effort of social construction, in other words, of Stalinism. All of that which today falls under the heading "Trotskyism" surfaced in Florinsky with immodest intensity, with a murky sincerity, to which his perverted nature lent an extraordinarily strong, spicy flavor. Everything included in the significance of the Goethean expression *bewegliche Gesetze* or "flexible laws," which the new Soviet society refused to obey, even if obeying them without knowing it in the darkest recesses of its consciousness, had no effect on Florinsky and the decadent communist society that was about to cede its place to the new Stalinist society, to the Marxist society to which the Five-Year Plans were about to give life. If I had to compare Florinsky and the society of his era to a historical figure and time, I would compare him to those unique characters of the Directoire period, such as Joséphine de Beauharnais, who had their small group of devoted followers. An old Marxist, a revolutionary of long standing, Florinsky still obeyed the agitation that the former czarist regime, the bourgeoisie, had left as a legacy, not to the men of the Revolution, but to the new communist society, or so-called communist society, produced by the 1917 Revolution. What I mean is that Florinsky was a contemporary of NEP, not a contemporary of the First Five-Year-Plan. He was decadent, in the ways that the communist society of those years was decadent—so trampled and polluted by the formidable, dangerous whiffs of Trotskyism, so fired up by passions, ambitions, and perversions. The significance conveyed by the word "Trotskyism" was not simply relevant to society, nor only to the moral collective, but to an individual's morality.

Florinsky's taste for the worldly life, his snobbishness, his penchant for forbidden pleasures, his sophisticated and perverted nature, his sophisticated egotism, his at once elegant and vicious cynicism, his skepticism—which was so apparent regarding the typical problems of Soviet life, but hidden and rigorous regarding the fundamental problems facing communism and the communist life—all of these traits were not exclusively his but were, in fact, shared by all of the Soviet nobility at the time. Some believed that he was the perfect embodiment of the societal decadence of "war communism" and a harbinger of its demise. He was, or he appeared to be, a Proustian character, complete with all that was missing from Proustian characters—that being a prophetic quality along with nostalgia, regret, remorse, and presentiment. The entire jumbled line-up of confused intricate existences that make up Proust's characters came together, like the four-in-hand reins in the grip of a coachman, in Proust's soft wax fingers and, arriving at the final page, were "steeped in the meek dimness of candlelight, nevertheless happy to believe in the sweet anguish of a pearl-gray and black dandy," were steeped in the "fumes of his fumigations, face and voice devoured by nocturnal use," in "the liquid darkness of his room," in the light from his lamp "pale and sticky like a jam," in his night full of "white gleamings of rare orchids and of Odette's gowns," of crystal "champagne glasses and chandeliers and the frilled shirt-fronts of General de Froberville," as he slowly fell asleep in his bed, slowly opened his closed fist. (And if here I cite Paul Morand and his particular version of Marcel Proust, it is for the exemplary value of Morand as a chronicler of his time, for his instinct for singular existences.) Florinsky was a Proustian character, just as Pushkin's Eugene Onegin might be considered a Proustian character, or Goncharov's Oblomov, all characters, that is, of a Proust who had grown up in Russia. Through his sexual perversion, Florinsky declared the tragic sunset of a revolutionary society that would soon be polluted and corrupted by their love of power, by their disorganized exercising of power, by their relatively inordinate ambitions, and by the particular immorality of the elite who had remained faithful to an unrealizable utopia. After some time, even Florinsky, that tragic and grotesque mask of the Soviet *ancien régime*, would have to disappear along with Radek, Zinoviev, Kamenev, Tukhachevsky, with the whole group of decadent Trotskyites, the "traitors." And for me Florinsky was the perfect mask of Trotskyism, that grotesque and lugubrious character with his rouged cheeks, his painted eyes, his shiny pink fingernails, who sat like a corpse in a corner of that old black landau dragged around the turbulent streets of Moscow by a poor old broken-winded nag who was all skin and bones.

Florinsky sat stiffly in the corner of the landau, his hands leaning on the pommel of his cane, the bouquet of flowers in his lap, munching on the chocolates while chuckling: "Hee, hee, hee!" He looked old, horribly old (he wasn't yet fifty), with his little head, ruddy and plump, his white skin, his small girl-like hands, his porcelain teeth. His gestures made a singular contrast with his otherwise rigid demeanor, his movements were soft and graceful, and he moved his hands while he was speaking, as if to the rhythm of some mysterious music, and every so often he stopped his hands in midair, his pink fingernails glowing in the shadowy interior of the carriage. His voice was shrill and seemed at some moments to be the voice of an old man, at others to be the voice of an irritable child. He spoke a refined, mannered, and gentle French with the accent typical of Russians from a good family, the one Turgenev said was the eighteenth-century French accent that had only survived in Russia and Poland. But what was surprising about Florinsky was that he spoke about these characters of the Soviet nobility, who were predominantly people who had come from nothing, without any sort of refinement and without *manières*, as if he were speaking about regulars of the Faubourg, the Jockey Club, or Grosvenor Square. He spoke of Tomsky, Radek, Voroshilov, and Lunacharsky with the same snobbishness with which in different times he would have spoken of the Countess of Noailles, of the Princess of Faucigny-Lucinge, or the Princess of Polignac; and he spoke of Stalin in the same way he might have spoken about Sosthène de La Rochefoucauld. He described to me Madame Lunacharsky's *négligées* as he might have described a Schiaparelli *négligée* worn by Barbara Hutton. He insisted on describing to me how Tomsky, the Soviet leader of the All-Russian Central Council of Trade Unions, comported himself at the dinner table in the same way and with the same impeccable manners as Boni de Castellane at the baccarat table. The lovers, the scandals, the affairs, the divorces of the Soviet nobility flowed through his discourse as if lifted directly from the scandal sheets of "The Upper Ten Thousand" from Edward VII's era or from the gossip columns about the *fleur de pois* during the time of Loubet or Fallières. What I mean is, he wasn't comparing Soviet society to that of czarist St. Petersburg, or to that of Paris or London, but he spoke of it as a contemporary of Edward VII might have spoken about the high society of his time. Florinsky's moral debasement, his decadence, manifested itself in the investment he made in laughing at communist society, without suggesting that it had been modeled after the czarist *ancien régime*. He was aware of his society's corruption and he laughed at it as if he could see before his eyes not the model of czarist society, which was also corrupt though splendid and of *grandes manières*, but a model of an ideal communist society that he judged by now unrealizable, failed before it was even born. This was, in fact, the substance of his Trotskyism. He spoke of various perverts among the Soviet nobility, without a nod to the unparalleled examples of Oscar Wilde's generation, instead focusing on those of the Marxist society prophesied by Lenin and by now unrealizable. Amazed, I asked myself what could possibly be, in Florinsky's eyes, the ideal of a pervert in a perfect Marxist society.

Perhaps his idea of a pervert was Karakhan, the famous Karakhan, famous for the Communist Revolution in China, then as ambassador in Ankara, and still then as Vice Commissar of Foreign Affairs: the handsome, mysterious, tall, and thin man with a jet-black Renaissance-style goatee and eyes veiled by spectacles. He was a fabulous tennis player, Karakhan, always wearing an impeccable white flannel suit, admired by all the wives of the foreign diplomatic corps who flocked around him on the tennis courts at the Spiridonovka Street mansion where the Foreign Commissariat held receptions, official dinners, and balls so that one could watch him play. Karakhan had something of the beast about him when he leaped onto the court, stretched out his arm, and then with a swift stroke dealt a resounding blow to the ball. He would only play with tennis balls he imported himself directly from Lillywhites in London. Also imported were his hats which, naturally, came from Lock, his ties from Whitelock in St. James's Street and Pall Mall, just as his white flannel suits were from Savile Row. Smiling, he would say that Russian balls had little bounce: "They are intransigent." Often, just behind him, watching his every move, coldly judging his every hit, was the Spiridonovka trainer, the famous Julianov, a handsome tall blond man with blue eyes whom all the diplomatic wives flirted with in order to get tennis lessons. At the time, Karakhan was much discussed in Moscow, and mostly the talk was about his love affair with the ballerina Semyonova, the most famous ballerina at the Bolshoi. The Moscow public, an immense proletarian crowd, packed the Bolshoi every night to see her, and forgave her every tantrum, her every bout of nerves, her every whim. Semyonova was a rather short woman, plump, with shiny blond hair, but she was tough, and had cold blue eyes. Her expression was invariably proud and insolent, and in order to understand how much premeditation there was in her tantrums, in her whims, how coldly calculating she was in her glacial movements of fury, all one needed to see was the turn of her head (she turned her head with a lizard-like jerking motion). And all it took was a small indecisiveness on the part of the orchestra conductor, the most tenuous dissonance of a violin, for Semyonova, in the middle of a pirouette, to stop the performance and hostilely remain perfectly still as marble at center stage. The public would then melt the ice of her capriciousness with heated applause to which she would bow with an insolent and arrogant condescension. "Semyonova," the British ambassador, Sir Esmond Ovey, once said, "is the only being on earth who would dare to dance upon a volcano." The German ambassador, Baron von Dirksen, had retorted: "You forget Karakhan."

Whenever Semyonova's name appeared on a poster announcing a ballet, Stalin didn't miss a performance. Every evening Stalin entered the small mezzanine box and sat near the back in the shadows. And in the box across from his sat Karakhan, the imperturbable Karakhan, rigidly leaning against the back of his seat, his profile insolent and cold, his head tilted slightly backward. The relationship between Karakhan and Semyonova was the subject of habitual conversation at every bridge table in the foreign embassies. Semyonova's name ran through the gossip mill of the Soviet

nobility much more often than that of, for example, Madame
Yegorova, the wife of General Yegorov, Chief of Staff of the
Red Army. She was a petite brunette, very beautiful, clad in
soft flab like a pearl in a velvet case and, like a pearl, she had
a damp, cold listlessness, a savage delicacy, a multi-shaded
gray sheen of indifference, a distracted, distant callousness.
Madame Yegorova brandished the most profound contempt
for the "beauties" of Soviet society, especially for Madame
Lunacharskaya, whose name appeared daily in the society
newspapers and tabloids. At the same time, Yegorova displayed a conspicuous soft spot for the wife of Marshal
Budyonny, the hero of the Red Cavalry, perhaps in order to
give greater significance and emphasis to her contempt for
the others. Madame Budyonnaya was a small brunette whose
provocative shape and pleasing vulgarity were unforgivable.

As Florinsky spoke about Madame Budyonnaya, he laughed
maliciously, "hee, hee, hee!" and held out his hand to show
how short she was, then widened his arms to show how
round and fat she was. "Her husband liked horses," he said,
laughing, and pulling his head down between his shoulders
like a tortoise. "Hee, hee, hee!"

But perhaps for Florinsky the ideal pervert in a Marxist
society was the Baron von Steiger. I had never before seen a
man so pale, so suspicious (and so suspect) as von Steiger.
He was about forty-five, short, hunched, thin, his face ashen,
his hands stubby and so bloodless they appeared transparent,
and at first glance it seemed as if his hands had been cut off
at the wrists. When he played bridge one could see his cards
through the flesh of his fingers. His teeth were ruined, his
smile a green glow, and he appeared to have a lizard darting
about in his mouth. Before the Revolution, von Steiger was
an officer in the Fourth Guards Uhlan Regiment and it

seemed he enjoyed a certain position among St. Petersburg's more sophisticated society. Now he was a functionary at the Commissariat of Foreign Affairs, and he devotedly frequented the foreign diplomatic world, where he often appeared at the side of Bubnov's wife. After the death of Lunacharsky, Bubnov took his place at the Commissariat of Education. Bubnova was a tall, athletic woman with thick dark hair. She was the manager of Torgsin, a store that sold art objects exclusively to foreign clients who were able to pay in foreign currency. Florinsky had a kind of timid admiration for von Steiger and many times I observed his eyes, full of an almost paternal loving tenderness, rest upon that former Officer of the Guard. Von Steiger was, along with Florinsky, one of the most assiduous tennis players of the Italian, British, and German Embassies, the favorite gathering places in the summer of the diplomatic community. In the winter, everyone went skiing in the Nikolskoye Hills, a village at the thirteenth verst from Moscow, or they met up at the British Embassy's *patinoire* where Lady Ovey—whom Edith Sitwell would have described as short, brunette, thin, and peppery, making sure to point out her Mexican origin—carried out the honors of the house while wrapped in a Caucasian black-goat fur coat in which she squirmed like a restless kid in the belly of its mother. Florinsky spoke of the foreign diplomatic community with grace, but lurking beneath the surface was a shy reticence mingled with malicious jealousy. He was, above all, jealous of the advisor to the British ambassador, William Strang, a young, tall, thin, and perpetually restless man with intense, restless eyes, their ironic, irritated shine slightly obscured by his spectacles. Later, when he eventually left Moscow, Sir William Strang suddenly revealed himself to be a close friend of Anthony Eden, one of his inner circle, and most recently became the political advisor to the British governor of Berlin.

"*Ce grand garçon*," Florinsky said, "this big fellow doesn't seem to be at home in Moscow." All of Florinsky's threatening maliciousness was expressed by these few words.

"*Pourquoi pas?*" I asked.

"He doesn't like von Steiger," Florinsky said.

"You're wrong," I said, "he doesn't like Helfand—"

"Helfand!" Florinsky said, with that indescribable hint of exquisite contempt.

"—and he detests Rubinin."

"Rubinin!" Florinsky said, with the same contemptuous tone he used to pronounce Helfand's name.

Sir William Strang was not wrong to not like Helfand. This Helfand, Chief of the Western Section of the Narkomindel, or the Commissariat of Foreign Affairs, was a thin man with slanting eyes and clammy hands. His excessive ambition, expressed through an introverted rancor aimed at colleagues more fortunate or better favored in their diplomatic careers than he was—due to luck, friendships, protection, and alliances—was further recklessly revealed by the often naive, often stupidly imprudent words of his wife, a tall, beautiful brunette originally from the Caucasus whose marvelously soft, white skin had a silky sheen. Her red eyes appeared to be made of enamel and were vivid, intent, full of a naive hatred, an innocent rancor, a stupid envy that betrayed the true, secret feelings of her husband. Helfand was later appointed Cultural Attaché of the Soviet Embassy in Rome, and from there he fled, with the help of Count Ciano, to Mexico. He was a traitor and a coward. Sir William Strang was not wrong to not like Helfand.

"Strang doesn't like Steiger," Florinsky repeated, his tone one of deep regret.

"*Et vous*, are you sure you like Steiger?" I asked.

"I am not at all sure!" Florinsky said. He laughed, and then after a long silence during which he tapped the base of his cane against the floor while looking out the window, he began to tell me about the ballerina Abramova, the black-haired, thin ballerina Abramova, whom he preferred to Semyonova, and about the new wife of the Swedish Ambassador Gullenstiern who changed his wife every six months, and about the German ambassadress, the tall, gigantesque Baroness Hilda von Dirksen, who had a ruddy face under a wing of white hair and with whom he was very friendly, often laughing with great pleasure and sophisticated grace ("*Florinsky est tout de même un monsieur*, Florinsky is, all the same, a gentleman," Monsieur Herbette, the French ambassador, who was already then the director of *Le Temps*, would often say) at her innocent delusions, at her pretensions to always win at tennis, at her unforgiving aversion to high heels, at the scolding she once gave Kulliky and Annalise Urbye, the daughters of the Norwegian ambassador, because their heels were too high.

"They are no different than Louis the Fifteenth's heels," the lovely Kulliky had responded, laughing; she was someone who knew how to shoot from the cuff.

"Ach! You are not going to get me to believe that King Louis the Fiftheenth wore heels the likes of yours," Baroness Hilda von Dirksen had responded.

There was only one woman in all of the USSR who would dare to wear high heels in the presence of the Ambassadress of Germany and that was Madame Lunacharskaya.

"*Ah, cette chère Hilda!*" said Florinsky, shaking his head. He was a good friend of the German ambassadress, and during the beautiful summer days when the members of the foreign diplomatic corps got together to row on the Moskva River at Nikolayevsky Bridge or at Kolomensky, a few miles outside of Moscow, it was rare not to see Florinsky and the Baroness sharing a boat, Florinsky the oarsman. The "*merveilleuses*" of Soviet high society also participated in that splendid sport and were accompanied by functionaries of the Narkomindel or by young cavalry officers with crew cuts wearing fashionable tall, rigid, knee-high Swedish boots, and many others wore copal boots in the manner of Marshal Budyonny, or those Cossack-style floppy ones made of sheepskin rawhide. High heels were very popular that year despite Baroness Hilda von Dirksen's objections and the *merveilleuses* of Moscow in 1929 made their Louis XV heels resound across the flagstones of the verandas of the *osobnyaki*, those wooden houses overlooking the banks of the river at Kolomensky, or across the asphalt of Nikolayevsky Bridge, in the same youthful, gay rhythm of the clink of the spurs of young cavalry officers. Many of the younger and more audacious women shielded themselves from the sun under parasols that had been smuggled in from Paris or Berlin through the Narkomindel diplomatic courier, and those red, turquoise, white, green, and yellow umbrellas on the banks of the Moskva, at the heart of Moscow, against a backdrop of the *osobnyaki* built out of ancient wood, resembled a thriving mold, a bronzed-green moss against a backdrop of smokestacks towering over the industrial outskirts of Moscow, against the green trees (or green and white birches along the banks of the Moskva River, or the white and olive birches of the North!), and the golden church domes lent a delicate light stain, a hint of Manet, to that Byzantine landscape in the style of the ancient wooden icons from the Trinity Lavra of St. Sergius and New Jerusalem monasteries, where impressionism was reduced to a decorative function. The breath of the river was sweet on the lips, a breath of tired wind that smelled of grass. The boats were gliding lightly across the green water, the immense clouds rested lightly upon the distant domes of St. Basil's Cathedral, arising in the heart of Moscow in deepest Asia, and on the crenellated towers of the Kremlin.

"*Daragaia, duscia maià*," Madame Lunacharskaya would cry, "my darling, my love," as she ran along the riverbank, lifting up the skirt of the Schiaparelli spring outfit she had borrowed from the Meyerhold Theater wardrobe. "*Daragaia, duscia maià*," said the slightly gravelly voice of the actress who was famous for her love affairs and scandals, as she made an invisible tear in the green and blue silk fabric of the landscape. The cold and haughty Semyonova, the jocular brunette Yegorova, the thin, dark Abramova, the Junoesque Bubnova, the small, fat Budyonnaya, the pale, hunched von Steiger, all of them turned to stare with desire or jealousy at the beautiful Lunacharskaya, her legs bare up to the knee, running along the river toward a group of cavalry officers gathered around a thoroughbred from the stables of Marshal Tukhachevsky. "*Daragoi, daragoi!*" The thoroughbred whinnied gently and the young officers turned their heads toward the beautiful woman. Marshal Tukhachevsky smiled, and said in a loud voice, "*Iddite, iddite sudà*, come, come here," and he moved a few steps toward the actress, extending his hand, smiling. And it was that last image of him that stayed with me, pasted on top of this horrible image of Marshal Tukhachevsky standing tall without his epaulettes or his decorations before a firing squad.

Of that era's Soviet high society, corrupt, always thirsty for pleasure, greedy for money, glory, and power, proud and snobbish, capable of any infamy in order to maintain their ephemeral power, ready to betray the people, the Revolution, communism, Russia, to deny their own revolutionary past, in order not to have to renounce the honors and privileges of their position, of that Soviet nobility corrupted by Trotskyism and Bonapartism, almost no one was still alive. *L'ancien régime* of the Communist Revolution, the new nobility that had emerged from the communism of the war and NEP, made up of men who believed they were heroes and were actually traitors, who believed themselves to be Marxists and were actually nothing but *krasni burjui*, red bourgeois, who believed they were the guardians of Marxist and Leninist theory but were instead Bonapartists, who believed they were leaders of the proletariat but were really leaders of the Trotskyite counterrevolution, had by then given up their positions to the *élites* of the Stakhanovites and the Udarniks, and to the Stalinist *élites* who were tough and lean but nevertheless more human and born of the Five-Year Plans. Of all the *merveilleuses* of the communist *ancien régime*, of all those men corrupted by ambition, hatred, jealousy, comfort, pleasures, and privileges, all that remains is memory: the "snapshots" firing squads caught of them in their supreme, ultimate moment, their pale faces turned toward the rifle barrels, their hands clenched in fists, their eyes widened, their brows enraged, the great wind of death unobstructed in the cold, squalid, magnesium light of the camera flashes that lit up, from some invisible height, the scenes of execution in modern Europe.

"Have you read the latest poem by Baltrušaitis?" Florinsky asked me. "It's a poem dedicated to Moscow, a glorification of Soviet life, an ode to the city of Moscow, not unlike the poem John Gay dedicated to London."

"No, I haven't read it," I said. Jurgis Baltrušaitis was the ambassador from Lithuania and a good poet whom the communist authorities honored as one of their own. And I declared: "Happy Augusta..."

"Baltrušaitis didn't leave a thing out of his poem. Anyone and everyone, as well as everything, in Moscow is in there," Florinsky said with gentle irony, chuckling in his shadowy corner.

"I hope," I said, "that he didn't forget to include the smell of Moscow." Moscow, and all of Russia, had a particular smell of onions, boiled cabbage, and that type of parsley called *ukrop* in Russian.

"As for *ukrop*," Florinsky said, his voice shrill, "there's far too much of it! Can you imagine anything that's truly Russian that doesn't smell of *ukrop*?" And laughing joyfully, he began to tell a story about when he was young and a student at the University of Petersburg (he said Petersburg, not Leningrad, and Marika, who had been obstinately taciturn and hostile, broke her silence in order to correct him: "*Ska-jite Leningrad, pajalusta, Tovarisch Florinksi*, Say Leningrad, please, Comrade Florinsky").

"Actually, when I was a student in Leningrad," Florinsky said, "I wrote a novel entitled *Ukrop*. It was a story in Gogol's style. The idea wasn't actually so bad. Have you been to the Stanislavsky Theater to see *The Bug*? Well my novel *Ukrop* very much resembled the comedy *The Bug*. In the comedy, there is a fellow who twenty years in the future happens upon a bug. You probably know that Russia is full of bugs. We have bedbugs here like you have ants. Hee, hee, hee! And yet you don't know what it's like. Anyway, after twenty years of communism, naturally all of the bedbugs have been destroyed, all gone. *Pas de punaises!* No more bedbugs! Can you imagine that? Not one bedbug in all of Soviet Russia. A colossal success for communism. Professors, scientists, naturalists, entomologists, specialists, rushed from every corner of Russia to study the strange insect that none of them had ever seen a specimen of before. It was certainly a rare specimen: imagine, a Russian bedbug! In my novel, *ukrop* replaced the bedbug. No *ukrop* in Russia! Can you imagine that? Not even the smell of *ukrop*. I didn't fault communism for what was still far in the future for us, but rather German philosophy, primarily of the Hegelian kind, which was at the time quite *à la mode* among young Russians. *Pas d'ukrop en Russie!* Hee, hee, hee! *Un vrai miracle*, imagine, a true miracle. Not even the smell of ukrop! A real miracle, hee, hee, hee!"

"Do you believe then, my dear Florinsky, that miracles are possible in Soviet Russia?"

"*L'hasard*, accident takes the place of miracles. Do you know of Marx's letter to Kugelmann? It was written in 1871. World history would have a mystical nature, wrote Marx, if accidents played no part. And he added that accident and human character, the character of leaders, had an enormous impact on events."

"*Sottises*, foolishness," Marika said, with profound contempt.

"The young women, *chez nous*, are often *délicieuses*," Florinsky said. "They aren't aware that it was precisely on Marx's letter to Kugelmann that Trotsky and all the others were betting their lives."

"You are disgusting, Comrade Florinsky," Marika said.

"Accident! The negation of Marxism," I said.

"Lenin was an accident within Marxism," Florinsky said.

"You are a dirty Trotskyite, Comrade Florinsky," Marika said, her voice bursting with indignation.

"*Je suis un sale bourgeois*, I'm a dirty bourgeois, isn't that what you mean? Still, I don't think any of these issues get in the way of the fact that Moscow is a marvelous city. *Regardez, donc*, look here, Malaparte. When I was young, I liked to wander through the streets of Moscow in the ghostly light of those white nights. I wrote poems about the city, full of love. Moscow was my Laura, my Beatrice. Now I am reduced to wandering about in this old carriage in order to secretly admire my poor Laura, my unhappy Beatrice. *Regardez donc*, Malaparte."

We were at the far end of Arbat, in a neighborhood of *osobnyaki*, those small moldy wooden houses surrounded by a garden with a tree right by the door, the inevitable tree that guards the doors of houses in all of the East. Birds were in every one of those trees and swallows' nests hung beneath the gutters of each *osobnyak*. The swallows flew through the air calling stridently, hurling themselves at our old landau almost as if they wanted to cross from one side to the other through the windows; stray dogs, little barking dogs with red fur ran along the picket fences around the *osobnyaki*, and every so often at the end of a *pereulok*, the cross streets that all flowed into the Arbat, one could see the high wooden scaffolding on the buildings under construction, the immense cranes on the worksites, the iron pylons rising out of dust clouds. Our carriage proceeded slowly forward at the pace of the emaciated horse's trot, and in the frame of the window, like a panoramic shot on the cinema screen, the green landscape panned across our window, showing the decrepit wooden houses of the old quarter, and the gashes in that gentle green landscape that were the construction sites, the cranes, the pylons, the high platforms of the scaffolding, the factory smokestacks on the opposite banks of the Moskva. At a certain point, while saying to me, "*Regardez comme c'est beau,* look how beautiful it is," Florinsky grabbed my arm and I was overtaken by a mild anguish. I felt as if I would never get out of that old lugubrious carriage, that the pink ghost, that pink ghost all dressed in white, would keep me prisoner in that old landau made of worm-eaten wood, would drag me along with him to who knew where. I freed myself from Florinsky's grasp and turned to look at him. The red light from the sunset, the green reflections off the trees, that gentle blue light that rained down from somewhere very high and pure, concealed and revealed the transparent shadows on his ruddy face, across his cheeks marked by tiny wrinkles resembling little white scars. Those painted eyes of his, those white porcelain teeth, that mouth with slightly swollen lips, that strange face that was at once a girl's and an old man's, the whole ensemble had something painful and cruel about it. He was the ghost of an entire world, the wax mask of an entire society.

Today, I wonder about that singular character and that extraordinary jaunt through the streets of Moscow in an old landau, about the story of his end which arrived unexpectedly some time later during the Great Purge. One evening, Florinsky found himself sitting at a bridge table in the home of the Greek ambassador, Policroniadis. It was not an "accident," as Marx had called it in his letter to Kugelmann, that Florinsky found himself sitting at a bridge table in the Greek Legation that evening. He went there quite often, almost every evening. Madame Militza Policroniadis (Militza Nicholayevich was Serbian: a tall woman, Junoesque, a redhead, with big black eyes) was seated at the same table with von Steiger and the Lithuanian ambassador, the poet Baltrušaitis. At a certain point, Mara Nicholayevich, Militza Policroniadis's sister, came over to the table and said to Florinsky: "Some gentlemen are asking to see you."

"Where are they?" Florinsky asked, placing his cards down on the table.

"In the next room," Mara told him.

Florinsky stood up and said: "Please play on. Replace me with a dummy." His face, as usual, was reddish but a thin veil of sweat had descended over his forehead. He pranced off in his habitual fashion. It was, perhaps, an "accident," but he neglected to say goodbye to the hostess. When he was at the door, he turned and stared at von Steiger. All in the room had turned their faces to the door and were watching him in silence. Florinsky lifted a hand, waved, and smiled. He went out, closed the door behind him, and disappeared forever. That smile made me think of Leon Feuchtwanger's account regarding Radek: During the second trial in Moscow when, after the guilty verdict, Radek was leaving the tribunal to head back to the Lubyanka Prison, he turned to his companions, all condemned to death, waved, and smiled.

"*Regardez donc*, Malaparte," Florinsky repeated. We had entered the Arbat which was at that hour very crowded, the crowd poorly dressed and flowing river-like down the sidewalk. The Bible often compared the people to water, to rivers. That crowd of people was similar to a muddy river that flowed with an oppressive, almost fearful sense of destiny between the houses which acted like embankments in the grand Arbat. A confused clamor arose from that badly dressed, badly fed multitude, who wore imprinted on their faces the gray masks of misery from the years and years they had suffered, from the hope, from the stubborn willfulness, from their faith, not in happiness but in a better suffering, in the triumph of their own suffering, of their own misery.

At a certain point, Florinsky grabbed my arm: "Look," he said. Two old convertible Rolls-Royces drove slowly up the Arbat, moving at the pace of the disorderly vehicles and crowd. In the first Rolls, next to the driver, sat Stalin. In the second were some GPU agents, their collars blue. Every day at that hour, Stalin rode up the Arbat in his old Rolls-Royce with its top down as he headed to his country residence, about ten versts from Moscow. The crowd turned to look at the car as it moved ahead and became lost in the turmoil. From the loudspeakers attached to the streetlamps along the Arbat, the thundering voices of the *besbozhniki*, the godless, began the transmission of their unremitting anti-religious campaign: "Comrades, read in this evening's *Vechernyaya Moskva* the poem by Demyan Bedny: 'Christ Died of Sleep.' Lenin said: 'Religion is the opiate of the masses.'"

"You never ran into God on the street?" Florinsky asked. "In Capri, I once ran into a God on the street and it was Apollo." After a long moment of silence, he then spoke to me of Capri where he had visited around 1910, about his time there together with Lenin, Lunacharsky, etc., in the Pension Weber near the small marina, and of the "communist school" founded in Capri by Lunacharsky. He asked me how Carmeniello was doing. I told him that Carmeniello, who at the time was a young fisherman as handsome as Apollo, was by now an old, wizened, toothless man. A grimace of fear and horror crossed Florinsky's pink, made-up face.

"*Pas possible!*" he cried, and he began to laugh, "hee, hee, hee!" with his shrill voice, shrinking back into the corner of the carriage as if he had just seen a ghost right before his eyes. "*Qu'il etait beau!* How beautiful he was!" he exclaimed suddenly lowering his voice. He dropped his head toward his chest and shuddered. That was the only time I ever saw him regret the past, and it wasn't just a regret for the loss of youth, but something more profound, and more irreparable. He wasn't in that moment the ruddy, sophisticated, grotesque, and refined Chief of Protocol of the Commissariat of Foreign Affairs who pranced ceremoniously across the Moscow train station platform as he met foreign ambassadors, or strutted gallantly among the tables at the Métropole or at the Scala or in the halls of the foreign embassies, he was instead a wrinkled and rouged old man who was afraid of the ghosts of Capri, the ghosts of Paris, London, Vienna, Venice, and Florence, afraid of his distant youth and the irreparable compromise he'd made with life, an error he now had to atone for. After a long silence he jolted out of his reverie, rummaged with his long fingers in the by now empty box of chocolates, and the amiable, elegant, malicious, grotesque, familiar Florinsky returned. Leaning out the carriage window, he cried: "*Regardez*, just look at Moscow, *quelle jolie ville*! What a pretty city!"

We were near the Church of San Salvatore, from the top of which the Kremlin could be seen in all its expanse, encircled by crenellated walls on the bank of the lazy turgid river tinted with delicate green reflections of the sunset's dull light. Behind the Kremlin towers and the bell tower of St. Basil's Cathedral, the sky appeared black, like a high, black wall. Against that black sky the red brick walls of the Kremlin stood out sharply, as if perched on the smoky wood base of an ancient icon. In that black, deep, and gloomy glow a small section of the golden domes flashed intermittently.

And the green, gleaming river emerging from the black cavern of night, penetrating the dusty city, still lit by the purple reflections of the sky at sunset, gave out a long, sad sound, that singular tone containing shades of green in a landscape of red and black. In the distance, toward the train station and the airport, the first lights were being turned on. As the landau descended at a trot toward the Kremlin, I imagined that old carriage painted black moving at the pace of the trot of a skeletal horse toward the turbulent heart of the capital of the USSR, in the febrile streets, red-hot with the anxiety, hope, and anguish of the First Five-Year Plan. Inside that landau were Florinsky, Marika, and I. I wanted to laugh and right away the vision of that black landau in the streets teeming with cars, trucks, crowds of workers returning from their jobs through the streets of the capital of the USSR, gave me a subtle feeling of fear, a cruel feeling of disgust. We entered Sverdlov Square and Florinsky, who up until then had been quiet, mumbled: "Would you like me to take you to your hotel?"

"Thank you," I said. "I can get off here. The Savoy isn't far and it would do me good to walk a little."

"*J'ai horreur de cette foule*, such a crowd terrifies me," Florinsky told me in a low voice, squeezing my leg. "I wouldn't walk in this crowd for anything in the world."

On a sudden cordial impulse, I squeezed his hand. He took my hand for a long time in his, perhaps not daring to caress it. All he said was: "*Vous avez une jolie main*, you have a pretty hand," and laughed. Then he added: "It's not worth it, having a pretty hand in Moscow."

"Oh, no," I said, "it's not worth it."

I descended from the carriage and stood still in the middle of the square, following with my eyes the old ghostly black landau as it slowly departed in the direction of Kitay-gorod in the midst of tumultuous traffic, the cars crisscross-ing every way possible.

"I'm afraid the bell doesn't work," said Litvinov, the People's Commissar for Foreign Affairs. He rang the bell for a third time, waited a little longer, then said, "Excuse me," stood up, went to the door, opened it, and with a tone of polite impatience, shouted: "*Pajalusta, tris stakan chai*, three cups of tea please," then came back, sat down behind his desk, and began to rub his hands together while looking at the Italian ambassador, Cerruti, who was smiling amiably. Lit-vinov was wearing a black *tolstovka*, the Russian shirt with the collar opening on one side and buttons running down from the shoulder to the chest. He was slightly hunched, leaning forward on both forearms, occasionally pushing his spectacles up the bridge of his nose with his open right hand. Litvinov was always especially kind to me, even protective, almost as if he'd promised himself to see to it that Soviet Russia left a good impression on me. He treated me, in other words, as a friend. My sympathy for communist Russia was already well known, as was my total intransigence when it came to intellectual and artistic freedom, not only as far as communism was concerned but also with regard to Mus-solini. I was grateful to Litvinov for the kindness and good will that made him try to satisfy my every legitimate desire. He had procured for me permanent authorization to visit any *rabotniki* club, or workers' club, gym, pool, tennis court, cinema, theater, proletarian dance club, and had given me permission to go on any collective outing organized by worker's organizations to places around Moscow. One

Sunday morning while in Leningrad, I took part in the October 27 Workers' Club collective visit to the Hermitage Museum. Another Sunday, I went to the Hermitage Treasury where the czar's treasure was kept, including gold jewelry, golden masks similar to those of Atreus, Scythian gold found in excavations in the Crimea, saddles, snuffboxes, swords, daggers, pistols, and Catherine the Great's caparisons. I visited the palaces of the great old imperial and noble families on the Fontanka Canal and the summer palaces of Tsarskoye Selo, the czar's village. During my long sojourn in Moscow, I had taken part in the collective outings of the *rabotniki* club of the chemical industry union to Prince Yussupov's palace in Arkhangelskoye some fifty kilometers from Moscow, and to the palace of the Counts Sheremetev where I had spent an extraordinarily free and happy Sunday in the company of young workers both male and female. We had gone skinny-dipping in the lake in front of the palace, then after the swim and a frugal dinner a party of young peasants from the nearby village joined us with their harmonicas and we danced until sunset. A tipsy worker who called me "*burjui*" (bourgeois) was severely reprimanded and forcibly removed by his comrades because I was a guest of the Soviet people and shouldn't be insulted. They were well-mannered, sincere, characterized by cordiality and a simple, frank civility. In the small theater on Sadovaya Street where I had gone to see a play by Mayakovsky, *Kvadratura kruga* or *Squaring the Circle*, I met some of the workers with whom I had been at the palace of the Counts Sheremetev and after a play we'd gone together to drink a *stakan chai* in a *stolovaya* just off Tverskaya Street. One of them, a mechanic, asked me if I knew Pushkin. What surprised me about those young workers of the *élites* was their strange predilection for

Pushkin, not for the Pushkin of *The Captain's Daughter*, which they rightly found inferior to Gogol's *Taras Bulba*, but for the Pushkin of, for example, the novel in verse *Eugene Onegin*, and other priceless poems among the most priceless and Byronic by that very great Russian poet.

"Yes, it's true, Pushkin is widely read by our people," Litvinov said, "especially by the young, and not only by students, but by the young workers. The popularity of Pushkin—certainly a most aristocratic Russian poet—among the proletariat was a surprise to the Soviet authorities and left them somewhat perplexed. Comrade Lunacharsky had his own explanation for this fact, but I won't tell it to you because by now it's the official explanation, and I know that official explanations are of no interest to you."

Laughing, I said: "I never know how to deal with them."

"I would like to hear," said Cerruti, the Italian ambassador, "Lunacharsky's thoughts."

"He thought that Pushkin's success among the proletariat was due to the extraordinary purity and musicality of his verse."

"Lermontov," I said, "is also highly successful among the workers, even if his poetry doesn't have the purity or musicality of Pushkin's. Lunacharsky's explanation doesn't satisfy me."

"Why not?" Ambassador Cerruti asked, squirming in his chair. He wasn't too pleased with how I freely expressed my opinions and he paled every time I opened my mouth. "Why not? Lunacharsky's explanation seems to me to be astute and accurate."

Smiling, Litvinov said: "You are very agreeable, *Monsieur Ambassadeur.*"

"His explanation is neither astute nor accurate," I said.

"It is, instead, convenient and politically opportune. I believe the reason for Pushkin's success among the proletariat is something else entirely. The younger generation of Soviets no longer accepts the official propaganda regarding the Russian aristocracy and is eager to understand it more intimately. Since today it is no longer possible to procure objective historical texts on the subject, the Soviet youth turn to poetry. That doesn't mean that the Soviet youth is sympathetic to the old Russian aristocracy or is nostalgic for the czarist regime: they are curious, not sympathetic. Undoubtedly, Pushkin's poetry reveals the spirit of that aristocratic society and regime, and he was its greatest, purest, most faithful interpreter, his work easily better than any Marxist treatise. As for Lermontov, his success confirms my opinion of Pushkin. Lermontov is a minor poet, a far lesser poet than Pushkin, his verse sickly-sweet, mundane, and sentimental. But apart from his purely poetical worth, it is undeniable that his poetry excellently captures the spirit of that society-in-decline from which emerged that small, liberal, bourgeois nobility behind Kerensky's Revolution. I believe this also explains the success of Tchaikovsky's music among the Soviet youth."

"So it would seem," said Ambassador Cerruti, nervously adjusting his bow tie. He regularly wore a bow tie and fiddled with it continuously whenever he was nervous or wanted to hide his discomfort.

"Tchaikovsky's success?" Litvinov said, visibly surprised. "Are you saying that the Soviet youth like Tchaikovsky's music for the same reasons they like Pushkin's poetry?"

"For the same reasons," I said.

"*Ça m'étonne!*" Litvinov exclaimed. "How surprising! I had no idea that today's youth appreciate Tchaikovsky!"

"Perhaps," said the Italian ambassador, "Malaparte is wrong.

Are you absolutely sure," he added, turning toward me, "that you mean Tchaikovsky's music? It seems impossible to me."

I laughed and said: "Rest assured there is nothing coun-terrevolutionary in what I am telling you. It's not implau-sible that the school of young Soviet musicians would one day become interested in Tchaikovsky and his aristocratic Westernism."

"Tchaikovsky," Litvinov said, "is the Turgenev of music, and I wouldn't say that Turgenev enjoys the sympathy of the school of young Soviet literati."

"Tchaikovsky's music," I said, "is full of friendly ghosts, of beautiful women who are pale and languid, of gilded furniture, young officers of the Guard, and parks in the moonlight. The people love these sorts of illusions. Why shouldn't the Soviet people also love them?" And I added that I had been amazed and touched by the workers' show of respect as they moved through the rooms of Prince Yussupov's palace in Arkhangelskoye. They had walked in silence, their eyes timidly skimming over the paintings, the *bibelots*, the Sèvres and Saxon porcelain, the gold enameled snuffboxes, the chandeliers from Murano, Bohemia, and Sweden, the Danish silver, the Italian and Flemish lace. They walked as if in a dream, as if finding themselves in a magic castle. At a certain point, a young female worker next to me had said, while contemplating a portrait of the young Prin-cess Irene Yussupova: "She's too beautiful. She can't be real. She's the invention of the artist."

"Her husband too," Litvinov said, glancing at me with an ironic expression, "Prince Felix Yussupov, Rasputin's assassin, was apparently gorgeous." And in a spiteful tone, he added, "Do you think he would have been able to assas-sinate Rasputin if he hadn't been handsome?"

"I met Irene and Felix Yussupov in Rome at Princess Nina Galitzine's home," I said. "I had never before seen a couple that beautiful. Irene was a stunning woman, her beauty cold, her aura blue and white. It pleases me to think that Rasputin was killed by a man as extraordinarily beautiful as Felix. It is Felix Yussupov's beauty that keeps him from being described as an assassin, even though he murdered Rasputin."

Litvinov chuckled cordially and Ambassador Cerruti, fiddling with his bow tie, said: "Yours is a literary conceit, dear Malaparte."

"Pushkin," Litvinov said, "would likely have agreed with him."

"When I was young," the Italian ambassador said, squirming in his chair, "all of Europe was rich with stunningly beautiful women, that type of beauty that by now has all but disappeared not only in Russia but throughout Europe." And then he added: "Princess Irene Yussupova, whom I met in Paris, must not be so beautiful anymore."

"Not only is that type of beauty disappearing," I said, "but the style of that beauty is gone. Aside from political and social considerations," I added, "I must say it's a terrible shame."

"In Russia," Litvinov said, "a new type is being created, and a new style of feminine beauty, which could be called a type of Soviet beauty. Russia is Sparta, not Athens. Spartan women must have been like Russian women today: solid, with strong legs, broad shoulders, a wide protruding jaw, a low, narrow forehead, big eyes, short muscular hands—a little like Picasso's women."

A servant finally brought in a tray carrying three cups of tea. Litvinov, while taking little sips of the boiling hot drink, asked me with a smile what it was about Soviet Russia that had made the biggest impression on me besides Pushkin, Tchaikovsky, and the Princess Irene Yussupova.

"Lenin's mummy," I answered.

"Lenin's mummy?" Litvinov exclaimed, visibly surprised. Ambassador Cerruti blushed and began to cough.

"It's not a mummy, perhaps? An embalmed corpse, then. You would have been better off burying or incinerating him and putting his ashes in an urn."

"That, in fact," Litvinov said, "was our plan at first. Then, and I don't know why, it was decided that he should be embalmed. The idea was . . ." and he stopped, as if pronouncing the name was repugnant to him.

"Trotsky's," I said.

"Yes, I think it was Trotsky's idea. If he had remained in power," Litvinov added with a smile, "Trotsky would have ended up embalming not only Lenin but all the rest of us as well."

I recalled that two years earlier when the fight between Stalin and Trotsky had become rather dramatic, rumor had it that Trotsky planned to sequester Lenin's embalmed body and to use the mummy as a kind of banner urging the people to rise up against Stalin.

"Trotsky is capable of anything," Litvinov said, "but I don't think he would have dared to desecrate Lenin's tomb. For the Russian people, Lenin is sacred. Peasants make pilgrimages to Moscow from every corner of the USSR to worship his remains. I wouldn't be surprised," he added, laughing maliciously, "if one day Lenin's remains become miraculous, even if miracles are prohibited in Russia."

"If Lenin starts working miracles," I said, "I don't think the Soviet government would dare, or even could, stop him."

"They would find a way to stop him," Litvinov said.

While we were riding back in the car toward Denezhny Pereulok, the street where the Italian Embassy is located, Cerruti said to me: "It's not true that in Russia miracles don't happen. They are prohibited, but they happen all the same. Come to dinner at my place tomorrow. I will introduce you to Paul Schaeffer. He will tell you the story of a miracle that occurred in Moscow a few months ago."

"A miracle?" I asked.

"Yes, a miracle," Cerruti said. "Do you think that strange?"

"You know that I came to Russia in order to see miracles happen, and you are hiding a miracle from me!"

"What do you want, my dear Malaparte? When dealing with miracles, one most go very slowly in Russia." He then added: "Don't you think Litvinov was very kind to you?"

"Very kind," I said. "I shall send him a bouquet of flowers."

"I hope," Cerruti said, a bit worried, "you are joking. Promise me that you won't send Litvinov a bouquet of flowers. You are quite capable of doing so."

"Why not?" I said. "Disraeli, before he left the Congress of Berlin, sent a bouquet of flowers to Bismarck."

"You are not Disraeli," said Cerruti.

"Oh, no," I said, "but Bismarck was charmed."

The next evening I went to dinner at the Italian Embassy. In addition to Paul Schaeffer, the Moscow correspondent for the *Berliner Tageblatt*, Ambassador Cerruti had invited the Polish ambassador, Patek. I had met Patek a few years earlier in 1920 in Warsaw while, for a long period of time, I was the attaché to the Director of the Italian Delegation. Up until the Communist Revolution, Patek was one of the most famous lawyers in St. Petersburg. Owing to his profession (he was the lawyer for the most important families of St. Petersburg's nobility), he had a perfect knowledge of czarist society and had cultivated friendships with several Bolshevik leaders whom he had defended many times in the courts of the *ancien régime*. During the meal we spoke for a long time about friends we had in common in Warsaw and I sang the praises of the Polish Minister of Foreign Affairs at the time, Prince Sapieha, a great Lithuanian man who had been educated at Oxford, and whom Patek evidently held in disdain.

"Yes, he was a great man," Ambassador Patek said, "but Europe will no longer tolerate being governed by great men."

The conversation then moved onto Piłsudski and Trąmpczyński, Marshal of the Sejm of Poland, and Patek asked me if I had drunk some of that marvelous Tokay that the Mislivsky Club, the Warsaw Hunting Club, reserved for Trąmpczyński's table.

"Naturally," I responded, "but I don't like to drink sweet wine with meals."

Patek observed that Trąmpczyński's entire political stance was that of a man who drank sweet wine with his meals, and he lingered over drawing a pleasant portrait of the Marshal of the Sejm, with his enormous potbelly, his fat pasty red face that resembled the ancient Polish "Pan."

"*Ce qui est drôle*," said Patek, "what's funny is that the best men, for one reason or another, were kept far away from holding any public position. The best Polish diplomat was Count Tarnowski, but the Foreign Minister, Prince Sapieha, never let him in the door on the pretext that Tarnowski had been an Austrian diplomat at Ballplatz. As you know, Tarnowski was Galician."

"It's not Sapieha's fault," Ambassador Cerruti said, "Tarnowski was kept out under pressure from the Italian government. The government in Rome excluded all the ex-functionaries of the Austrian government."

"I know," Patek said, "but I prefer to blame Sapieha," and laughing, he brushed his palm over his bald head.

"Were you in Warsaw with Minister Tommasini?" Madame Cerruti, the wife of the Italian ambassador, asked me.

"Ah, my dear Tommasini!" exclaimed Patek, and he began to speak about Minister Tommasini's wife, Donna Muzzoli. He described her extravagances, her obsession with organizing luncheons, outings, and teas, and he recounted a horrific escapade arranged by Donna Muzzoli for a group swim in the Vistula during which a French diplomat and his sister drowned. "Donna Muzzoli was enthralled by it," said Patek.

"Don't be horrible to Donna Muzzoli," I said. "Even she risked dying in that incident."

"*Oui, je sais,*" said Patek. "I know it wasn't her fault but don't you find it extremely funny, knowing Donna Muzzoli, to accuse her of this drowning?"

"Extremely amusing, I'm sure," I said.

"*N'est-ce pas?*" Patek said, laughing his heart out.

"You are a horrible man," said Madame Cerruti.

"I liked the Tommasinis very much," Patek said, "*beaucoup.* Minister Tommasini was a first-rate man, entirely first-rate," and he started to recount how Minister Tommasini had the habit during the luncheons, and especially during official luncheons, of taking off his shoe in order to massage with his unshod foot the ankles of his female neighbor. One evening at a gala dinner held in the ballroom of the Italian Embassy, the Countess Maurice Potocka, who was seated next to Minister Tommasini, had, with a swift kick, sent his shoe flying into the corner of the room. And when all of the diners had risen from the table, the Italian minister was compelled to cross the room hopping on one foot in order to retrieve his shoe. "An admirable scene worthy of Racine!" Patek exclaimed.

"Why Racine exactly?" asked Madame Cerruti, who was, before she married Cerruti, one of the most famous actresses in the Hungarian theater.

"Why? *Mais c'était tragique!* Quite simply tragic!" Ambassador Patek exclaimed. He took extraordinary delight in narrating such stories and lost himself in a thousand little details, as the Polish do whenever they tell a story.

"Do you remember," he asked me abruptly, "the Canoness Waleska and her charming nieces? They are all married now," and he described stone by stone the little lane where the Canoness Waleska lived in Theater Square in Warsaw, directly facing the theater, and, with the same meticulousness, he painted the portraits of the Canoness's young nieces, with identical care described the genealogy of the nieces' husbands, and finished by saying—who knows why—that those young husbands would have been worthy of being among the group of Polish gentleman who had accompanied Maria Leszczyńska, the Queen of France, wife of Louis XV, to Paris.

"Do you remember their names?" I asked

"Their names?" Patek asked. "That's of no importance."

"They also would have been worthy of accompanying Marina Mniszech to Moscow," said Madame Cerruti ironically, referring to Marina, the wife of False Dmitriy, the mysterious adventurer who takes over the throne in *Boris Godunov.*

"*Parfaitement!* Perfectly!" exclaimed Ambassador Patek,

and he began to speak about Moscow, Leningrad, the czarist nobility, the scandals at court, as if he were talking about
people and events that had occurred the day before, and as
if the Communist Revolution had never happened. Places,
circumstances, anecdotes, parties, scandals, affairs, duels,
the entire marvelous procession of Venus and Mars that had
accompanied the last czar, Nicolas II, in front of the firing
squad, passed through Patek's words with a light and bemused
elegance, and the women, alive and light and bemused, also
passed through leaving in their wake the fragrant and warm
atmosphere of that happy time free of foreboding. Every so
often Patek slid the palm of his hand over his shiny bald
head in a gesture of refined vulgarity. It seemed that, with
this gesture, he chased away events and characters from his
mind like a croupier who with his long stick rakes the *louis
d'or* across the green felt surface of the gambling table. And
every once in a while Patek let out a shout, a small, shrill
shout of surprise, or admiration, or reproach, and a name
would exit his lips: "Ah, *la petite* Zamoyska! And the Princess Bariatinskaya! And the young Naryshkina! Ah, the
Countess Sheremeteva!" and he would immediately, as if in
a great hurry, pursue those names like an old man in a ballroom who breathlessly follows a woman among the dancing
couples and, reaching her, bows then grasps her little hand
bringing it to his lips with that entirely inimitable Polish
gallantry that the Polish nobles brought home from the
Court of Versailles and which they jealously maintained in
their manners, and he would exclaim: "*Ah, chère Princesse!
Ah, chère Comtesse.*" He would say her name then climb
"through the branches" of her family tree like a spider climbing across a silk dress, retracing the meandering genealogy,
recounting where she was born, whom she had married, and

he explored her allies, the key events in her life, her scandals, the rumors that accompanied her triumphs in St. Petersburg and Moscow society, of *that* St. Petersburg, of *that* Moscow. His maliciousness was so impartial, so gratuitous, that even the nastiest piece of gossip became a compliment on his fleshy, moist blue lips. Finally, after name upon name, year upon year, rumor upon rumor, he ended up in a discussion of Moscow and the Soviet nobility of that current year of 1929. He spoke about it without any sense of time passing, as if the Revolution actually hadn't caused a change in the players and Litvinov was Izvolsky, Semyonova was Kschessinskaya, Abramova was Pavlova, and Madame Lunacharskaya basked in the worldly glory of Princess Naryshkina.

"Ah, Florinsky, dear Florinsky!" Patek cried suddenly, and with a gentle, high-pitched voice, with quick movements of his wizened hand in the air, like that of an artist, like that of Renoir in the last years of his life when he painted with a brush fastened to his paralyzed hand, Patek painted in the air a portrait of the Chief of Protocol of the Foreign Ministry looking upward as if he really and truly had a canvas before him and was carefully observing an invisible model, comparing it to the painting that was slowly materializing. Florinsky was already there, standing, flushed and handsome in his white linen suit, each of us believing that the static portrait would soon begin to move and talk, when with another sudden movement of his hand, Ambassador Patek erased Florinsky's features from the canvas and exclaimed: *"Ah, cette chère* Madame Lunacharskaya!"* and he began to paint on the invisible canvas a portrait of Commissar Lunacharsky's beautiful wife.

Patek's voice, as he was narrating the last bits of gossip about Madame Lunacharskaya (he said *Madame* with the same emphasis he once used to say *Princesse*), became deep, a little hoarse, sliced knifelike by a thin edge of sensuality. From her final amorous scandals, he moved on, not stopping to mention the public reproach *Pravda* had stirred up against Madame Lunacharskaya for having taken part in a masked ball wearing one of the *négligées* the theater directors had ordered from Paris which were to be worn exclusively on stage. But suddenly, abandoning Madame Lunacharskaya, Ambassador Patek turned to Paul Schaeffer and asked him if he knew the final sequence of events in the struggle between Stalin and Trotsky. "It seems that Tomsky…" Tomsky was the Secretary General of the Unions.

"Tomsky was a lost man," Schaeffer responded with a hint of disdain.

"Ah, certainly, he was a lost man. But that isn't what I meant. You know, of course, the charming Tatiana G——," and Patek said the name of a young and beautiful actress from the Stanislavsky Theater. "They say she was involved in Tomsky's misfortune. Today, a leaf doesn't rustle without Trotsky being somehow invoked. But this time Trotsky was not involved. It rather appears that Stalin doesn't like certain worldly behaviors of the Soviet nobility, nor does he like scandals involving women. Stalin, at heart, is a puritan. *Drôle de chose*, funny that, a Soviet puritan! The other night, seeing numerous luxury cars in front of the Bolshoi for performances of *Krasni Mack, The Red Poppy*"—and here he turned to me and said, "*allez le voir*, you must see that famous ballet," then continued his story. "Seeing those cars, Stalin gave orders for all of them to return to their garages. That night, the most illustrious names of the Soviet nobility, all the most beautiful women of Moscow, had to go home on foot in the rain. *Est-ce que cela n'est pas drôle?* Isn't that amusing?"

"Such a gesture," Madame Cerruti said, "would be far more meaningful coming from Queen Victoria than from Stalin."

"Oh, yes, Queen Victoria and Stalin, they have something in common," Patek said with a radiant smile, almost entirely without malice. "I don't know what it is, but they do have something in common." This was his way of being caustic.

We had in the meantime moved to the library, and Patek, who was twirling his glass of whiskey in his pudgy hand so that the ice would melt more rapidly, began talking again about Lunacharsky and Madame Lunacharskaya with a persistence that revealed a personal interest as opposed to the usual aloof stance required for these society conversations.

"I wonder," Patek said, "if Lunacharsky will succeed in getting by this time too."

"He doesn't seem to be acting any worse than usual," Madame Cerruti said indifferently, sensing that there was in Patek's unrelenting gossip something hidden, repressed, a kind of nasty grudge. Even so many years after having abandoned the theater in order to marry Vittorio Cerruti, who at the time of their marriage was only a Legation Secretary but afterwards became one of the last great representatives of the classic European diplomatic tradition, something had remained in Madame Cerruti of that mysterious flair that is refined in actors, and even more so in actresses, by rehearsals. To her, it appeared that people and events didn't have secrets: they were part of a script of which Madame Cerruti knew not only the plot, but all the lines, word for word; and she seemed to follow the progress of the action on stage as if she had rehearsed the scene of this drama or comedy who knows how many times, but now found herself the spectator of the theater of life. Even if her name had disappeared long ago from the marquees and theater posters, and nothing about her, not the way she dressed, nor her voice or movements, outwardly revealed the actress inside, something had remained of her passion for everything to do with the theater. The playwrights, the directors, the actors and actresses still defined her personal world, her forbidden world in which she took refuge in her mind and heart every time she was assailed by the splendid tedium of her social life. Even gossip about actors and actresses elicited her keenest attention, graciously mingling her interests as an actress and her weaknesses as a woman. While living in China at the Italian Embassy in Peking, she had learned a Chinese proverb that wonderfully described the reason for her interest in, curiosity about, and faithful devotion to the theater: "The world is one gigantic theater in which the spectators are the actors, the actors the spectators." Madame Cerruti watched the spectators perform, and her perfect worldly grace, her amiable skepticism, her detachment from people and events, her secret bitterness, and her bitter irony all originated in her long and studied experience as spectator.

"I don't agree with you," Patek said. "You already know, of course, what happened today, only a few hours ago, to Lunacharsky. All of Moscow is talking about it. It will be for all of us a welcome antidote to that boring story about Trotsky and his squabbles with Stalin."

"All this gossip, in the end, is so exhausting," Madame Cerruti said. "I don't see how the private matters of Madame Lunacharskaya are entertaining."

"*J'adore* this kind of story," Patek said. "It's gossip worthy of Tallemant des Réaux. You will agree with me that a Tallemant des Réaux in Soviet Russia is more interesting than an official Thucydides. After all, Madame Lunacharskaya is a spirited woman, and she is the first to laugh at what is said about her. What are they actually accusing her of? Of being beautiful? Ridiculous. Of being elegant? Ridiculous. Of going out in public, to balls and dinners dressed in Schiaparelli outfits that she's only meant to wear on stage? Of using the theater's costume department as if it were her own private wardrobe? Ridiculous, *sottises*, nonsense. Of having lovers? And which pretty woman from the Soviet nobility doesn't have her lovers? Karl Marx did not forbid lovers. There are more amorous intrigues, scandals, sexual and romantic machinations among the Soviet nobility than in all of Choderlos de Laclos, with just a tad more vulgarity than in the *Liaisons dangereuses*. But what does it matter? Madame Lunacharskaya is not a vulgar woman. An adulteress is never vulgar, except in special cases."

"Very special," said Madame Cerruti.

"I would like to know more," Ambassador Cerruti said, "about the special cases."

"*Mon Dieu*," Patek said, "I forgot to specify that an adulteress is only vulgar and immoral when she forgets that she has a leading role in the good morals of society, and if she does not exhibit a comportment appropriate to the political and social circumstances. No one will condemn Madame Lunacharskaya for having lovers. Her grave error has been to choose her lovers from among the Officers of the Pervaya Moskovskaya Proletarskaya Division, in the same manner as the *grandes dames* of the czarist regime chose their lovers from among the Officers of the Guard."

"Is this the only thing she's being reproached for?" asked Madame Cerruti.

"She's being reproached for comporting herself in the

same manner as the *grandes dames* of the *ancien régime*, and not in the manner of the Communist Revolution."

"I would like to know," Schaeffer said, "just what might be the proper comportment of an adulteress in a Marxist regime?"

"The proper comportment of an adulteress in a communist society," said Patek, "is what might be called the American way: to try to please men without showing one's own pleasure; to be as impersonal and indifferent as possible; to give no significance to the sexual act. Madame Lunacharskaya gives far too much meaning to her affairs, to her own pleasure. For this, they won't forgive her. *Elle met trop d'individualisme dans la volupté.* Her sensual delight is altogether too personal."

"*Pauvre femme!*" exclaimed Madame Cerruti. "I pity her with all my heart."

"I pity her husband," Patek said. "What happened to him today is very significant and very interesting with regard to comportment in a communist society. The Moscow Soviet Assembly was called to a special session to address this subject today at five o'clock. Lunacharsky, the Soviet People's Commissar of Education and member of the Moscow Soviet, received a summons to appear before the Assembly and he couldn't refuse. On the Assembly's agenda there was only one issue up for discussion: the public conduct of Comrade Lunacharskaya. The Assembly met in a theater on Sadovaya Street. A huge crowd thronged the room. All of the speakers who went up to the podium repeated the same arguments: 'Your wife comports herself in a manner unworthy of a communist Comrade. Her conduct is contrary to Marxist morality and offends the proletarian sensibility. That your wife has lovers is not our business. However, Comrade Lunacharskaya publicly exhibits herself together with her lovers on the streets of Moscow in your official automobile, which should be used only by you, as People's Commissar, and only for the requirements of your job. Furthermore, she flaunts jewelry and luxury outfits that belong to her theater's wardrobe, and she has publicly declared on numerous occasions, at official luncheons with diplomatic representatives from capitalist countries, that she would like to leave "tedious" Moscow to go live in Paris. The responsibility for your wife's conduct is not yours, Comrade Lunacharsky, but you must choose between your wife and the Communist Party.'

"A very pale Lunacharsky stood up. He began to say that he was one of Lenin's oldest Comrades and collaborators; that they had gone into exile together and had shared the dangers of clandestine struggle for the liberation of the Russian people; that Lenin had chosen him in October of 1917 as one of the first of the People's Commissars and he had indisputably earned through merit his titles with regard to the Revolution and the proletariat; that it was also thanks to his efforts that the Russian artistic and cultural patrimony had not been destroyed or dispersed during the upheaval of the Revolution; that the magnificent success of the Revolution in terms of the people's cultural development was also thanks to him, and so on, and that for all these reasons he asked his Comrades of the Moscow Soviet to consider his case with leniency. 'I love my wife,' he concluded. 'I am afflicted by this weakness and I ask you to forgive me this weakness. My wife Comrade Lunacharskaya will understand the reasons for your dissatisfaction and I am sure that in the future she will adjust her conduct to conform with your directives. But I beg you to forgive me for the shameful weakness I have shown for my wife.'

"'Divorce or departure!' shouted the crowd. Lunacharsky,

white as death, tried to appeal to the people's human understanding. It was entirely futile. 'Divorce or departure!' And this was the political novelty of the evening: tomorrow morning it is expected that the People's Commissar of Education Lunacharsky will divorce or depart."

"He won't divorce or depart," Madame Cerruti declared. "It's said that Stalin was once Madame Lunacharskaya's lover."

"No, I don't think she was Stalin's lover," Patek said, his hoarse voice raised slightly. His face suddenly flushed and he seemed strangely agitated.

"Why not? What's wrong with it?" Schaeffer said, smiling.

"I refuse to believe it. We do not have the right, *mon cher ami*, to attack . . . please forgive me," he added, his voice suddenly softening as he wiped the palm of his hand across his bald head. "The truth is this woman means nothing to me. I feel pity for her, that's all. *Voilà tout.* The days are numbered for this entire sorry Soviet nobility. And Madame Lunacharskaya's disgrace is a bad sign. When the people attack women that's because the men are in danger. But she wasn't and has never been Stalin's lover. She is too intelligent a woman to commit such an error. If it were true, she would be lost. Perhaps it is also the case in Italy with Mussolini's lovers?"

"I've never heard it said that Mussolini has lovers," Ambassador Cerruti said, squirming in his chair and fiddling with his bow tie. And to change the direction of the conversation, he turned to me and added, "Have you heard, Malaparte, the story about this chair? It was in this chair that the German ambassador, Mirbach, was assassinated. There is still a bloodstain on the backrest."

"A bloodstain?" I said, "I thought all bloodstains were washed away in Russia."

"It's difficult to get a bloodstain off leather. One would

have to scrape it and it would be a shame to ruin a leather chair for a little bloodstain, don't you think?" Madame Cerruti said, laughing.

"It's right here where I am resting my head," Cerruti said, "and it may just be this bloodstain that is causing me to lose my hair."

"*Oui*, I remember," Patek said. "Mirbach was killed right in this room. Lenin used the opportunity to accuse the socialist revolutionaries of the crime and they were executed as provocateurs."

"This was the location, up until a few years ago, of the German Embassy," Cerruti said. "Then the Italian government bought the building to use as our embassy and the furniture came with it. I knew, of course, the story of Mirbach's assassination, but I hadn't investigated which actual chair was the one in which he was killed. One day I dozed off in this chair and I had a strange dream: I dreamed that two men came in through that window and shot me with a pistol twice in the head. I woke up with a jolt, highly disturbed, but I didn't tell a soul about the dream, not even my wife. One evening a short time later, I invited to dinner the Lithuanian ambassador, Baltrušaitis, who had been in Moscow for many years. I told him about my dream and Baltrušaitis laughed and then told me that this was indeed precisely the armchair in which Mirbach had been killed. And to prove it to me he showed me the bullet holes in the chair's headrest, along with the bloodstain."

"This armchair will bring you happiness," Patek said.

"This armchair will not be my ticket to becoming the Minister of Foreign Affairs," Cerruti said, laughing.

"I am certain," Patek said, "that a few seconds before he died, Mirbach had the same dream. He had dozed off in this armchair and dreamed that two men entered the room through the window and shot him twice with a pistol and then, in fact, two men came in through the window and killed him. Throughout time, Russia has always been the country of dreams, of visions, of mystical revelations."

"And of miracles?" I asked.

"And of miracles, naturally."

"Malaparte," Cerruti said, "came to Russia in order to witness miracles. He believes that in a Marxist society there is also room for the supernatural, that Marxism can't stop miracles."

"Have you seen a miracle in Russia?" Patek asked.

"Not so far," I said.

"I'm sure one will come your way," Patek said. "Russia is truly the country of miracles. Once upon a time, the Russian people didn't believe in miraculous things, and I don't think much has truly changed. Some time ago, Zinoviev told me that the peasants, at heart, perceive the enormous successes of Soviet policy's construction of the Socialist State as miraculous. The pilgrimage to Lenin's tomb mimics the pilgrimages to the tombs of saints. In 1914, in order to announce the war, police officers dressed up as archangels were sent around the White Russian countryside: they held swords in their hands and wore wings on their shoulders, and even their horses were winged. They stopped in the village squares and read the czar's *ukaze*, or proclamation, for mobilization. The communist leaders haven't escaped the morbid atmosphere characteristic of the Russian people either. Of course, you've heard of Yurovsky, the assassin of the imperial family. You've surely run into him at the Métropole or at the Scala. *C'est un charmant garçon.* A charming boy, yes, and an entirely serious man. He's about forty-five years old, tall, blond, and burly. A real Russian type with peasant roots. He's a clerk at the Commissariat for Foreign Trade, a low-level clerk of no importance. Assassins, *vous savez*, never get rich. One must never kill, not even a tyrant. Can you tell me how it ended up for Judith? Very badly, I imagine. I believe she had a hard time finding a husband. Yurovsky is a very sensitive man and a sad one. They say he cries all the time about nothing. It's certainly not due to remorse. Imagine that! If I didn't know what he'd done, I would say that he wasn't capable of killing a fly. A while ago he had a dream in which the czar appeared and asked: 'Where is the czarevitch. What did you do with the czarevitch?' You know, just like in Pushkin's *Boris Godunov*. 'Where is the czarevitch, Yurovsky? What did you do with him?' And so from that day on Yurovsky was obsessed by that dream. He lived in a nightmare in which the czarevitch was still alive. There had been a prediction that Yurovsky would be killed by a child. A few nights ago, on his way home, Yurovsky was assaulted by a band of *bezprizorni*, homeless children. One of them stabbed him in the stomach with a knife. Yurovsky, in a delirium, cried out that the boy was the czarevitch."

"Are you sure that it wasn't the czarevitch?" Schaeffer asked.

"One never knows, in Russia," Patek said, shrugging.

"You witnessed a miracle," Ambassador Cerruti said, turning to Schaeffer. "Tell Malaparte about the miracle you witnessed."

"I didn't witness a miracle," Schaeffer said, "but I can say, alas, that I was mixed up in this ugly story," and he laughed oddly, throwing his head back to reveal his pink palate, the vibrating uvula at the back of his rosy-purplish throat, and the red hollows of his hairy nostrils.

The way Paul Schaeffer laughed disturbed me, and I observed him closely. He was a man of medium height, stocky, broad-shouldered, thick-necked, and round-headed. He was the only one of us—we were all in gray—who was wearing a tuxedo. His black jacket, the shiny whiteness of his starched shirt, the dull sheen of his silk lapels, lent a grotesque aspect to his red face, his white hands, the gleaming skull beneath his thinning hair. It was that same grotesque and profoundly cumbersome aspect that one finds in the people painted by Lucas Cranach in which the pink German skin speckled with golden reflections becomes dulled ivory spotted with greenish reflections and assumes, in contrast with the black clothing, that pallor of decomposing flesh that is the fundamental color of every German moral landscape. Schaeffer's arms were a little short, a trait common in Germans, and he had a slow, heavy, and insistent gaze that landed on objects and people like the warm and sweaty palm of someone's hand. Paul Schaeffer was the Moscow correspondent for the *Berliner Tageblatt*. (He'd married a Russian and was of all the foreign correspondents certainly the one who best understood Soviet Russia and the Russians; he understood them even better than Walter Duranty, the American who'd had the bad taste to possess a sense of humor, since a sense of humor is of no use in Soviet Russia.) Schaeffer was well liked by the foreign diplomatic corps and the Soviet authorities esteemed him for his seriousness. I liked and esteemed him not for his seriousness—the renowned German seriousness is a form of their stupidity, their seriousness the source of their greatest defect, common to all serious Germans, which was to think all other men frivolous and stupid. I liked Paul Schaeffer because he analyzed Russia without a sense of humor, which is the only way to objectively analyze or understand the place. He was the only foreigner I had met in Russia who understood communist Russia and who did not joke about communism. I met him again in London a few years later, in the spring of 1933. He'd been transferred there as the correspondent of the *Berliner Tageblatt* after his expulsion from Russia. The reason he had been expelled from the USSR was this: The Soviet authorities had strictly forbidden foreign correspondents from mentioning in their papers anything about the experiment held in the Medical School at the University of Leningrad—that is, the coupling of a woman who was a prisoner in a penitentiary with an orangutan. Schaeffer had submitted to *Berliner Tageblatt* a long piece on the subject. When I met him in London at Cecil Sprigge's house near Putney Bridge, if I remember correctly, I asked him if it was true that he had been expelled from Russia for that reason. He told me that it was true, but he seemed annoyed by my question. Perhaps he suspected that what I wanted to know was if he had been on the side of the woman or the orangutan. I didn't have any need to ask him. I knew perfectly well that Schaeffer was like Disraeli, always "on the side of the angels." His mistake had been his failure to understand that in Russia one always had to be "on the side of the apes."

"I beg of you, my dear Schaeffer," Cerruti said, "tell us the story of that miracle."

"*C'est une sale histoire*," Schaeffer said, "*n'est-ce pas*, don't you think, *Monsieur L'Ambassadeur*, that it's an ugly story?"

"An ugly story, yes," Patek said.

"I don't like ugly stories," Schaeffer said.

"*Moi non plus*," Patek said. "Me neither."

"I don't like to tell ugly stories," Schaeffer said.

"*Moi non plus*," Patek said, "I like to listen to them."

"You came with me this morning to Professor Obolensky's house. He was your friend, Professor Obolensky. You've known him for thirty years, *n'est-ce pas?*"

"Yes," Patek said, "we've been friends for nearly thirty years. We met in 1902 when I was a young lawyer in St. Petersburg and he already had a reputation for being a great surgeon."

"I've known him for only two or three years but we immediately became good friends." And turning to me, Schaeffer continued: "Professor Obolensky was the greatest surgeon in Moscow. He's old now, about seventy, and he dedicated his entire life to the good of humanity. I have never before met a man who worships, as he does, goodness. Before the Revolution, he had the best patients in Moscow. His clinic was open to all, rich and poor. He was loved by the people because he treated the poor for free. He was a poor man, and he would have been rich if he hadn't given all he had to the poor. Naturally, he too had suffered a great deal for the Revolution. He lost his only son, a doctor, in a field hospital, shot in Kiev by the Makhno Band. His wife died of starvation during the terrible 'Naked Year,' as it was called by Pilnyak. After the Revolution, he was reduced to living in a miserable little room in a poor house in the Bolshaya Pirogovskaya District. But since the Revolution needed doctors, and the Medical Schools of the Soviet Universities were only able to give the hospitals third-year students, and, above all, because in the field of surgery the need was enormous, Professor Obolensky was given permission to continue to work in his clinic, which had been by then incorporated into the new Polyclinic complex the Soviet state had built on the far side of the Khamovniki District. And despite the open hostility directed at him by the young communist doctors and surgeons who saw him not only as an old bourgeois reactionary and so on, but also as an old rival (not an old master, but an old rival) who, enjoying the fruits of all his years of study and practice, had become the official surgeon of the new Soviet nobility, Professor Obolensky had been able to preserve intact his immense prestige and his position as a preeminent scientist. He lived a poor man's life in his miserable room in Bolshaya Pirogovskaya and to avoid rubbing his position in the faces of his colleagues, both young and old, to avoid their envy and jealousy, to avoid providing any fodder to the sectarian and self-interested hatred of the young doctors at the Polyclinic, and to avoid any pretext for them to rail against him, he had even renounced those few privileges that his position gave him. He was too old to visit his patients at home, as he once had. The influx of patients at the unit of the Polyclinic that had once been his private clinic was enormous, since he never refused his help to anyone, rich or poor. He had only one defect, and for a doctor it was a grave one: he was very religious. His faith was his weak point. He knew it, but he believed in God, and he wouldn't renounce Christ in order to comply with the antireligious propaganda that had erupted all over Russia, rigorously reinforced by all means necessary, right at the moment in time that this ugly story took place.

"One night last winter around two o'clock in the morning, Professor Obolensky was sleeping when he heard a knock at the door. He got up from bed, put on his bathrobe, and went to open the door. On the doorstep stood a child of about ten, a working-class girl dressed in rags, her shoulders wrapped in a torn goatskin covered in snow. The girl threw herself at his feet, hugged his knees, and cried: 'Oh, *babushka*, come save my mother. Oh, *babushka*, oh, *babushka*, come save my mother. *Mamushka* is dying! *Mamushka* is dying!'

"Professor Obolensky picked up the little one from the ground, brought her into his miserable room, closed the door, and said: 'I'll call my assistant immediately and tell him to run over to your house. I'm too old, my assistant is faster than I am, and in five minutes he can be at your house. What's your name? Where do you live?'

"'Ah, *babushka*,' cried the girl, 'you come, you come, *mamushka* said that only you could save her, come, come, *mamushka* is dying!' And she pulled him by the hem of his robe with her poor little bony corpse-like hands purple with cold.

"'My assistant is better than I am. I'm too old. I'll call him now and in a few minutes he can be at your house and will save your mother. Come now, don't cry, and let me go to the phone.'

"'No, you must come, it must be you!' the girl cried, throwing herself down onto her knees while crying and banging her forehead against the floor. Professor Obolensky lifted her up off the ground and while he was saying the words, 'My assistant . . .' and reaching for the phone, the girl stood up and in a fury began to pummel the old man with her bony little purple hands shouting: 'Ah, cursed, cursed *burjui*, you don't want to come because my mother is poor, you won't come because my mother can't pay you, you won't come because my mother isn't a rich *burjuia*!'

"Professor Obolensky was upset by her unexpected violent outburst but even more so by the pale, furious face of the child; and perhaps out of prudence, or pity, or because of the strange feeling that had arisen in his heart at that wan, enraged face, he said: 'Alright, I'll come. Run home, I'll dress, and in five minutes I'll come to your house.'

"The child bowed to the ground, kissed his hands, and ran off. The old surgeon dressed in a hurry, wrapped himself in a fur coat, grabbed his doctor's bag, and went out. It was snowing and terribly cold. A few minutes later he reached the street the child had indicated to him, found the door, and entered into the hovel where she lived. On a bed in a corner lay a woman who was already almost entirely drained of blood. Blood drenched the bed and had formed a large black puddle on the floor. The surgeon didn't waste a second, rolled up his sleeves, and got to work. He stopped the hemorrhage, gave the dying woman an injection, revived her, and while he was drying his hands, said to her: 'If I had arrived five minutes later, you would have been lost.'

"'Thank you,' said the woman, 'I owe you my life.'

"'You owe your life to your daughter, not to me,' the surgeon said. 'If your daughter hadn't persuaded me with her tears to come myself, without a doubt my assistant would have arrived too late.'

"'My daughter?' asked the woman.

"'Yes, your daughter. You owe your life to her, not to me. She came to get me.'

"'It can't have been my daughter,' the woman said. 'Look behind that screen.' The doctor looked behind the room divider in a corner of the hovel and saw lying on a miserable straw mattress the girl who had come to get him.

"'It wasn't my daughter,' the woman said. 'She died yesterday morning.'

"Word of that prodigious occurrence spread quickly throughout the neighborhood and the next morning a crowd of poor people gathered outside of Professor Obolensky's home, hurling themselves into the snow, shouting: 'It's a miracle! It's a miracle!' The police immediately rushed in and brutally dispersed the crowd, arrested some of the most fanatic, closed off the street to traffic, and arrested Professor Obolensky. 'You'll learn to perform miracles,' said a police officer to Professor Obolensky. 'Don't you realize that this story might cost you your life?' The charge was very serious: the old surgeon was charged with attempting to spread superstition among the people by way of a false miracle with the intention of eliciting counterrevolutionary sentiment. The charge was very serious, especially since at the time the anti-religion political campaign had just been initiated.

"As soon as I heard the news of the painful affair, I went directly to Professor Obolensky's house. All of us foreigners were his friends since he was the doctor for the diplomatic corps and all of us were very fond of him. When I arrived, two police officers were stationed in front of his house and awaiting their orders. They would not let me go in.

"'Call your superior and tell him that I am Doctor Paul Schaeffer of the *Berliner Tageblatt*.'

"'*Niemojna*, not allowed,' said the officers.

"'Please call the Lubyanka and ask that they give me permission to speak with Professor Obolensky,' I said. 'I am Schaeffer of the *Berliner Tageblatt*. I beg of you, call Comrade Kalinsky and use my name, he knows me, he will grant me permission.'

"'*Karasciò*, alright,' said an officer and he went to call. I was on the doorstep and waited. Suddenly from inside the room, Professor Obolensky called me by name through a closed door.

"'My dear Schaeffer,' he said, 'don't insist, don't try to see me or talk to me. It's useless. There's nothing that can be done. I'm lost. Thank you, my dear Schaeffer. I thank you for your generous attempt on my behalf, but don't risk yourself, there's nothing that can be done. Good-bye, dear Schaeffer.'

"'I will attempt the impossible,' I shouted through the door. 'I'll send a telegraph to the *Berliner Tageblatt* in order to raise support and protest from all German doctors. You'll see, dear Professor, the Soviet authorities are presently very sensitive to foreign public opinion. They have initiated the Five-Year Plan and the Soviet State needs foreign capital. Don't despair, leave it to me.'

"'It's useless, dear Schaeffer,' said the old surgeon. 'If it had been a true miracle, perhaps I could have been saved, I could have shown that it wasn't my doing, but God's. The truth, sadly, is another thing altogether. Last night I slept in my bed as usual and no one came to disturb me, no girl came to knock on my door, I did not leave my room, I did not cure any woman. It was all a story designed and diffused by young communist doctors in order to ruin me, to take my patients from me, to make me disappear. That's the whole of it. Do you understand now, Schaeffer? Do you understand now that there's nothing to be done?'"

"There was nothing to be done," Patek said. "I learned the other day that Professor Obolensky died last month somewhere in the Solovetsky Islands."

The Shame of Death

THEY WERE seated one next to the other in front of the immense crowd that filled the Bolshoi Theater auditorium. Some of them had their arms crossed over their chests, others rested their hands on their knees, others clutched dossiers. All of them had a vague look of engagement. I stared at Lunacharsky. He was pale, his cheeks slightly flushed, his forehead sweating, and every once in a while he wiped it with a handkerchief. Kalinin appeared to be sleeping, his eyes half closed behind his glasses. The President of the USSR looked as if he had been carved out of old, dusty wood. His beard was white and bushy. I looked at their feet, their shoes. It seemed a natural thing to observe their shoes. In the paintings by fifteenth-century Italian artists, the ambassadors and the nobles kneeling before the pope or kings, emperors, and lords all appeared to be examining their masters' shoes. They wore ironic expressions since the painter was being ironic. They all appeared to be observing how the shoes were made, how they were sewn, if the leather was good, the shoelaces durable, the soles thick, the studs well crafted. What competent shoemakers, those courtiers! In some Florentine paintings only the tip of the papal slipper was visible sticking out from under the vast landscape of his white robe, and on that slipper tip the courtiers' gazes were all fixed with extraordinary concentration, as if the fate of the world resided on the tip of that slipper. Here the shoes were coarse, Soviet-made, inelegantly cut and sewn. Some wore Russian boots, others walking shoes, others shoes made in Germany. A radio tripod resembling a dentist's tool stood directly in front of Kalinin, and like a patient in a dentist's chair, Kalinin's head was slightly tilted to the side and backward. It occurred to me that the pageant must have been orchestrated by a director: white light from reflectors fell perfectly on their faces, accentuating their eyebrows, noses, cheeks, and lips. Their chalky faces in deep, dark shadow had features like those on the faces of the dead in certain American photographs. Displayed before me was an Expressionist tableau. The faces were like those of gunned-down gangsters, like those on the dead in a morgue as might be rendered by a Flemish painter such as Bosch. And to my horror, I suddenly observed that among those heads there were, actually, a few faces of the dead, of corpses, similar to the cadaverous green face bulging out from behind Christ's left shoulder in the Hieronymus Bosch painting in the Royal Museum in Amsterdam. Indeed, behind Kalinin's left shoulder bulged a green, cadaverous face, the face of Lunacharsky. Kalinin's face had a similar look. And then, suddenly, I saw Stalin's face. He had entered silently, almost secretly, behind the backs of those gathered and had seated himself in the last row from where his pale face now emerged, shadowed by his large mustache, his bushy eyebrows, his protruding lips. Where was Trotsky's face? If in that moment Trotsky's face had insinuated itself between shoulders, like in a Bosch painting, how everyone would have been struck by terror and wonder.

The day before I had seen a funeral procession making its way through the streets of Moscow. It was the funeral of a high-level functionary of the Soviet trade unions whose name I don't remember. A group of the dead man's colleagues walked behind the coffin with their hats in hand. At a certain point, the coffin disappeared behind a tram stopped in the middle of the street and for a moment before our eyes was the funeral of a tram. An acute, confident, cool, proud, stern indifference was painted onto the faces of all those present. It seemed as if they were accompanying an empty coffin to the cemetery. They were accompanying it to the crematorium. A few days earlier, while I was on a tram, a proletarian's funeral had taken place right next to me outside my window. It was a funeral still in the orthodox style: the coffin was open, and in the open coffin there was an old man with a large white beard. His eyes were open and he was staring at the sky. The tram was stopped and when the coffin passed next to me, the dead man looked right at me. It was an ironic, malicious stare, the look that Axel Munthe must have had on his deathbed. His hands were crossed over his chest, in the Russian fashion, and the fingers of his hands were entwined. He was wearing boots and dressed in black, not in the style of the workers, custodians, and peasants, but in the style of Gogol's clerks. His suit most certainly had come to him from the closet of some long-dead employee. If I had stretched out my hand, I could have caressed his face. There was a certain peace about his face, an ironic Tolstoyan peace, that peace I'd searched for, in vain, in the faces of the living that year in Moscow. Peace on the faces of the dead or living is not necessarily a sign of justice or liberty. Peace, the serenity of the faces of the dead, is the ultimate bourgeois hypocrisy. But there was also an ironic peace, the sign of a life lived with the consciousness of one's own responsibility, the peace that glows on the faces of those who have lived their own lives, who have sinned on their own, who have practiced a pleasing virtue on their own, or who have sinned on purpose on their own. Life is cruel, hypocritical, unjust, ugly, and vile, say the faces full of peace. And only on the faces of the murdered will one find the century's expression. Whenever he was in Paris, Horace Walpole took the opportunity to visit the morgue in order to see the murdered and the suicides, and he was always present at public executions. In those faces, in those atrocious grimaces, he was searching for the portrait of his era, the expression of the people of his time. In every face there was surprise, the unexpected, the same astonished, frightened expression found on dead animals and on certain fish—a stunned and secret wonder, a round world in a round eye encircled by red.

When I asked Litvinov if he would be so kind as to grant me permission to visit Moscow's morgue, he looked at me in amazement. "A morgue in Moscow? I don't think there is one." He pushed a button and asked the functionary who had rushed in if there was a morgue in Moscow.

"A morgue?"

Litvinov spent the next five minutes explaining to the functionary what a morgue was. Finally, after a few telephone calls, everyone agreed that there was no morgue in Moscow. The dead were sent to the University where they were preserved under refrigeration for use in anatomy lessons. I went to the University and a young physician's assistant showed me the corpses lined up in the refrigerators. The cold had stiffened their protruding toes which were bent backwards like the legs of a crab pushed up onto its back; their eyes were glued shut by a thin crust of ice; their flesh was blue with occasional purple patches. I asked the doctor if, given the low temperature during the night, the dead's teeth chattered.

"Certainly not," he said. "Our dead know their place."

I asked him who these dead were, if he knew their names, their social statuses, their jobs, their addresses, who their families were. He told me that the dead came to the University from prisons and hospitals, and many were workers who had suffered job-related deaths, though the drowned or those excessively damaged by their wounds were buried by the administration. The dead who came to the University didn't have names.

"Besides," he added, "why would I be interested in their names?"

"There's no reason for you to be interested in their names," I said, "but it might be somewhat more human if they did have names, if they weren't anonymous, if they were corpses of men, not mere carrion."

The doctor smiled. "You believe corpses are important, am I right?"

"All Christians think corpses are important," I said. "For a Christian, a dead person is much more important than someone alive."

"Christ said: 'Let the dead bury the dead,' am I right?"

"Yes," I answered. "That is what Christ said."

"Christ was horrified by the dead," the doctor said. "He thought of them as trash, as carrion, junk to throw on the garbage heap."

"He preached pity for the dead," I said.

"Ah, no!" the doctor said, nearly shouting. "Don't come to Russia and tell your old stories. The image you have painted for yourselves of Christ is a convenient one, all sugar and honey, a poor pederast with an unhealthy attachment to his mother and father. Christ taught us pity for the people who are alive, not for the dead. Did he or did he not say to let the dead bury the dead?"

"Yes, he said that, but . . ."

"Did he say it, yes or no? And if he said it, do you know what he meant by it? He wanted to say that those alive should not worry about the dead, about their insignificant rotting flesh. Leave the dead alone, throw them in the garbage, do not busy yourself with them. They will dig their own graves if they want to be buried. They will help each other, they will bury each other. Don't you think," he said, "a spectacle in which the dead bury the dead is a beautiful thing?"

"A very beautiful thing," I said.

"Imagine the scene as if painted by Breughel, Bosch, or any Flemish painter. I visited Holland; I've been to Leiden and Amsterdam; I saw *The Anatomy Lesson* at the Hague; I saw *The Enraged Swan* in Amsterdam. Imagine those tiny dead figures, deformed, hunchbacked, scrofulous, cross-eyed, their faces disfigured with sores, swelling, leprosy, some busy dragging their fellow dead by the legs, by the arms, others grabbing them up by the arms, the legs, the skin of their necks, the hair, and viciously swinging the dead, jettisoning them into a deep pit which in the meantime the other dead have dug with shovels and hoes. Pity for the dead is an issue for the dead. The live Christian does not have, nor should have if he is a true Christian and a follower of Christ, anything but a profound disgust, a supreme disdain for the flesh that humankind leaves behind on this earth the moment he rises into heaven or descends into hell."

I stared at the doctor and thought that watching the dead bury the dead must indeed be a magnificent spectacle to watch; as was watching, above the hills, Christ rising into heaven, his left foot brushing against the earth while his right foot was already taking flight. I was born in a village in Tuscany where the living had a horror of the dead. And ever since I was a boy, whenever the sight of something dead offended me, I told myself that Christ must hate everything that was dead, all that signified death. I told myself that vice was something akin to a corpse and sin something already dead, while virtue was alive and something full of life. I always told myself that pity for corpses offended Christ, that he hated corpses because to do so was the triumph of life, of eternal life.

I stared at the doctor and smiled. Abruptly, I asked: "What do you do with the remains of the dead?"

"We burn them," the doctor said.

I then went to the glue factory on the outskirts of —— District. In the factory courtyard there was a mountain of dead animals—cats, dogs, horses, and rotting horse and ox hides. A nauseating smell emanated from that mountain of rotting flesh. The duty of modern civilization is to transform dead things into materials for common use—into creams, soaps, glue, perfume; into odorless, colorless, tasteless chemical matter. I wondered when that industry of dead things had begun and I was amazed by the fact that it had coincided with the birth and discovery of photography. The discovery of photography had inundated the world with terrible images. Until then, the images that humankind had of the world and of human life were images born of art, created from the imaginations of painters and illustrators. All that man saw of himself and of the world had been thought about, seen, interpreted by way of genius, by way of the artists' imagination. Sculptures, paintings, these were the images of man and his world that art offered to human eyes. No image by a painter, no matter how filthy, no matter how disgusting—the poor in Magnasco, the grotesque in Breughel and Hieronymus Bosch, the old women and the monsters in Goya, the corpses in Goya—none of them was as revolting as the images of the deformed and dead fixed onto the photographic plate. Art does not surprise nature but transforms it and helps to cover its face. Art is a mask that covers the face of nature. But photography surprises nature by revealing what is most exposed, blatant, obvious, visible, most spectral, and I would say, most dead. A portrait painted by an artist is the portrait of a living man. That surprise, produced by the camera, is a portrait of a dead man, or better yet, the instantaneous portrait of what is most ephemeral, most dead, most macabre, in a human, the thing in a human that portends the future corpse. The features of a face are much more harshly delineated: eyes appear wide open and full of a solid white light and the gaze shows astonishment and terror. The teeth, if the mouth is smiling, appear crooked and broken, and the shadows between one tooth and another and beneath the gums suddenly become black, and even the purest, whitest, most beautiful teeth appear to be rotting and full of cavities. Nostrils appear as black, hairy holes. Ears stick out, noses stick out, lips stick out, and seem to be harshly rendered in a hard, pasty material. Even a smile appears to be a grimace of fear and disgust. What the photograph has revealed to us about humankind is a terrible thing; and the extent to which the photographic image—the mechanical reproduction of the face, the voice, human gestures—has influenced the sensibilities and taste of the modern generation is incredible, though many are unaware because by now the spectacle of humankind mechanically reproduced is a common, everyday event. The macabre accompanies the ridiculous in every

photograph and, little by little, the ridiculous takes prece-
dence over every other element until only the ridiculous
remains and is supremely evident in old photographs and
films. This ridiculousness does not, however, appear in paintings that reproduce, thanks to the paintbrush of the artist,
those same scenes, those same faces, frozen in the eternal
moment of art. Instead, on a photographic plate, the cadaverous is the strongest aspect on a human's face, especially
when reproduced in the candid photographs taken without
the studio setup of artificial shadows and soft light. The
modern sensibility is by now used to seeing humans through
photography, their mortal, deathly, and cadaverous aspects
collected in this form. *Tout se tient*, the French rightly say,
everything is contained. And it is not only due to philosophy
and certain political and social ideologies that we owe the
great modern disdain for the living man, for human life, but
also to this sensibility, entirely modern, born from the mechanical representation of man, of nature, of life in all its
forms. The modern man is used to thinking of mankind as
already dead, as a harbinger of the corpse. And it is not
reckless or arbitrary to assert that the distance from the
discovery of photography to Dachau, to the concentration
camps, to mass killings, is one and the same step and that
step a short one. We see the world and humankind today in
black and white, and if we close our eyes and recall any
image—a train moving down a track, a man, a horse, a tree,
a corpse—we see it in black and white, macabre and demonic.

Staring at the members of the Supreme Soviet lined up
on the stage at the Bolshoi Theater, I was aghast. I thought
they were dead. I thought that they would wind up in the
garbage, ashes removed from the incinerator. I thought of
the corpses under refrigeration at the University, the enor-

mous pile of animal carrion, of rotting hides heaped in the courtyard of the glue factory on the outskirts of the Dorogomilovo District. I looked at Kalinin and thought: "Where will this end?" I looked at Lunacharsky and thought: "Where will his cold ashes be tossed?" I looked at Stalin, sitting behind the others, his face bulging forward, his large black mustache glued across his face, and I thought: "Where will be the resting place of his eternal sleep?" The crowd behind me was breathing heavily and their hot breath warmed my back and neck. Every once in a while, I heard a murmur run through the audience and I thought: "Where will this crowd end up? In what grave, in what urn, in what crematorium?" Ever since the utilization of man, of his remains, his detritus, became a conquest of the modern world, nothing now in the whole human spectacle will ever counter the belief in the chemical utilization of his remains, his corpse, his hair and nails, his fat, the calcium from his bones, the sugar and starch from his flesh. For the first time in the history of humanity, in human civilization, human corpses were used scientifically, chemically; the fat, the pus, the bones, the hair were made into pills, medical ointments, pharmaceuticals. Death is disgusting. It doesn't elicit fear anymore or give hope. It's disgusting, repugnant. We abhor corpses. We are ashamed of corpses, like the excrement humans leave behind themselves. We are ashamed of corpses, as if humans leave nothing behind themselves on this earth except for a pile of shit. Modesty and the particular brand of puritanism characteristic of the modern world makes us blush at the sight of a corpse. We don't know what to do with it. We no longer even have the courage to honor a human corpse, to bury it with dignity. The modern world is ashamed of death. The modern world is ashamed of having to die, of our own mortality. Death is a denial too difficult, peremptory, brash, decisive, of all the theories about human happiness, about human intelligence, it is a too-open denial of the soul's mortality. Modern man, revolutions, Marxist governments hide death. Marxism is ashamed of death. The corpse of a man is nothing but a residue of a combustion, a bit of ash, a bit of excrement. To the garbage heap! If God doesn't exist, why should death? That blush, that shame of death, where are its roots? In the Germans. In the German soul there is a profound disdain for the corpse. A dead man, for a German, is nothing but a carcass, a bit of rotting meat to be thrown out as soon as possible, buried in a mad hurry, hidden away immediately from the human eye. Or, perhaps, in the German soul there is a profound indifference to the dead man, to the corpse. In German art, there isn't a great difference between the dead and the living. I always wondered why Lucas Cranach painted Venus and Eve as decrepit old women, filthy, wrinkled, and crusty-eyed with sagging bellies and breasts. Why paint Venuses who look like dead Venuses, their corpses still warm? I wondered why Matthias Grünewald painted men and Christ already full of worms. And Dürer painted them already as skeletons, already desiccated, mummified by the arid breath of the tomb. Why in all of German medieval art, as well as in Dutch and Flemish art, in all of European painting, even in Italian and French, dominated by Gothic inspiration, do the living man and the dead man appear almost identical? Not because of those cultures' love of the macabre, but because of their disdain for the dead and death; not because of their fear of death; not because of their love of death, like the Etruscans, or the Spanish; not because of their pity for the dead, like the ancient Greeks (Antigone); not because of that love of death that for the Spanish, the Sicilians, the Neapolitans, and the Calabrians contains something sensual, including an emotional sensuality, beginning with envy. Rather, the identification of the living with the dead was due to a real disdain, an indifference to death and to the dead man. It was not a love of the macabre, but disdain and indifference to the corpse, that feast in the presence of the corpse, that sleeping on the edge of battlefields. And later, during the war between Germany and Russia in 1941, every time I saw German soldiers sleeping, or eating, or drinking, or sitting around chatting next to some horrendous and already rotting corpse, I was stunned by that indifference, by that disdain. These attitudes then mutated in the modern spirit into the shame of death; almost as if death were proof of the frailty of all things human, of man, and therefore of his philosophy, his politics, his morality, almost as if death were a denial of his pride, revealing as a lie all of his promises for happiness, all of his promises for a future. It was almost as if death for man was a limitation to his life and work; and in a Marxist society death appeared as a denial as well as a danger, a threat, and a contradiction, and even more importantly, as an evil, a sin, a guilt. In Marxist society death gave rise to feelings of guilt, not because one had sinned, but because of one's frailty, one's inability to create a new, eternal world without God. The shame of death in a Marxist society expressed itself as a feeling of disdain for the living man. Death in a Marxist society was an individual event, not a collective one, thus a return to individual feeling. Death kills individual by individual, not by group or mass. And still the shame of death in our own modern world, and especially in the Marxist world, is a revelation and proof of man's poverty (capitalism) and his insufficiency (communism). Capitalist Anglo-Saxon and American countries don't fear death, they are rather ashamed of knowing how poor, how abject, how nude they are, ashamed to see how easy and fast it is to pass from the greatness of American wealth to the squalid abject poverty of death. Society then demands funeral parlors and enterprises of the sort that one can call up to request that a dead body be removed from one's home and taken to a funeral parlor where the body is washed, the face made up, the lips rouged (and a small piece of wood placed between the lips in order to open them into a smile revealing white teeth), and when the corpse is all dressed up in a fancy suit, his face bright, his lips smiling, then come the visits, the drinks, the softly playing music from a gramophone in the corner of the room only a few steps from the smiling corpse lying on a bed of satin and flowers. Even in death the corpse is rich, even dead he is rich and happy. America is the country of the rich and happy dead, the mecca of corpses. Ah, those greedy and insatiable capitalists! In communist countries, everyone is ashamed of death, ashamed to admit that at the end of Karl Marx Boulevard or Lenin Boulevard or Stalin Boulevard, just as at the end of Roosevelt Boulevard or Wilson Boulevard or Marshall Boulevard, there is death, a smooth cement wall without doors or windows that is death. They are ashamed to have to recognize that communism can't change man's ultimate destiny—death; communism can do nothing against the supreme wretchedness, the supreme nakedness, the supreme loneliness, the supreme degradation of death.

While in Moscow, I felt this impotence of communism in the face of death and the shame of death profoundly. I almost never came across a funeral procession in the street. The churches were closed with the exception of the Chapel of Saint Nicholas on Nikolskaya Street. Funeral ceremonies were invisible. In the Soviet newspapers *Pravda* and *Isvestia* funerals were invisible; there were no obituaries, no funeral announcements. Only occasionally would there be mention of the death of some high-level functionary or revolutionary, but it would be in an anodyne form and would never include the verb *umiral*: to die. In the entire official communist literature the word "death" never appeared; not even one page addressed death, even as a problem. Lenin is silent. Stalin is silent. Trotsky is also silent. And Bukharin, the philosopher of the October Revolution, spoke of death, but only in passing, as something of negligible "political" or "social" importance. I had come to a strange country, a country in which death did not exist.

During my early days I felt as if I had been freed from the obsession with death that persecutes Europeans. Then, slowly, under the fear of the police, so enduring in Russia, and not only in communist Russia, I began to notice the classic Russian disregard for death, as well as the Marxist shame of death, their shameful hidden burying of the dead. Even communist society produced their share of waste, corpses, etc., etc.

Modern death is disinfected, polished, nickel-plated—a streamlined death, a *rostfritt* or stainless death. It is an aspect of the mechanized life, a crankshaft, a cylinder, a spark plug, a valve, an aspect of the generator life, a spare part. A man is a spare part. But the presence of death, the feeling of death is the most vile feeling that exists in a communist society. Nothing in a perfect communist society should make one think of death. Death is a capitalist invention, an invention of bourgeois philosophy. A communist society must liberate itself from the slavery of death. Death is the legacy of centuries of bourgeois obscurantism, tradition, philosophy, and a falsified capitalist culture. In Soviet theater, circus, and cinema there is never any allusion to death. The glorification of life—that is Soviet art. In Europe, I was the offspring of Western culture. In no way did I feel trapped by the idea the Western world, the bourgeois world, had fashioned of Soviet communism. The idea that communism was an expression of the "Antichrist" made me laugh. Everything for a bourgeois was "anti-Christ" if it didn't fit into the framework of his interests and cultural ideas. Communism returned Christianity to its deep, programmatic, fundamental contempt, not of death, but of the corpse, of the dead man. Communism replaced the Western fear of death with the shame of death. But this wasn't a characteristic of communism alone, it was a characteristic of the modern world. Even the Americans, who in certain respects came closest to the communist mentality, were ashamed of death. The idea that Christ liberated us from death meant only the death of the soul and sin. Christ could do nothing to implement the human myth of freedom from physical death: immortality. Christ accentuated in the world the horror of physical death unknown in many respects to the ancients. Christ introduced into the classic world the horror of death. Communism took it further by introducing into the Christian world the shame of death. As such, communism was a characteristic of modern life.

At a certain point Kalinin, the President of the USSR, stood up and was greeted by loud applause. He slowly rose from his chair and slowly moved to the microphone. He closed his eyes and with closed eyes he looked around. Looking around, he began to speak. He spoke with a dull voice which despite the amplification of the microphone maintained his weak, faded, almost extinguished tone. I thought about Kalinin's corpse and I wondered what they would do with it. A few days earlier, I had gone again to visit Lenin's mummy. It was the tenth time I had gone to visit Lenin's mummy. In front of the wooden mausoleum in Red Square, stretching away from the mausoleum door there was a long line comprised of mostly old peasants, workers, women, and most of those had come from the remotest provinces of the Soviet empire. The crowd was silent, poor, squalidly dressed. Men and women wore worn-out boots; the women had large scarves over their heads, tied beneath their chins; the men wore caps with shiny black leather visors; some who had come from the Asian provinces, from the Upper Volga, wore gray sheepskin caps; and others wore the Tatar skullcap embroidered in red and green. The old men had long reddish beards interwoven with streaks of white and long hair cut like a mop in the old Russian style. The young had shaven heads, strong jaws, large cheekbones, wide prominent foreheads, and eyebrows that jutted out like horns. Those who imagine Russians as the characters depicted by Tolstoy or Dostoevsky or Gogol, the *mujiki* with noble faces and large bright eyes full of kindness, docility, and wit, the ones with their faces darkened by long brown or red beards, and then see today's Soviet *mujiki* with their shaved faces would be surprised and disappointed. Now we see what those Russian beards were hiding! Strong-jawed, hard-boned faces with large cheekbones, the brutish, vulgar faces of butchers. And their shaved heads revealed a lumpy skull, not round, but oblong and undulating with protrusions here and there. The vulgar, brutish expressions on those faces were disconcerting. And already those faces were making inroads every day among the old faces of the functionaries, the intellectuals, the Russian officials, the noble, sad, pale faces which were each day mixing in with the crowds of new faces and disappearing. And already at the front of the crowd were the Soviet faces, almost German faces, but those from German Expressionist films and paintings made fashionable by Lambrecht and Sternberg, Fritz Lang, Murnau, Lasar Segall, and Grosz. A new race was arising in Russia: the Marxist race. Alongside the shaven *mujiki*, a new race was arising, a young race of eighteen- to twenty-year-olds who would be thirty when the Germans invaded Russia. It was the modern race, born out of capitalist decadence, out of the rise of the new Marxist society that had already invaded Europe, England, and America.

Finally we entered Lenin's crypt. We went down the narrow stairway divided into two short flights and arrived at a small door flanked by two Red Army soldiers armed with fixed bayonet rifles. I was pushed to the threshold where I was stopped by the two guards who crossed their rifles over the door. From where I stood I could study the crypt in detail: Lenin's mummy laid out in the glass coffin, the *mujiki* filing around the mummy. The crypt was small, entirely built of wood and simply decorated with a few red flags. The coffin in which Lenin lay was made of glass. He lay on his back, his right hand down along his side, the left folded onto his stomach. He was dressed in black. His face was very pale, slightly enlivened by a touch of rouge on his cheeks along with rose-colored freckles scattered across his white face. His beard was red. In photographs his beard, mustache, eyebrows, and the sparse hair around his temples appeared to be black. In reality, Lenin had red hair and a white face with freckles, the uncertain, delicate, almost shy face of a redhead. Lenin smiled. It was the ironic smile of one who knows a great deal. He had no rhetorical grandiloquence on his face. In *Le bonhomme Lénine*, I told the story of Lenin's life by drawing a portrait of him. One cannot understand the underlying meaning of the Russian Revolution if one hasn't seen Lenin, either dead or alive. He rests in the sleep of death, a squalid mummy. Everyone knows in Moscow that the embalming of Lenin was performed in a hurry and badly. The illness he suffered from had ruined his blood and the corpse had rapidly decomposed. The embalming happened too late. After a few months of lying in his glass coffin, it became clear that the mummy was decomposing, crumbling, becoming flaky, soft to the touch, damp and spoiled.

NOTES

3   *the famous ballerina Semyonova:* Marina Semyonova (1908–2010) was the first Soviet-trained prima ballerina. She worked in the Kirov ballet from 1925–1930 when she was transferred by Stalin to the Bolshoi Theater in Moscow. She was briefly married to Lev Karakhan.

Karakhan: Lev Karakhan (1889–1937) was a Russian revolutionary and Soviet diplomat who served as Soviet Ambassador to Poland, China, and Turkey and served as the Deputy People's Commissar for Foreign Affairs from 1927–1934. He was executed in 1937 during the Great Purge.

Florinsky, Chief of Protocol: Dimitry Florinsky began his career in the czar's diplomatic service and served as Imperial Russian Consulate in New York. He was Chief of Protocol of the People's Commissariat for Foreign Affairs from 1927–1934. He was exiled in 1935. His brother was Michael Florinsky (1895–1981) who fled Russia in 1921. A Columbia University professor of economics, Michael was also the author of many books on Russia and Europe, including his renowned two-volume *Russia: A History and an Interpretation.*

4   *those who gathered around Barras:* Paul François Jean Nicolas, vicomte de Barras (1755–1829), was a notoriously corrupt and amoral politician who aligned himself with Napoleon Bonaparte.

Langeron: Legrandin.

Albert Thibaudet: Thibaudet (1874–1936) was a French essayist, literary critic, and professor at the University of Geneva.

7   *Lunacharsky:* Anatoly Lunacharsky (1875–1933) was a Russian Marxist revolutionary and the first Soviet People's Commissar of Education and Culture. He was also an important and prolific literary and art critic. His most notable book is his memoir, *Revolutionary Silhouettes.*

8   *"A Dangeau who became Saint-Simon":* Philippe de Courcillon, Marquis de Dangeau (1638–1720) was famous for his diary kept

during the reign of Louis XIV, which Saint-Simon described as "of an insipidity to make you sick."

8   *a* Cyrus *and a* Clélie: *Artamène, ou le Grand Cyrus* and *Clélie* are lengthy novels by the French author Madeleine de Scudéry (1607–1701).

11   *Kschessinskaya:* Mathilda-Marie Feliksovna Kschessinskaya (1872–1971) was a prima ballerina of the St. Petersburg Imperial Theaters and mistress of Nicholas II. She moved to France after the Russian Revolution.

15   *Stanley Owen:* The name of the British Ambassador changes from Owen Stanley to Stanley Owen (accompanied by Lady Owen) finally settling on Edmond Ovey. The actual name of the first British Ambassador to the Soviet Union was Sir Esmond Ovey, which is also used.

16   *S'enivrait en marchant:* In English, "While walking he was intoxicated by the pleasure of seeing." (Malaparte misquotes Racine here. The actual quote is "S'enivrir en marchant.")
      Giraudoux: Hippolyte Jean Giraudoux (1882–1944) was an important French dramatist as well as a novelist, essayist, and diplomat.

17   *Ilya Ehrenburg:* Ehrenburg (1891–1967) was a prolific Soviet author of novels, poetry, essays, and journalism. His most famous works are the novel *The Thaw*, describing the post–Stalin era, and the *Black Book*, edited with Vasily Grossman and containing documentary accounts by Jewish survivors of the Holocaust in the Soviet Union and Poland.

18   *Tairov:* Alexander Tairov (1885–1950) was a leading innovator of the theatrical arts during the Soviet era. He founded the Kamerny Theater in 1914.
      Marshal Yegorov: Alexander Ilyich Yegorov (1883–1939) was a Soviet military leader appointed Deputy People's Commissar for Defense and Chief of the General Staff of the Red Army in 1931. He was one of the first five Marshals of the Soviet Union, the supreme military rank created in 1935. He died in prison, victim of Stalin's Great Purge of the Red Army.

19   *women boyars:* A boyar was a member of an old order of high Russian nobility ranking immediately below the princes. The order was abolished by Peter the Great in 1711.
      "Old Believers": A group of Russian religious dissenters who separated from the official Russian Orthodox Church after 1666 in protest

against church reforms introduced by the Patriarch Nikon of Moscow.

20 *Fallières:* Clément Armand Fallières (1841–1931) was president of the French Republic from 1906 to 1913.

21 *Litvinov:* Maxim Maximovich Litvinov (1876–1951) was a Russian revolutionary and prominent Soviet diplomat. He was appointed People's Commissar for Foreign Affairs by Stalin in 1930. In 1933 he persuaded the United States to recognize the Soviet government and facilitated the USSR's acceptance into the League of Nations. Due to his Jewish heritage, in 1939 Stalin replaced Litvinov with Vyacheslav Molotov.

22 *Borodin:* Mikhail Markovich Borodin (1884–1951) was a prominent Comintern agent. He negotiated the First United Front between the Chinese Nationalist Party and the Chinese Communist Party.

23 *Chateaubriand:* François-René, vicomte de Chateaubriand, was a French writer, historian, and royalist who in 1792, during the French Revolution, was forced into exile in London. An amnesty allowed him to return to Paris in 1800.

Giuliano Sorel: Probably Albert Sorel (1842–1906), the highly respected and influential French diplomatic historian distinguished for his major work, the eight-volume *Europe and the French Revolution*. Sorel is now considered by revisionist historians to have been something of an apologist for Napoleon.

24 *Trotsky, Kamenev, or Bukharin:* Leon Trotsky (1879–1940) was a Russian Marxist revolutionary and founder of the Red Army. He was an early dissenter of Joseph Stalin's policies, which led to his expulsion from the Communist Party in 1927 and his exile to Mexico in 1929. He was assassinated in Mexico on Stalin's orders. Lev Borisovich Kamenev (1883–1936) was a Bolshevik revolutionary, prominent Soviet politician, and Trotsky's brother-in-law. He was one of the Old Bolsheviks in the Trial of the Sixteen (1936), the first of the Moscow Show Trials in which defendants were forced to confess to myriad crimes. Nikolai Ivanovich Bukharin (1888–1938), also a Bolshevik revolutionary and Soviet politician, wrote extensively on revolutionary theory. Once known as the "Golden Boy" of the party, he was condemned to death in one of the Show Trials. His performance and confession during the trial inspired Arthur Koestler's novel *Darkness at Noon.*

Fabrice del Dongo: The main protagonist of Stendhal's novel *The Charterhouse of Parma.*

28 *Marshal Budyonny:* Semyon Mikhailovich Budyonny (1883–1973) was a Red Cossack, a Soviet military commander, a politician, and a close ally of Joseph Stalin. He was made one of the first five Marshals of the Soviet Union in 1935 and was one of two Marshals to survive the Great Purge of the late 1930s.

Sollogub's: Count Vladimir Alexandrovich Sollogub (1813–1882) was a minor Russian writer of novellas and plays who hosted a well-known literary and musical salon in St. Petersburg.

29 tolstovka: A traditional Russian shirt, also known as the *kosovorotka*, or "skew-collar," because it opens on one side of the collar. The shirt is long-sleeved and reaches mid-thigh. The *kosovorotka* came to be known as the *tolstovka* or the Tolstoy shirt because in his later years the author Leo Tolstoy often wore one.

mujik: A Russian peasant.

30 toilette de guillotiné: On the evening after Baudelaire was convicted on obscenity charges for writing *Les Fleurs du mal*, he appeared in a Parisian brasserie *en toilette de guillotiné*, that is wearing a shirt without a collar and a shaven head.

Stanisław Patek: Patek (1866–1944) was an activist in the Polish Socialist Party and served as Polish Minister of Foreign Affairs from 1919–1920. From 1926–1932, he was Polish ambassador to the Soviet Union in Moscow, and from 1936–1939, the Polish ambassador to the United States in Washington, DC. He was involved in protecting Jews after the German invasion of Poland and died of injuries sustained during the Warsaw Uprising.

the Thermidor: Thermidor is the eleventh month of the French Republican calendar and the month in which Robespierre and his cronies were arrested and executed. The word "Thermidor" has come to mean a retreat from more radical goals after a revolution. Leon Trotsky referred to the rise of Stalin and the postrevolutionary bureaucracy as the "Soviet Thermidor."

32 *the Putilov Plant:* A major machine-building plant established in 1789 and employing 12,400 people by 1900. That year the company began to produce artillery, becoming a major supplier to the Imperial Russian Army. In early 1917 strikes at the factory led to the February Revolution.

33 *the First* Pyatiletka: Five-Year Plan for the National Economy of the USSR. Instituted by Stalin in 1928, this was the first in a series of plans for rapid economic development with the aim of transform-

ing an agricultural subsistence economy into a modern industrial economy.

33 *a sousoff:* A noncommissioned officer.

34 *Dollfuss, Schuschnigg, and the Anschluss:* Engelbert Dollfuss (1892–1934) was Federal Chancellor of Austria from 1932 until his assassination by Nazi agents. Kurt Schuschnigg succeeded Dollfuss as Chancellor until Nazi Germany's annexation of Austria, known as the Anschluss, in March 1938.

38 *Marshal Tukhachevsky:* Mikhail Tukhachevsky (1893–1937) was Commander-in-Chief of the Red Army (1925–1928) and a Marshal of the Soviet Union. He also was a victim of Stalin's Great Purge.

Ambassador Cerruti: Vittorio Cerruti (1881–1961) was a diplomat who was the Italian ambassador to the USSR from 1927–1932.

40 *Zinoviev:* Grigory Zinoviev (1883–1936) was a Bolshevik revolutionary, a Soviet communist politician, and head of the Communist International. Along with Lenin, Kamenev, Trotsky, Stalin, Sokolnikov, and Bubnov, he was a member of the first Politburo in 1917. He was also convicted in the Trial of the Sixteen and immediately executed.

45 kolkhoz: A collective farm in the Soviet Union.

46 *Nepmen and kulaks:* Nepmen were businessmen in the new Soviet Union who engaged in private trade and small-scale manufacturing made possible by the New Economic Policy. Kulak, in Soviet terminology, was the word for an affluent farmer who owned land and livestock.

Grosz: George Grosz (1893–1959), a German artist known for his cartoons and drawings satirizing Berlin life in the 1920s.

rabotniki *clubs:* Workers' clubs that proliferated throughout the USSR within a few months of the installation of the Soviet regime. They were run by trade unions or political organizations, often local, and were set up in former private houses, in converted churches, in sheds, almost anywhere. Soviet architects soon designed and built many of these workers' clubs, which remain outstanding examples of Constructivist architecture.

47 *Jacques Mornard:* The pseudonym of Ramon Mercader (1913–1978), a Spanish communist and KGB agent who assassinated Leon Trotsky in Mexico City in 1940.

Marshal Zhukov: Georgy Zhukov (1896–1974) was a Soviet

officer in the Red Army and the most highly decorated commander in the history of the Soviet Union and Russia.

48 *Steicher:* Up until now he has been called Steyer. The same character will later appear as von Steiger, or simply Steiger.

49 *the Lubyanka:* The familiar name for the KGB headquarters and affiliated prison on Lubyanka Square in Moscow. A large Neo-Baroque building built in 1898 to house the All-Russia Insurance Company, it was seized following the Bolshevik Revolution.
Shchusev: Alexey Shchusev (1873–1949) was a renowned Russian and Soviet architect who worked predominantly in the Constructivist style.

51 *Scriabin's pale ghost:* Alexander Scriabin (1871–1915) was an innovative and controversial modernist Russian composer and pianist.

52 *Boris Pilnyak:* Pilnyak (1894–1938) was a Russian writer whose anti-urban views brought him into disfavor with communist critics. His most famous works, which all concern revolutionary or postrevolutionary Russia, are *The Naked Year* (1922), *Mahogany* (1927), and *The Volga Flows into the Caspian Sea* (1930). He is also the author of *Okay! An American Novel* (1931), an unflattering travelogue of his 1931 visit to the United States. He was tried and executed by the People's Commissariat for Internal Affairs in 1938.

53 *Patriarch Tikhon:* Saint Tikhon of Moscow (1865–1925) was the eleventh Patriarch of Moscow and All Russia of the Russian Orthodox Church in the early years of the Soviet Union (1917–1925).
Metropolitan Sergius of Nizhny Novgorod: Patriarch Sergius of Moscow (1867–1944) was *de facto* head of the Russian Orthodox Church from 1925 to 1943 and the 12th Patriarch of Moscow and All Russia of the Russian Orthodox Church for less than a year from 1943 to his death.

54 *Tiflis:* The capital and largest city of Georgia; renamed Tbilisi in 1936.
Technique du coup d'état *and* Le bonhomme Lénine: *Technique du coup d'état* was first published by Grasset in France in 1931. The English translation, *Coup d'État: The Technique of Revolution*, was published by E.P. Dutton & Co. Inc. in 1932. *Le bonhomme Lénine* (That Good Man Lenin) has never received a full translation into English.
Mikhail Afanasyevich Bulgakov: Bulgakov (1891–1940), born in

Kiev, was a Russian writer and playwright who is now best known for his novel *The Master and Margarita*.

55   *Piscator:* Erwin Piscator (1893–1966) was a German theater director and producer, renowned for his promotion, along with Bertolt Brecht, of "epic theater" that emphasized the sociopolitical content of drama.

57   *Simon Ushakov:* Ushakov (1626–1686) was a renowned Russian icon painter and a favorite at the court of Czar Alexis.

     Church of Our Lady of Georgia: Better known as the Church of the Trinity at Nikitniki.

58   *Metropolitan Alexius:* Saint Alexius of Moscow (1296?–1378) was a Metropolitan of Moscow and All Russia and is a patron saint of Moscow. He was Bishop of Vladimir and a government advisor to Dimitri Donskoi.

59   *Sukharevskaya Bashnya:* Sukharev Tower, built by Peter the Great, was one of Moscow's most famous landmarks. It was destroyed by the Soviet authorities in 1934.

     Demyan Bedny: Bedny (1883–1945) was the pseudonym for Efim Alekseyevich Pridvorov, the prolific and popular Soviet writer who wrote anti-religious works. His poem *The New Testament Without Shortcomings* possibly inspired Bulgakov's *The Master and Margarita* as a rebuttal.

     Bezbozhniks: *Bezbozhnik*, which means "godless," was an official Soviet literary journal devoted to anti-religious propaganda. Its founder and publisher was Yemelyan Mikhailovich Yaroslavsky (1878–1943).

60   *Sverdlov Square:* So called between 1919 and 1991. It is now called Tetralnaya (theater) Square.

61   *"tunic, so soft that it fitted him like the skin of an onion":* From Book XIX of Homer's *The Odyssey*.

80   *the poet Mayakovsky:* Vladimir Mayakovsky (1893–1930), a Soviet poet and playwright, was a prominent figure in the prerevolutionary Russian Futurist movement.

81   *"the men of fire William Blake saw rise…":* Mayakovsky is probably referring to William Blake's poem "America, A Prophecy" (1793).

     Sergei Yesenin: Sergei Alexandrovich Yesenin (1895–1925), a lyric poet, was hugely popular among the Russian people during his lifetime and remains so today. There is strong evidence that his suicide was staged and he was instead assassinated by the Soviet Union secret police.

82 *Barbara Hutton:* Hutton (1912–1979) was a socialite and heiress of the retail tycoon Frank Woolworth. She was one of the wealthiest women in the world and renowned for her beauty. She married seven times, including several European princes and the actor Cary Grant. Known for her extravagant spending, both on luxury goods and philanthropy, by the end of her life she had burned through most of her inheritance of over a billion dollars.

85 *"You pig":* In English in the original.

87 *the satirical magazine* Krokodil: Named after the satirical short story "The Crocodile" by Dostoevsky, the magazine was founded in 1922. At the time there were many satirical magazines published in the Soviet Union, but under Stalin nearly all of them disappeared except for *Krokodil.* It lasted until the dissolution of the Soviet Union in 1991, but was reinstated in 2005.

Kremlin's "Upper Ten": "The Upper Ten Thousand," often abbreviated to "The Upper Ten," refers to a city's upper circles and was coined by American poet Nathaniel Parker Willis when he used the phrase to describe New York City's elite.

cuisse légère: A French idiomatic expression used for an "easy" woman. A slut. The term literally means "light thigh."

88 Sov-cocu: Soviet cuckold.

93 *the Kolomenskoye:* A former royal estate several kilometers outside of Moscow, overlooking the steep banks of the Moskva River.

97 *Sokovino:* Sovkino was the name of the central cinema organization from 1925–1930. It was preceded by Goskino (1924–1925) and followed by Soyuzkino, which lasted until 1963.

99 *"It is a tree, self-born, self-grown…":* Lines 694–700 in *Oedipus at Colonus* by Sophocles translated by G. Theodoridis.

101 *the Streltsy rebels:* In 1698, during Peter the Great's reign, an uprising among the Moscow Streltsy regiments occurred. Some of the Streltsy secretly contacted Peter the Great's sister Sophia Alexeyevna at the Novodevichy Convent in hopes of installing her in her brother's place. When their campaign failed, the Streltsy rebels were tortured, then executed or sent into exile.

103 *the historian Solovyov:* Sergey Solovyov (1820–1879) was a renowned Russian historian who published nearly thirty books, including his

220 · NOTES TO PAGES 103–140

magnum opus *History of Russia from the Earliest Times.* He was Dean
of Moscow University and tutor to the future Alexander III.

103 *Krapotkin's grave:* Pyotr Krapotkin (1842–1921), geographer, zo-
ologist, anarchist.

127 *how Sophocles depicted Alcestis:* The tragedy *Alcestis* was, in fact,
written by Euripides in 438 BCE.

128 *the GPU:* Shorthand for State Political Administration *(Gosu-
darstvennoe Politicheskoe Upravlenie)*, the intelligence service and secret police founded in 1922 under the Russian Soviet Federative
Socialist Republic.

130 *the playwright Ostrovsky:* Alexander Ostrovsky (1823–1886) was
the author of forty-seven plays, which were among the most widely-
read and frequently performed dramatic works in Russia. He is cred-
ited with bringing realism to the nineteenth-century Russian stage.
A contemporary of Tolstoy, Dostoevsky, and Turgenev, he remains
little known outside Russia.

136 *the Goncourt brothers:* Edmond de Goncourt (1822–1896) and
Jules de Goncourt (1830–1870) were French novelists renowned for
being inseparable and for writing all their works together. They were
also known for their disdain of revolutionary tendencies in politics.
Countess Potocka: Probably Countess Emanuela Potocka (1852–
1930), an Italian noblewoman who married the Polish Count Potocka.
She moved to the Hôtel Potocki in Paris and hosted a renowned literary and artistic salon famously frequented by Proust, who also wrote
about her.

139 *Count Pálffy:* Probably Fidél Pálffy (1895–1946), a Hungarian
nobleman who founded the Hungarian Nationalist Socialist Party.
He was executed in Budapest in 1946, condemned by the communists
for being a Nazi sympathizer.

140 *the slap Skirmunt gave the Princess Betka Radziwill:* It is unclear
exactly whom Skirmunt slapped as earlier he describes the recipient
of Skirmunt's slap as Countess Potocka. Given her age at the time it
is unlikely that it was Princess Betka Radziwill (b. 1917), the daughter of an American heiress, Dorothy Deacon of Boston, who married
Prince Albert Radziwill; then after her daughter's birth, had the marriage annulled and married Count Fidél Pálffy, also mentioned in this
scene.
the slap Sciarra Colonna gave to Pope Boniface: The incident

immortalized in Dante's *Divine Comedy*, Purgatory, XX, but apparently the slap actually occurred in the nearby Anagni Palace.

142 *Joséphine de Beauharnais:* Josephine Tascher de la Pagerie, later de Beauharnais (1763–1814), was the first wife of Napoleon Bonaparte, who crowned her Empress of France in 1804. She had been arrested and imprisoned during the Reign of Terror due to her first husband's counterrevolutionary activity.

143 *Paul Morand:* Morand (1888–1976) was a French diplomat who wrote short stories, novels, plays, essays, poetry, and memoirs, and was considered an early modernist. He was a great friend of Marcel Proust, with whom he often dined at the Hôtel Ritz. His poem "Ode à Marcel Proust," which Malaparte quotes from here, is included in Morand's poetry collection *Lampes à Arc.*

147 *Sir Esmond Ovey, once said… "You forget Karakhan":* Earlier in the novel these quips were attributed differently. The French ambassador said the line about the volcano and the British ambassador made the retort about Karakhan.

155 ukrop: Dill or fennel.

The Bug: A play by Vladimir Mayakovsky first performed in Moscow in 1929.

164 *the play by Mayakovsky:* The playwright was actually Valentin Kataev (1897–1986). *Circling the Square*, also translated as *Quadrature of the Circle*, was written in 1928. It is a satire describing the effect the housing shortage has on two married couples who share a room.

166 *Kerensky's Revolution:* Alexander Kerensky (1881–1970) was a key political figure of the Russian Revolution of 1917 and served as the second Minister-Chairman of the Russian Provisional Government from July to November of 1917. His government was overthrown by Lenin and the Bolsheviks in the October Revolution.

170 *the Congress of Berlin:* The congress (June 13–July 13, 1878) took place following the Russo-Turkish War of 1877–78 and was a meeting of the six major European powers and the leaders of the Ottoman Empire as well as of the Balkan states. The goal was to establish the territories of the states in the Balkan peninsula. German Chancellor Otto von Bismarck led the Congress and engaged intensely with British Prime Minister Benjamin Disraeli, who caused an uproar by making his opening address in English rather than in French, the accepted language of diplomacy.

171 *Prince Sapieha:* Eustachy Sapieha (1881–1963) was Polish Minister of Foreign Affairs from 1920–1921, successfully negotiating several agreements with Western powers during his short tenure. Apparently he wasn't educated at Oxford but in Zurich (1900–1904) where he studied forestry and earned a degree as an engineer.

Piłsudski and Trąmpczyński, Marshal of the Sejm of Poland: Józef Piłsudski (1867–1935) was a Polish revolutionary and statesman who served as the minister of military affairs and the de facto head of state from 1926 until his death in 1935. Wojciech Trąmpczyński (1860–1953) served as Marshal of the Sejm of Poland (the Sejm is the lower house of the Polish parliament) from 1919–1922 and of the Senate of Poland from 1922–1928.

172 *Count Tarnowski:* Adam Tarnowski (1866–1946) was a Polish-born Austro-Hungarian diplomat who briefly served as ambassador to the United States until the outbreak of World War I.

174 *Ah, la petite Zamoyska! And the Princess Bariatinskaya! And the young Naryshkina! Ah, the Countess Sheremeteva!:* Countess Maria Carolina Zamoyska (1896–1968) was the sixth child and youngest daughter of the Polish nobleman Andrzej Zamoyski and Princess Maria Carolina of Bourbon-Two Sicilies; Princess Bariatinskaya was probably the actress Lydia Yavorska (1869–1921) who married Prince Vladimir Bariatinsky in 1896; Princess Naryshkina was likely Princess Liubov Alexandrovna Obolenskaya, who married Prince Sergei Obolensky; Countess Sheremeteva was probably Yekaterina Pavlovna Sheremeteva (1849–1929).

179 *Tallemant des Réaux:* Gédéon Tallemant, Sieur des Réaux (1619–1692), was a bourgeois Frenchman who wrote a series of biographies of prominent figures of his class. The profiles were renowned for their maliciousness but deemed accurate. They were collected into a book entitled *Historiettes* (1836).

183 *the German ambassador, Mirbach:* Wilhelm von Mirbach (1871–1918) was a German diplomat. He was appointed the German ambassador to Russia in April 1918. Mirbach was assassinated by Yakov Grigorevich Blumkin at the request of the Central Committee of the Left Socialist-Revolutionaries, who were attempting to incite a war between Russia and Germany.

185 *Yurovsky, the assassin of the imperial family:* Yakov Mikhailovich Yurovsky (1878–1938) was an Old Bolshevik who executed Czar Nicholas II of Russia and his family in July 1918.

188 *the Makhno Band:* Nestor Makhno (1888–1934) was a Ukrainian anarchocommunist revolutionary and the commander of an independent anarchist army in Ukraine during the Russian Civil War of 1917–1922.

194 *Kalinin:* Mikhail Ivanovich Kalinin (1875–1946) was a Bolshevik revolutionary who served as head of state of the Soviet Union from 1919–1946. He was one of the few members in Stalin's inner circle who came from peasant origins. He survived the Great Purge by keeping a very low profile and by remaining submissive to Stalin.

196 *Axel Munthe:* Axel Munthe (1857–1949) was a Swedish physician and psychiatrist who lived in Italy and often treated the poor. He was also, at one point, physician to foreign dignitaries in Rome. He had a house, the Villa San Michele, on Capri and is best known as the author of *The Story of San Michele*, his autobiography.

TITLES IN SERIES

For a complete list of titles, visit www.nyrb.com or write to:
Catalog Requests, NYRB, 435 Hudson Street, New York, NY 10014

* *Also available as an electronic book.*